Praise for

Murder Uncorked

"All the sparkle, complexity, and romance of a fine champagne. This mystery is one you'll want to read right through with a bottle of good wine and some of the author's tasty canapés at your side. I loved it and look forward to more installments."
—Nancy Fairbanks

"A superb amateur sleuth tale starring an upbeat heroine and a fabulous prime suspect."
—*Midwest Book Review*

"A perfect blend of murder and page-turning fiction!"
—Holly Jacobs

"The first in a series that has great potential . . . The Napa Valley is a lush setting, and foodies will drink in the wine lore and will savor the recipes for tasty tidbits."
—*The Mystery Reader*

The Wine Lover's Mysteries by Michele Scott

MURDER UNCORKED
MURDER BY THE GLASS
SILENCED BY SYRAH

The Horse Lover's Mysteries by Michele Scott

SADDLED WITH TROUBLE

Silenced by Syrah

MICHELE SCOTT

BERKLEY PRIME CRIME, NEW YORK

THE BERKLEY PUBLISHING GROUP
Published by the Penguin Group
Penguin Group (USA) Inc.
375 Hudson Street, New York, New York 10014, USA
Penguin Group (Canada), 90 Eglinton Avenue East, Suite 700, Toronto, Ontario M4P 2Y3, Canada
(a division of Pearson Penguin Canada Inc.)
Penguin Books Ltd., 80 Strand, London WC2R 0RL, England
Penguin Group Ireland, 25 St. Stephen's Green, Dublin 2, Ireland (a division of Penguin Books Ltd.)
Penguin Group (Australia), 250 Camberwell Road, Camberwell, Victoria 3124, Australia
(a division of Pearson Australia Group Pty. Ltd.)
Penguin Books India Pvt. Ltd., 11 Community Centre, Panchsheel Park, New Delhi—110 017, India
Penguin Group (NZ), 67 Apollo Drive, Mairangi Bay, Auckland 1311, New Zealand
(a division of Pearson New Zealand Ltd.)
Penguin Books (South Africa) (Pty.) Ltd., 24 Sturdee Avenue, Rosebank, Johannesburg 2196,
South Africa

Penguin Books Ltd., Registered Offices: 80 Strand, London WC2R 0RL, England

This is a work of fiction. Names, characters, places, and incidents either are the product of the author's imagination or are used fictitiously, and any resemblance to actual persons, living or dead, business establishments, events, or locales is entirely coincidental. The publisher does not have any control over and does not assume any responsibility for author or third-party websites or their content.

PUBLISHER'S NOTE: The recipes contained in this book are to be followed exactly as written. The publisher is not responsible for your specific health or allergy needs that may require medical supervision. The publisher is not responsible for any adverse reactions to the recipes contained in this book.

SILENCED BY SYRAH

A Berkley Prime Crime Book / published by arrangement with the author

PRINTING HISTORY
Berkley Prime Crime mass-market edition / March 2007

Copyright © 2007 by Michele Scott.
Cover art by Cathy Gendron.
Cover design by Rita Frangie.
Interior text design by Stacy Irwin.

ISBN: 978-0-425-21452-7

BERKLEY® PRIME CRIME
Berkley Prime Crime Books are published by The Berkley Publishing Group,
a division of Penguin Group (USA) Inc.,
375 Hudson Street, New York, New York 10014.
The name BERKLEY PRIME CRIME and the BERKLEY PRIME CRIME design are trademarks belonging to Penguin Group (USA) Inc.

PRINTED IN THE UNITED STATES OF AMERICA

10 9 8 7 6 5 4 3 2 1

Chapter 1

Nikki Sands was going to die. She squirmed, knowing that her eyes were dark with fear. Her stomach tightened into a knot, making her feel like she was about to heave, as a barely audible sound escaped from her lips—like a faint cry for help. She did the only thing a woman in her position could. She smiled. The two men she had feelings for walked toward her: Derek Malveaux, her boss, and her maybe, kind of, boyfriend, Andrés Fernandez.

She snapped her attention back to the group of people in front of her, pouring another taste of wine for each of them and recommending a recipe for an appetizer that would match the wine. This time the wine was the Malveaux Estate Syrah, also known as Shiraz. "The nice thing about the Syrah grape," she said to some of the many people she'd spoken to that day, "is that it pairs well with just about every kind of food." She received nods and praises from the folks tasting the wines. "The chef has paired the Syrah with what is called a Pissaladiere, which is a French style white pizza. Feel free to take a copy of the recipe."

Nikki pointed to a pile of cards with various recipes

created for the day's event by the vineyard's chef, Georges Debussey. She tried hard not to look at Derek or Andrés, who had now joined the small audience. Hopefully the damn tremor in her voice was unnoticeable.

With voiced approval from the group, she finished up. "I'm sorry to say, ladies and gentlemen, that's all I have. If you would like to order any of the wines you've tasted here today, please go into the gift shop, where you'll find a table with the discount prices. We appreciate your coming out to Malveaux and hope you will enjoy the wines. If you'd like to go back and retaste any of today's wines, feel free; and don't forget, the spa and hotel are offering half-price packages this weekend for accommodations and services."

"And," Derek Malveaux added as he and Andrés neared the table, "remember that tonight is the opening of Georges on the Vineyard. We'll look forward to having you." He flashed his brilliant smile at them, his blue eyes lighting up his face.

The group walked through the courtyard of the new Malveaux Inn and Spa, set on the back forty of the Malveaux Estate and Winery where Derek, the owner of the vineyard, had been convinced by his brother Simon to build the mission-style boutique hotel and spa. They had been in operation for a little over a month now, but the opening of the restaurant had been behind schedule due to interior decorating conflicts.

Derek faced Nikki. "It looks to be going well," he said. "I ran into Andrés here and told him that I knew where you were." He gave Andrés a friendly, guy kind of pat on the shoulder.

Nikki smiled, knowing the quiver at the corner of her lips had to be giving her away. They're just men, not anything out of the norm here. But talk about opposites. And, because she was either weird, demented, or probably a combination, and truth be told it had been quite some time since she'd shared her bed with anyone—not that just anyone would do—she craved both of them. What the hell was wrong with her? Derek was as blond and golden as if he had leaped straight from a Tommy Bahama ad, and about the most down-to-earth man she'd ever met. Andrés, well, "luscious" would fit nicely. Passionate, artistic, sensually dark all the way to the brown, almost black eyes that the Spaniard, at that moment, had turned her way. Not good. How to weigh charming and grounded against luscious and creative? "Great. So you decided to stop by, then?" Nikki asked.

"I did. I want to be certain we were still planning on dinner *esta noche*. I couldn't reach you by cell, and I have to go take care of some business in the city for a couple of hours," Andrés said. "So, when I saw Derek finishing up a tour of the hotel, I asked him to help me find you."

"I had it turned off, my cell, because I'm working. I can't take calls when I'm doing a tasting." Did she sound like a dope or what? *Confidence. Exude confidence.* "Yes, yes. We are on for tonight. You betcha. I know it'll be wonderful. Georges Debussey is a master. I've eaten at his place in San Francisco, and the food is divine. And the cookbook he's been working on with Derek is going to be great." She looked at Derek. "I took notes on the wine information for the book. Georges is a little nutty." She shrugged. Right now she got the distinct feeling that she was looking a little cuckoo herself, rattling on and on, but she couldn't stop. She had to fill the air with something. "And the poor designer. I caught her walking to the car last week in tears because he wanted something different for the drapes and she just let it all go on me. Telling me she didn't think she could do it, and that her kid had been sick with the flu, and that she'd have to work overtime to get it all done. I thought she was going to kill him." *Take a breath.* "In fact, I have a meeting with Georges at the restaurant here in a little while, because I got a message that he wanted me to come into the kitchen and talk about the wines and what they would work with tonight. I just hope he doesn't yell at me. With that temper of his . . ." *Shut up. Shut up. For God's sakes quit rambling*. She realized both men were watching her as if she'd landed from another planet. She couldn't help wondering about it herself.

The band that Derek hired for the event started playing and saved Nikki. Ah yes, the fluted sounds of Peruvian music filled the air. She reminded herself to breathe again, and this time did so. "Pretty music."

"It is," Derek said and looked almost as uncomfortable as she felt. "Well, it's nice to have seen you, Andrés. It looks like you'll be here tonight, so I'm sure I'll get a chance to visit later on. Right now I need to see how things are running over at the spa."

Andrés shook Derek's hand. "Yes. Thank you for leading me to this beautiful woman."

Derek nodded at the two of them. "Nice work, Nikki. Thanks."

She watched him walk away. If that wasn't weird . . . Sure he was only her boss, but he'd also been her friend over the last couple of years since she'd come to work as the Malveaux Estate Winery manager, and his assistant. Then there were those moments when their eyes lingered a little too long on each other, or a joke told between them insinuated something. Something ever so slight, but it was there. Wasn't it? Could it all be a matter of hallucination on her part? Maybe Derek Malveaux simply enjoyed the art of flirting. She'd given him plenty of opportunities, and he hadn't grabbed one. But when she'd reached out to Andrés, he'd not only taken it, he'd run with it!

Andrés cleared his throat. "This looks to be going nicely. Are you having a good time?"

She shrugged. "It's work, you know."

"Uh-huh. And, Derek? He's only your boss?"

"What does that mean? Of course, he's only my boss."

She tossed back her hair, which lately she'd allowed to grow long and started coloring a medium brown. She'd done it at first for fun, but then had received a lot of compliments and also found that the old adage about blondes and brunettes was true. Blondes may have more fun, but she'd found in her case that as a brunette people seemed to take her more seriously, and she liked that. Blonde had also been *the look* she'd clung to when she lived in L.A., pursuing an acting career that flowed about as smoothly as a roller coaster ride, until she'd finally decided to get off and get a *real* job. Crossing her arms over her fitted striped blouse, she took a step back from Andrés. Now the job was stable, but the relationship stuff—another trip altogether.

"I'm sorry. He looks at you as if there is more there, and maybe I'm jealous."

She reached out and touched his shoulder. Strong shoulders and arms, the kind she liked wrapped around her—a man who worked the vineyard. Andrés was a winemaker down the road at Spaniard's Crest. "There is nothing between me and Derek. Nada. Nothing." There wasn't. A wink, a smile, typical flirtation, right? But nothing in terms of it meaning anything. "Okay?"

"Fine." He made an attempt at laughing. "It's my nature to be, uh, maybe protective, or as you might say in English I have a bit of that green-eyed monster lying within."

"Tell the monster to relax." She took his hand and squeezed it. "So, you're going into the city? Why?"

He looked down and then away from her. "Some business."

"What kind of business?" There was something he wasn't telling her. She could see it. She'd known him long enough to know that Andrés didn't lie well or hide things for that matter. In fact, his straightforwardness was one of the things she liked about him. They'd been friends before they'd ever decided to venture further into this new territory of dating. And, one day he'd laid it on the line for her, telling her that he had feelings for her and wanted to be with her. As much as there had been chemistry and flirtation with Derek, there had been honesty with Andrés. She'd decided to take a chance. And, so far so good.

"Nikki, yoo-hoo." Nikki glanced over to see Derek's

brother Simon waving at her from the corner of the courtyard. She waved back.

"He would drive me loco," Andrés said.

"He's sweet and harmless."

"If you say so, but he would still drive me loco," he re-
peated.

She stuck her index finger into his chest and gave it a
slight jab. "He's my friend. You be nice."

Andrés shook his head. "I have to go anyway. I'll see
you tonight."

"You're keeping something from me, aren't you? Your
business in the city, what's it about?"

He kissed her on the cheek. "We speak tonight. Go and
see your friend. He appears as if he is about to wet his
pants." He laughed.

Nikki glanced back over at Simon, who was doing some
kind of little dance. She figured it was to the Peruvian beat.
For a gay man, Simon had zero rhythm. He waved her over
and before she could stop Andrés from leaving and question him further, he headed out of the courtyard. She made
her way over to Simon.

"Hi, Goldilocks. I saw you over there talking to your
Spaniard. He is so divine." He puckered his lips and kissed
the air.

Nikki smacked him on the arm. Andrés *did* have a point
about Simon being annoying. The one thing about Derek's
brother was, even though she loved him and he'd become
one of her best friends in the last year, he really could be as
irritating as nails on a chalkboard at times. "Do you like
my new do? I think it's kind of Stingish. He's so sexy. I
bought his new album the other day. You should get it. It'll
put you in the mood."

Nikki rolled her eyes at him.

"Oh, oh, oh. Wait a minute. What is this? News flash!
No!" He ran his hand through his newly platinum spiked
locks and made a face. "You and the Spaniard *haven't* been
playing nasty, have you? What in God's name is wrong

with you? I would have had him swinging on a chandelier by now. My God, you've been seeing him for what, two months, at least? Goldilocks. I guess I can't call you that anymore. Hmmm, maybe Snow White. Oh God, why did you change your hair? It's totally ruined my nickname for you. Anyway, you need to get busy, girl. I hate to say it, but you aren't getting any younger and some other Miss Thing is gonna come along and get with it."

Yep. Just like nails down a chalkboard. "My sex life is none of your concern."

"Hmmm. I think it is. You need some lessons in love, Goldilocks. I'm still gonna call you that. Even with the dark hair thing going on, which I have to tell you *is* working. Really it is. So, vamp the rest of it up and let's get that love life in full swing. All you need is a pep talk and there are no two people better than me and my Marco to give you the facts of life on what men want and need." He shook a finger at her. "Oh yeah, baby. I know you have that innocent thing going for you with those green eyes, your flawless complexion—what do you use on that skin of yours anyway? And your knit sweater sets that add to the girl-next-door image have got to go, because I know lurking behind all of that fluff is a woman, a *W.O.M.A.N.*"

"Don't you have to go and give someone a spa treatment or something?"

"Oh God, no. I run the place. I don't do treatments. I do host the nine a.m. and four p.m. meditations, though. You should come. We can do a visualization thingy. The Guru Sansibaba says that anger is only pent-up sexual anxiety. Once you get in *touch* with that inner Goddess you'll be free. Free to fly like the wind, my friend," he sang out.

"I need a glass of wine. I told you I don't want to hear that Guru Sansibaba crap," Nikki replied. The Guru Sansibaba was a New Age kook that Simon and Marco found while on hiatus in Sedona, Arizona. They'd gone in as two materialistic, pompous gay men and had come out as two materialistic, pompous gay men who now believed they could balance people's chakras and spout New Age wisdom courtesy of their famous guru. Man, if she could ever get her hands around that freakazoid's neck . . . However, their return from Sedona prompted them to get more involved at the winery and vineyard, and they'd even come up with the idea of opening the hotel and spa on an area of land where the grapes didn't grow too well.

"You don't need wine, honey. You need to get busy with the Spaniard."

"Can we talk about this later?"

He sighed and looked at his watch. "I think we're going to have to. Marco has me scheduled for the grapeseed facial."

"Wait a minute, you're going to get a spa treatment while people are coming in and out of here like this is a zoo? I'm sure your help is needed."

He gave her a kiss on the cheek and squeezed her hand. "Oh Goldilocks, I tell you, it pays to be the boss. There are perks. And, to run a tight ship in the spa, which is my job, I should probably try out the treatments on a regular basis to make sure it's what we want here at the Malveaux Inn. See you at that meditation; we'll work through that pent-up angst." He winked at her.

Blah! Not just nails on a chalkboard, but the alarm clock on the nightstand at the crack of dawn, when Jose Cuervo was the best friend of choice the night before.

Another thought crossed Nikki's mind. Was Simon so annoying with his suggestions of taking her relationship to another level with Andrés because maybe he had a point? Was it time to give up her crush on Derek and take a leap with Andrés? Too much introspection to deal with at the moment. She had an eccentric chef to tend to. Hopefully, things were running smoothly at the restaurant and no one had pissed Georges off on opening day, or vice versa. Georges wasn't necessarily known for his couth, and already a handful of employees who'd originally been staffed at the restaurant had either been fired by Georges or had quit. Napa Valley was basically a small town in the scheme of things and Georges was quickly becoming the topic of choice for the gossip circles. It was one way to attract customers—come to Georges on the Vineyard and meet the quirky chef. Hmmm, one could cross her fingers and hope everything would go off without a hitch tonight, but the knot in the pit of Nikki's stomach told her it was doubtful.

Pissaladiere with Clos du Bois Shiraz

Hosting your own wine tasting can be a lot of fun. Nikki would say that the best tastings go well with friends. Invite a dozen friends and ask that each bring a bottle of wine. Suggest on the invites which varietals, so that you don't get a dozen Chardonnays. Also ask if everyone could bring an appetizer that they might pair with the wine. If your guests aren't sure what that might be, then do the homework for them. There are many sites online, including ones from the various wineries that also have recipe sections that make suggestions for the wines. Have each guest bring the dish and a copy of the recipe so that you all go home with twelve new fabulous recipes and wine pairings for future reference.

When hosting a wine tasting remind your guests to use all of their senses. In a well-lit room, hold your wine glass up to a white background. The color of the wine should be clear and intense, coming from the contact of the juice and grape during the wine-making process. Whites, depending on varietals, can be light green, clear, straw yellow, or gold with a slightly brown hue. Sweeter white wines start off with a deeper yellow.

Red wines may be purple, ruby, or blood red. As red wine ages, it will lose color and appear more brick brown. Blush wines like dry rosés or white zinfandels are pink.

For the special event at the Malveaux Inn and Spa, Nikki paired the Estate Syrah with a Pissaladiere, a.k.a. French-style, white pizza. Since Malveaux Estate Wines can only be found in Nikki's world, another she suggested trying with this recipe is Clos du Bois Shiraz. The Sonoma County Shiraz is a full-flavored wine that pairs well with a wide range of foods. It's reminiscent of the Australian Shiraz, with rich flavors of berries that include raspberry, blackberry, and a hint of blueberry. On the back palate the wine leaves the impression of spice, fennel, and black pepper.

     1 (6.5 oz) package "Alouette Garlic et Herbes"
     10- to 12-inch ready-made pizza crust
     1 medium sweet onion, thinly sliced
     6–12 Nicoise or black olives, pitted and sliced
     2 tsp olive oil
     1 tsp "Herbes de Provence" (or combine ¼ tsp each
         basil, rosemary, marjoram, savory, and thyme)
     1 tbsp grated Parmesan cheese

Preheat oven to 400°. Spread Alouette on pizza crust. Arrange onions and olives on top of cheese. Sprinkle with olive oil, herbs, and Parmesan. Bake for 10–15 minutes. Cut into 8 slices and serve immediately. Serves 4–6.

Chapter 2

Nikki walked through the lobby of the inn on her way to meet Georges at the restaurant. The inn resembled a Mediterranean villa with a central cloistered courtyard that served as a reception area, lounge, café, and wine bar. The rooms were mainly on the second story, all with sweeping views of the estate's vineyard. There were thirty rooms divided and located among three separate courtyards. The pathways at night were lit by candles on patio stakes, bouncing shadows off the sand-colored walls. To walk through the serene gardens and past the waterfalls throughout the courtyards was nothing less than spectacular.

A pianist played one of Norah Jones's hits in the golden lobby of the inn. Outside the lobby was a stone pathway that led up the hill to the restaurant. As Nikki entered Georges on the Vineyard, she caught sight of the view through the windows. The restaurant had been built on the hillside to take full advantage of the vistas a few hundred feet from the hotel. Patrons could hike the steep path up to the restaurant or choose to be chauffeured in one of the vineyard's golf carts. Nikki had chosen the hike, having missed out on her morning run. As she stepped into the foyer, she turned to look out at the view. She sighed. It never ceased to amaze her: the greens, golds, ambers, and shades of red and purple that took hold of the valley and brought it to life like an earth-toned rainbow, never to be duplicated by man's hand.

The clinging and clanging of pots and pans coming from the kitchen broke her reverie. She entered the kitchen to the scene of a half dozen men and women, their heads topped with chef beanies, working at a frantic pace chopping and dicing, and Georges Debussey yelling at all of them. *"No, no, noo!"* he hollered at a young woman at the pastry counter, who appeared to be blending cream. "Sacre bleu. You do not beat le crème? Where did you go to school? Are you an *imbecile*? I do not remember you. Did I hire you? Who are you?" The young woman looked up at him, her dark eyes brimming with tears. *"No, no, no.* Do not cry in my kitchen." He took the blender from her. "Like this. You do it like this. *Oui?"* He rolled his eyes.

"Yes, monsieur," the young woman said, and as what seemed to be an afterthought, "My name is Bridgette."

"Ah, well, Bridgette, you must do as I do in my kitchen. *Comprends?"*

"Yes, I understand," she replied.

Georges moved on and stood over a man rinsing dried porcini mushrooms. "Nice. *Bon.* Good. Those will be perfect in the *Daube de Boef aux Cèpes et à l'Orange."* He then turned and caught Nikki's eye. *"Mon Dieu.* Who do we have here?" He spread his arms out as if he'd just seen a long lost friend.

Nikki had learned that this was the way Georges greeted everyone. She'd become his "new best friend" after working with him on the cookbook he'd done in conjunction with Derek. Nikki's participation in the project had been to take notes for Derek about the vineyard, winery, and wines produced at Malveaux, compile them, write them out in text format, and pass them on to Georges, who then took the notes and fit them into the cookbook. It had been a fun project to work on and Nikki had discovered during it that writing was something she enjoyed. She'd had to meet with Georges at his restaurant in the city a few times in regard to the book, and although he'd always been a bit off the wall, he'd also been fun to be around. He always had a mischievous twinkle in his hazel eyes, even when scolding the underlings working for him. Right now that look was directed at Nikki. He licked his thin lips.

"It is so good to see you, Mademoiselle Nikki," he said, his French accent rolling off the end of each word.

She went to shake his hand. He took it and kissed it instead and tucked a piece of salt-and-pepper hair back into his ponytail, revealing a large diamond stud earring. Nikki found him sort of cute in a weird, over-fifty, eccentric, French chef kind of way. Maybe it was the dimples when he smiled, or that twinkle. Whatever it was, even with his offbeat behavior, she thought Georges charming.

"It is soo difficult to maintain control here. My partner is late. I will kill Baron when I see him. Never have an Irishman as your partner."

Nikki had only met Baron O'Grady twice before and he came off as the quintessential Irishman, brogue included.

"Baron is likely off drinking whiskey on the job," Georges continued. He waved a hand through the air. "Enough of that, though. Come on, you are here to tell me about the *vin* and I am here to look at those green eyes of yours. *Oui?*"

No. But whatever. He looked around. "Janie! Where is Janie?"

A young twentysomething woman walked around the corner. She was petite, pretty, with long blonde hair, huge blue eyes, and freckles dotting her nose that made her look childlike. She came up next to Georges. "I was making sure the escargot you ordered from the city had arrived."

"*Oui*. You have met my *assistant*, Janie Creswell. My angel from God."

"Oh Georges, don't lie to Nikki. I am not an angel."

Nikki smiled as the two of them laughed at the comment. "Nice to see you again, Janie."

Georges said, "You are an angel."

Nikki had not figured these two out yet. It was weird because they bantered back and forth and seemed to share a certain intimacy, but he still flirted with every other woman around, and Janie wore an engagement ring.

"Why don't we go into the bar and go over the wines for this evening?" Nikki said.

"*Oui*. Janie?"

"Right behind you," she replied, notebook in hand.

Nikki had never seen the girl without a notebook.

They entered the bar, elegantly painted in Tuscan tones of gold, champagne, sage, and burgundy. Malveaux Estate wines sat on glass shelving behind the bar, reflected in the mirror that covered the rear wall.

"You tell me about the *vin* and I tell you more about Georges," the chef said.

Nikki tried to laugh. Janie gave Georges a dirty look. "I am only teasing," Georges said.

"I'm sorry. He's incorrigible. I do try to keep him in line," Janie said.

"Keep me in line. *Blaspheme*. I do not need to be kept in line. I am a good boy. Very *bon*." He winked at Nikki.

Okay, robbing the cradle and trying to get two women in his bed.

"Georges," an attractive woman seated at one at the end of the bar called out.

"*Oui*, Lauren?"

"I have some questions. I'm meeting with Rick and we need to ask you a few things before we go forward on some of these campaigns. He'll be right back; he went to the men's room."

"Is that not why I hire you? To do the job? Get it done. You are the best. I have been told that. I was not lied to, was I?" he snipped. "I do not have time for questions now. Do your job. *Oui?*"

"That's true, but we are dealing with *your* money here, and Rick and I need some approvals, and he needs to show you a few things on the books. Can we get five minutes of your time?"

Georges sighed. "Come, Mademoiselle Nikki. Meet Madame Lauren Trump."

"No relation to The Donald," Lauren replied and stood to shake Nikki's hand. She had a firm handshake—all business. She wore a cream-colored suit and peach blouse, and had recently spent time in either a tanning booth, the sun, or in a spray-tan booth. She had silvered hair, cropped short in a pixie, and there weren't any visible lines on her face. Classic, elegant type of beauty. Either one helluva plastic surgeon or someone who aged really well, because she had to be in her fifties and it had nothing to do with the silvering of her hair, but rather there was a glint of wisdom in her eyes that reminded Nikki of Aunt Cara, who had raised her. The kind of glint that only comes from many years of living, loving, and learning. "Lauren Trump. I'm Georges' marketing director for his restaurant in the city and now I'm going to be doing some things here at the vineyard for this restaurant. I also work for Rothschild, Georges' publisher, but only on Georges' books."

"I see. Nice to meet you. I'm Nikki Sands, the winery's manager." A spicy, mandarin scent wafted her way. Must have been Lauren's perfume. Strong, but fitting for the woman.

"Fantastic. Maybe we can meet up soon and discuss some kind of campaign with the winery. I know you've been helping Mr. Malveaux with the notes on the book and passing them on to Georges. I think that's wonderful. I'm surprised we haven't met before. Granted Georges and I usually conduct our meetings in the city, but I'm certain

I'll be spending more time out here in the wine country seeing how Georges' new restaurant will be the hottest thing around." She turned to Georges and winked; he smiled and winked back at her.

"Absolutely. Give me a call." Nikki handed her a card. She knew when Derek had set out on this venture that the restaurant would be an almost separate entity. Sure it was in conjunction with the vineyard, but Derek and the rest of them had no clue how to run a restaurant. That was why he'd brought in Georges and his partner, Baron, and had given them control in that department.

"Oh, good afternoon, Mr. Debussey. I see Lauren got your attention."

A slight man walked into the restaurant, he, too, wearing business attire—a charcoal suit. His hair, the color of sand, was almost shade for shade the color of his skin. Quite a contrast to Lauren Trump's tan. He wore wire-rimmed glasses and as mean as Nikki knew the thought was, and as hard as she tried to shove it away, the word "nerd" popped into her mind. Knowing that was not nice, she stretched out her hand and introduced herself before Georges had a chance to.

"Hello," he replied. "I'm Rick Moran. Hello Ms. Creswell." He nodded at Janie, who briefly glanced up from her notebook to reply.

Funny how Ms. Trump hadn't even looked Janie's way, even though Janie stood behind Nikki, almost as if she were trying to hide.

"I'm Mr. Debussey's accountant," Mr. Moran added.

Accountant? Yep. That fit. Jeesh! She really had to stop thinking in terms of stereotypes.

"Rick, stop calling me Mr. Debussey. I am Georges. Now what is the problem?"

"Maybe it would be a good idea to discuss financial matters in private," Rick said and gave Nikki a half-hearted smile.

"Actually that's not a problem for me. Janie? Why don't

we go in the other room and talk about the wines together and you can fill Georges in?" Nikki suggested.

"Sure," she replied with cheerleader enthusiasm.

Georges sighed and faced Rick Moran. "Make this quick." He waved a hand at Janie and Nikki. "I will be with you in a moment. I am so sorry."

Nikki and Janie walked outside to the patio dining area. This place was definitely going to be a hit. Nikki breathed it all in. This was where she and Andrés would sit tonight, right out here. But would that be too romantic?

They had just sat down when Georges came outside.

"That *was* quick," Janie said.

"Bah. They did not need me to make the decision. Conservative." He looked at Nikki and smiled. "Accountants are *conservateurs*, and Lauren, she is not and I am not. I take *risque* and Lauren *comprends* this. Rick no. I make the *décision* that I know Lauren wants to hear and Rick, he will have to make the money work out. Nikki, Lauren will phone you next week. I want to have a grand campaign over the next few months and she thinks that we need to include the Château, as do I. You will discuss this with Derek, *oui*?"

"Sure." Nikki had learned Frenchlish over time. Most of Georges' words were easy to follow and she'd learned that Château was Georges' word for winery, as that is what they're called in France. "Is Lauren still here? I can maybe get some thoughts from her before I leave today and speak with Derek tomorrow."

"I told her to have a visit at the spa. Maybe tonight you will see her at the fete." He laughed. "I did not invite Monsieur Moran. He would not spend the money on a gourmet dinner, and I do not want to treat him."

"Georges, he's your financial advisor and accountant. Don't you think you should invite him tonight?" Janie suggested.

Georges rolled his eyes. "I am irritated with Monsieur Moran. He has made some errors as of late and I am considering replacing him anyway. Enough of that. Let us open a bottle of *vin*, and you tell me what we will *recommendons* for the soiree at Georges on the Vineyard."

"Actually, I thought we would do a tasting rather than having a bottle right now. You know, sample each one. I can give you my recommendations on what to pair the wine with and you can decide from there. Let me grab a spittoon. And get someone in the bar area to bring out the wines."

"Spit? I do not spit. *Je bois. Ouvre le vin.*"

Janie touched his hand. "Georges. It's a really big night. Maybe you should wait to start celebrating, you know."

It was then that Nikki noticed the addition to the ring on Janie's finger. Along with the small, delicate, not-even-one-carat diamond ring—but pretty and simple like the young woman—was now a gold band. Nikki also noticed Georges' eyes soften as Janie touched his hand. Wait a minute. Were they married? Janie had to be at least half his age.

"Fine. No *vin*." He patted her hand and smiled. "Mademoiselle Nikki, write down the list for me. I know the servers are versed in the *vin* already. If you look at my menu for the night, and tell me what to have the servers recommend, that is what I will do."

"Sure. I can do that. You don't want to do a tasting, then?"

"I cannot simply taste *vin*, mademoiselle. You tell me which to have the waiters *servirant*, and I *boirai* later." Georges looked at his Rolex. "Where is Baron? Janie, phone him!"

"Did ya call me name?" A round-shouldered man approached them. He wore a light green T-shirt that matched his eyes and a pair of jeans that met the T-shirt at the hem. His paunch of a belly showed through as he extended his hand to Nikki. "Nice to see ya again, Miss Sands. The Frenchy givin' ya fits?" Dark Irishman down to the brogue and black hair. "Lauren tole' me where I could find ya."

"Lauren is not gone, yet?" Georges asked. "I told her to go take a spa treatment."

"She was in the lobby in the hotel when I passed her

twenty or so minutes ago and she tole' me where ya were."
He blushed. "It took me that long to take the walk up here.
Phew, mighty steep that trail is."

"Where have you been?" Georges roared.

"I'm sorry, old man. Calm down and don't have yerself
a heart attack. Who would take care of ya if that happened?
Not me. I was on the telephone with me ma back on the
Emerald Isle. She's a wee bit lonely, today being her birthday and all and me pa gone now. I couldn't hang up with
her crying in me ear. Ye know."

"*Oui.* You and your *mère.* It is late. You are lucky I think
of you as my *ami.*"

"Oh yeah, mighty lucky to be yer friend. Ya should see
the way he treats those he don't care fer." Baron winked at
Nikki. "Listen Frenchy, why don't ya take a load off and
go for a spa treatment yerself like ya told me ya was gonna
do when we talked on the phone this mornin'."

"How could I go to the spa? You were not here. I had to
cook and watch over the imbeciles in the kitchen. Did you
hire that Bridgette? She does not know what she is doing."

Baron laughed. "I'm here now. Go on to the spa with ya.
Bridgette is fine and she's a good helper."

Georges let out something that sounded like a growl.
Janie smiled at him. She turned a page in her notebook.
"Baron is right. Take an hour to rest. You are scheduled for
one of those Syrah bath splashes at the spa. Between the
two of us and Nikki to help with the wine, we shouldn't
have any problems."

"Hmmm? *Oui.* I do love the baths at the spa—relaxing
and invigorating at once. I will go. Do not make mistakes.
I will have *no* mistakes." He took Nikki's hand again and
kissed it. "Mademoiselle, it has been nice to see you again.
Tonight you will dine on food meant for the kings and
queens." He nodded at Baron and Janie, and stood.

"I better get in the kitchen," Baron said. "Good day,
miss."

With the two men gone, Janie turned to Nikki. "He's a

handful. They both are. Oh God, working with them can drive me crazy, but they're really great. And together, well, they might fight but you know what, it works. They've been cooking together for years. They really love each other. The best of friends. Baron is the only one I've seen who can get away with any crap, except for me."

Nikki couldn't help but ask. The girl had opened the door, after all. "You and Georges are . . ."

"What?"

Nikki looked at the ring. Janie caught on. "Oh my God, no. Georges is like a father to me. I've worked with him for about a year. I'm married. Almost a month now." She blushed. "My husband is in law school in San Francisco. We're debating what we're going to do because he clerks for a firm there, and now with Georges opening the restaurant here, I don't know. I mean I'm the one making the money right now, so it's not like I can afford to lose the job. Plus, I really love it, you know? I mean it's totally cool but hard on me and Trevor. I don't know. He's coming to visit this weekend and we're gonna have to talk to Georges and see what he says."

What to say? Old standby. "Good luck. I'm sure it'll work out."

Maybe Lauren was Georges' lover? None of her business anyway. He was so intent on making certain that Lauren took time out for a spa treatment.

"I know. Georges is cool and Baron is the best. He's gonna run the restaurant in the city, so maybe I can go back and forth and help both of them. I don't know. Well look, I need to make sure the oysters are here and being refrigerated, and Georges wants only lilies on the tables, so I've got to check and make sure the florist will be on time. Do you think you can write up a list of those wines and leave it at the hostess' desk? I'll pick it up on my way out. The menu for tonight is right here." She flipped back a few pages in her notebook and took out a piece of paper with a handwritten menu on it. Some pages fell out. Nikki bent to

pick them up and hand them to Janie. She couldn't help notice that they included Georges' day-to-day schedule on
them for the past week, today included. "Jeesh, thanks. I
don't know what I'd do if I lost this. I keep track of both
my and Georges' schedules in here. I tried one of those
Day-Timer things, but they're so bulky and complicated. I
have my own system, but I don't know, maybe the spiral
notebook thing isn't the best idea. Look, I'd stay, but
there's still a ton to do."

"Not a problem. I can do this for you and Georges."

"Nice talking with you and thanks for the help. Georges
can sometimes drink too much and that would be bad for
tonight. So, it's good we didn't do a *tasting*. Besides, it
would have run into his bath time at the spa, which he kind
of needs. I'm really glad they're on the spa schedule. I've
arranged it with Simon for Georges to take a daily bath before coming into the restaurant in the evening. He will have
to meet with people since he's the chef, and sometimes, he,
well, he . . ." Janie wrinkled her nose.

Nikki stifled a laugh and held up her hand. "No need to
explain. I'm sure the Syrah bath splash will take care of
everything."

Janie nodded. "Thanks again for doing this."

The young woman walked out of the room and Nikki
sighed, sinking down in her chair. What a day. And it was
barely past two in the afternoon. She reflected on what had
already taken place. Derek-blue-eyes Malveaux had brought
Andrés out to find her. Andrés seemed to have something
to hide. Simon railed her and maybe nailed it on the head
when he'd told her she needed to get busy between the bed-
sheets. But she did have this three-month rule. Even though
she was thirty-five. Okay, thirty-six, but who's counting? A
girl still had to have some standards, even as that time
clock chimed on.

Boy, what a day. It really had been a strange afternoon in
a sense. Nikki couldn't completely figure out why she felt
that way. Probably the chain of events and all the *characters*

involved. But more so than feeling disjointed about the day, she couldn't help thinking of the evening to come. There was this itch prickling at the back of her neck, as if someone stood behind her whispering a secret—and the secret was not a good one.

Beef Daube with Porcini and Orange with St. Jean Cabernet Sauvignon

When life gets crazy, do as Nikki and the French do and fix a gourmet meal and have a bottle of *vin*. The recommended pairing for Beef Daube with Porcini and Orange is Chateau St. Jean 2002 Cabernet Sauvignon as it is similar to the bold reds of the Bordeaux region in France. The wine is an interesting, delicious blend of berries, black cherry, raisins, chocolate, and hazelnut. It's a complex wine with a satisfying finish. This is a wine to savor over an elegant dinner.

4½ lbs stewing beef, cut into large pieces
4 carrots, peeled and cut into rounds
3 medium onions, coarsely chopped
2 garlic cloves
1 sprig fresh parsley
1 celery rib, thickly sliced
3 bay leaves
1 tbsp fresh thyme (1 tsp dried)
¼ cup Cognac
1 bottle sturdy red wine
¼ cup plus 1 tbsp extra-virgin olive oil
1 tsp whole black peppercorns
3 whole cloves
3 tbsp unsalted butter
2 oz dried cèpes, soaked and well-rinsed (Cèpes are a type of wild mushroom and can usually be found in gourmet grocery stores or in the specialty aisle at your local supermarket.)
1 tbsp tomato paste
salt and pepper
grated zest and juice of 1 orange

One day before serving the stew, in a large bowl, combine meat, carrots, onions, garlic, parsley, celery, bay leaves, thyme, Cognac, wine, and 1 tbsp olive oil. Tie peppercorn and cloves in a piece of cheesecloth; add to the bowl, toss well, cover, and refrigerate 24 hours. Let meat and vegetables return to room temperature. Remove meat from marinade. Set vegetables aside. Transfer liquid and cheesecloth bag to a large pot. Bring to a boil over medium-high heat. Boil for 5 minutes to reduce slightly. Remove from heat. In large skillet, melt butter and ¼ cup olive oil. Brown meat on all sides; with slotted spoon transfer meat to the liquid in the pot. In the same skillet, sauté the vegetables about 7 minutes and transfer them to the pot. Add mushrooms to the skillet and sauté about 5 minutes; set aside. Stir tomato paste into pot. Bring to a simmer and cook meat until very tender over very low heat, about 3½ to 4 hours. Stir in salt and pepper to taste, mushrooms, and the orange zest and juice. Discard cheesecloth bag. Serves 8.

Part II to hosting your own wine tasting party—smell. Yep, if it don't smell good, don't drink it! That's what Nikki would say. She'd also tell you how to smell the wine. Swirl the glass to release the bouquet. The bouquet refers to the odors that are the result of the wine-making decisions made on blending, alcohol content, and so forth. The aroma is the odor that is associated with the grape's varietal used in the wine. As the wine clings to the glass, more aromas are released. As you take in the bouquet, what is the first thing you think of? Pears, tobacco, grapefruit, leather, bacon, melons . . . the list can go on. Much of it is in the impression of the wine lover—as in the eye of the beholder. Cheers!

Chapter 3

Four thirty and Nikki's day finally had that wind-down feeling to it. The festivities of that Saturday had come to a halt, and the sun cast shadows across the vineyards, giving the valley an ethereal quality. Heaven on Earth.

The spa remained open but would close soon, and the opening of Georges on the Vineyard would be in full swing within less than two hours. She needed to hustle back to her cottage to get ready to meet Andrés. She decided to first stop by the spa and see how things were going for Simon and Marco.

Marco stood at the front desk singing with Andrea Bocelli over the speakers in the spa's lobby, which continued, like other areas of the inn, the traditional, rustic Italian theme. Marco's voice was almost as beautiful as Bocelli's, and she could've listened for hours.

Marco smiled when he saw her. "*Bellisima*. How are you?" His Italian accent was as melodic as the music.

"Good. Long day. How about you?"

He sighed. "It is hard to do the spa. People can be difficult. 'I want this.' 'I want that.' 'That cream the therapist put on my face is much too oily.' I say I am sorry. I give more of a discount. Ah!" He waved his hand in indifference. "It is a problem to make people, how you say? *Lieto*. Happy. *Sí*."

She laughed. "Yes, I'm sure it can be difficult. What about what you learned from the Guru Sansibaba? Wouldn't he have something to say about relaxing under stress?"

He frowned. "Thank you for reminding me." He came around the counter to give her a kiss on the cheek. He smelled of lemon verbena and clove. His light green silk shirt made his olive skin appear almost golden. "You look beautiful today. I am thinking you know that." His dark eyes, the color of espresso, sparkled.

What a flirt. "No. But, thank you. You always know exactly what to say to a girl. I feel frazzled." She went on to tell him about her day, knowing that she could trust him. Simon was not nearly as trustworthy. She'd tell him something and he always blabbed it, even though she knew his intentions were usually good. But Marco knew how to keep a secret. He'd told her that discretion meant everything with friendships, and he'd held to that.

"It is hard to love two men," he said.

"Whoa, slow down. I do not love two men. I don't even love one man. I . . . oh crap, I don't know."

He took her hand and they walked outside into the garden area, where a water fountain sprinkled crystalline droplets onto the Saltillo tiles, and jasmine crept up a trellis, casting its heady fragrance throughout the area. Nikki breathed it in. Shadows of the vines on the trellis danced on the tiled ground as the descending rays of sunlight splashed through the courtyard. They sat down on one of the benches under an orange blossom tree. "What you have to do is find out why you can not or do not want to love either of these men. Have you considered the possibility that you love them both, but you are too afraid to admit that? Loving one may be frightening enough, but if you love two, you will terrify yourself in such a way that you may not have either one."

She sighed. "Love? That's so huge, and I don't know if I've ever been in love. I know I *want* to be in love. I think I do, but there are so many complications. Derek is so good-looking and grounded. He's smart and witty, very thoughtful of his employees, friends, everyone."

"Derek is a good man. I know there is some chemistry there. I can see it when the two of you are together. Simon and I have spoken of it."

"Yeah, I know." The two of them had tried hard to play matchmaker, but it had never panned out. "But, then there's Andrés."

"*Sí.* There is Andrés. Beautiful man."

She nodded. "I know. And he's crazy, as in fun crazy. I mean, we have so much fun. We go to art exhibits. We take hikes. We play together, you know, and he's got a joy for life." She sighed and, clasping her hands together in a fist brought them to her chest. "Sometimes maybe too much. He can almost be exhausting." She looked down at the tiles. "I know he wants a family and I think I want that, too, and he is so passionate. So alive."

He took her hands and uncurled them. "It frightens you, *bellisima.* You are afraid to let go with him because it is that intense. You find Derek safer and that is why you stay attracted to him. But you cannot have someone to love who is so safe that he cannot let go of whatever pains himself inside. Do you not see? You cannot love Andrés because his passion is a fire burning out of control and you need to maintain it to feel safe in loving him. Derek sees you that same way. A vicious circle."

"You're good. I think. I don't know if I like what you're saying, because that's not exactly an answer and I want an answer."

"Do not live life, as you Americans would say, half-assed. Live it with passion."

"Something the Guru Sansibaba would say?"

"No. Something I would say. I can only do so much as

your friend, Nikki. Your heart must do the rest." He tapped his chest. "You will know what man you want."

"Thanks. Thanks a lot. So, in your opinion, which of these men has my heart?"

Before Marco could answer, Simon came running into the garden. "Oh, oh, oh." He was out of breath. "There you are. I need help now. Come on, Goldilocks." He grabbed her hand and started to drag her. "Marco come on. You too."

"What is going on?" Nikki asked as she followed him inside the spa and down the hall to the treatment rooms.

Simon pointed at one of the doors that had a plaque on it reading, Vineyard Bath. "He has been in there for an hour. He was supposed to come out twenty minutes ago. Charlotte, who has been giving him the treatment, can't get an answer from him."

"Who?" Nikki asked.

"Georges Debussey. You know him. Right?"

"Yeah. So? We all know him. He's been coming over here for months getting the restaurant ready."

"Exactly. But now he's in there taking a Syrah bath splash and he won't come out."

"What do you mean he won't come out?" Nikki asked.

"I've knocked. Charlotte has knocked. I even went outside and yelled up at him. I'm sure the French doors were open."

"You couldn't tell if they were?" Nikki asked.

"No. Not without climbing up a hill over there and using a pair of binoculars," Simon replied.

The bath area had been set up to be extremely private. It was at the end of the spa, and the room was the only one built onto the second story, with French doors that opened out onto the vineyard so that the bather could take in the view while bathing. No one could see in, as the bath room was on a separate level and also situated remotely.

"His assistant and his partner have been calling, saying

that he's needed in the kitchen," Simon continued. "But he won't answer. I think he's asleep. He did take a glass of wine in there with him."

"This is not good," Marco said. "He could drown in the tub."

"I don't think so, love. He's a pretty big man and even if he did drink that glass of wine, it wouldn't be enough to get him so schnockered that he wouldn't know if he went under. He's asleep, or he has the earphones on and is listening to music. I think he's lost track of time. Go in and get him, Nikki."

"Me? Why me?"

"Duh. He's naked."

"Okay. But you are a man and you have seen naked men before. So what is the big deal?"

Simon looked away. "Tell her."

Marco shook his head. "You tell her."

"No," Simon replied.

"Yes."

"Tell me what?" Nikki asked.

"I don't like nakedness. It freaks me out," Simon blurted.

"What?" Nikki tried not to laugh.

"He cannot look at a naked body."

"Oh please," Nikki said.

Simon gave her a dirty look. "We all have our issues."

Nikki clucked her tongue. "Wait a minute, that's why you don't give the treatments."

Simon nodded.

"And, can I ask you two something? Don't you see each other naked?"

They both shook their heads. "Lights off. Always," Marco answered.

"What about you? Are you afraid of nakedness?"

Marco shrugged. "What can I tell you? Simon and I met at a circle."

"He means group therapy," Simon interrupted.

"*Sí.*"

"I thought you met at a fashion show," Nikki said.

"We've always told a lie about how we really met. It is called nudophobia. The thing that we have. The, uh, issue," Simon replied.

"Oh my God. I wonder what the Guru Sansibaba would say." She looked at Marco and placed her hands on her hips. "Crazy. And, weren't you the one who just told me to go out and live my life with passion? You two are nuts."

Simon's cell rang. He looked at the incoming call. "It's that Janie girl again. Shit."

"Give me the key. We'll talk about this later." Nikki grabbed it from Simon's hand and unlocked the door.

She walked inside the room, which was lit by candles. It looked like a pile of towels was bundled up in the corner by the French doors, which were closed, making the room quite dark. She could see the back of Georges' head. "Georges?" Nothing. "Um, Georges? Time to go. Wake up." She clapped her hands. "Big night, my friend. You're late." No reply. She took another step closer and saw that Georges had dropped what looked to be an almost full glass of red wine on the floor. Maybe he'd grabbed a bottle of the wine he'd wanted so badly at the restaurant before coming over to the spa and gone ahead with a precelebration. "Georges, let's go. Hustle. Move out. Wake up. Alrighty, then."

Just reach out and shake him on the shoulder. No biggie. It's only a naked man in a bathtub. That's all. It's not as if she'd never seen a naked man before. Well, it had been some time. But it wasn't like her two pals, who had nakedness phobia. What a weird thing. Nudophobia? Please! Who knew there was such a thing? *Take a step closer*. There are bubbles. That was a good thing. A naked man in bubbles. All she had to do was tap on his shoulder, shake him a bit maybe. "Georges," she said louder.

"What's he doing, Nikki?" Simon asked from behind the door.

"I don't know. He's sleeping."

"Wake him up," Marco said.

"I'm trying." *Just go for it. If his* thingy *comes into view, well, it is only an appendage. Right? Yes.* Nikki walked around to the front of Georges. Oh, no. "Georges?" she said, only this time her voice was small and came out sounding distant, almost outside of herself. But she knew he wouldn't be answering. She closed her eyes and blinked a few times to try and focus, to see if what she was viewing was real. It was.

She ran out of the room, bile burning the back of her throat. Simon caught her as she started to sink to the floor. "Goldilocks? Honey? What is it?"

She faced her friends and somehow choked out the words. "He's not asleep. He's been shot to death."

Pampering and Sofia Rosé

Everyone deserves a little pampering at times, and one of the nicest things Marco might suggest doing for yourself or a loved one is running a grapeseed bath. Grapeseed oil can be found at many grocery stores and in your local health food market. Add a couple of tablespoons to your bath with your favorite aromatherapy oil—lavender for relaxing, grapefruit for revitalizing, and ylang-ylang for a little boost in the love life department. Pour yourself a nice cool glass of rosé and enjoy the softening properties of grapeseed. One of Nikki's favorite rosés comes from the Niebaum-Coppola Winery. It is the Sofia Rosé, which is perfect for enjoying while taking a grapeseed bath on a summer day. The wine is delicate and sensual, at the same time being dry in style yet refreshing and juicy, making it a romantic, versatile wine.

Chapter 4

It was Marco who dialed 911. Simon paced across the slate tiles that covered the spa floors, completely beside himself, and it was Nikki who had to pull him together.

"Stop this. Stop it," Nikki told him. "We need to sit down and relax. You could be contaminating evidence."

Simon halted and gave her a hard stare, hands on hips. "Oh my God. There was a murderer here. Walking the hall. What if he's still here? What if he comes and kills all of us? Oh, shit. We have to get out of here now. We have to get everyone off the vineyard and out of here. He could be lurking, waiting to attack his next victim."

Nikki placed a hand on his shoulder and almost forcefully pushed him down atop the waiting area's purple velvet sofa. "The murderer is probably long gone. The spa isn't huge. There are what, ten treatment rooms and a locker area? Anyway, my guess is that whoever killed Georges didn't travel through the spa. The French doors leading to the verandah were closed, but I'll bet that's how the killer got in."

"Then he'd have to have a key to the place," Simon said.

"Not necessarily. I know that Georges has been here a few times in the bath treatment. Do you know if he usually keeps the doors open?" Nikki asked.

Simon and Marco shrugged. "It is hard to say," Marco said.

"Okay, but the bath treatment room was located where it is and on the second floor for a reason. When you guys designed it, it was with the mindset that whoever was in there taking a bath could keep the doors open and look out on the vineyard," Nikki said.

"That is true," Simon replied.

"Okay, so that's established. I'll bet that the doors were opened by Georges when he first settled into the bath. Maybe Charlotte knows. She might have opened them herself."

"She is gone for the day," Marco answered. "She left saying that she had another commitment and that she'd stayed overtime waiting for Mr. Debussey. I couldn't stop her. I told her to go and that we would manage taking care of Mr. Debussey."

"How do you think the killer got in? There's no staircase leading up there, and to go through the spa, someone would have likely seen him or her," Simon said.

"I'm not sure," Nikki replied. "There's a trellis out there. I don't know. The police will figure it out I'm sure. But I don't think you need to worry, Simon. It's unlikely that whoever killed Georges is a serial killer."

"How do you know?" Simon asked.

Marco had gone and retrieved a bottle of Zinfandel. He brought back three glasses and was behind the counter uncorking the bottle. They all needed something to calm the nerves. Nikki doubted the liquid grape would do the trick. Not after what she'd seen. A tranquilizer, maybe, but a glass of red wine? Doubtful. Besides what the hell kind of wine could be paired with murder? Oh, brother, she was losing it, to even think such a bizarre thought at a time like this.

Nikki fiddled with her pearl earring, twisting it as she spoke. "I know because of my aunt. She's a former homicide detective with the LAPD." Nikki glanced over at Marco. "As much as I know everyone would care for a glass of wine, we probably should hold off on it, Marco. The police will take note of that."

Simon sucked in a deep breath. "Right. The cop, your aunt. The one who raised you. Oh, no! And, *the* cops will be here." He put his face in his palms and shook. "This isn't good. We were all here. What if they think one of us did it?"

Nikki placed a hand on his back. "They'll question us, but we all know none of us did it. I know enough about investigations to guess that the police won't be targeting us. We barely knew Georges. I mean, I suppose out of the three of us, I knew him the best. But when it comes to killers, Aunt Cara filled me in, and from what I remember, when someone is, um, shot"—she gulped—"in the head like that, it is usually a crime of passion, and God knows, I liked Georges fine, but trust me fellas, there was no passion going on there."

Two uniformed deputy sheriffs entered the spa. Nikki glanced at Simon. Oh no. He was going to cry. His blue eyes were as big as saucers. She nudged Marco, who took notice of his partner's trembling lip and grabbed his hand. Simon sighed and sucked back his emotion.

"We received a 911 call."

Nikki stood and walked over to the deputies. She told them what she'd discovered and where they could find the body. They told her to have a seat. It wasn't long before she heard their radios from down the hall confirming her report, and it didn't take much longer for more sheriff's deputies to come rolling in, along with what had to be the detective on the case.

Talk about Mr. Cool. Wow! The detective coming through the front doors didn't take his dark sunglasses off until after speaking with one of the deputies and making his way over to the three of them, still seated and not saying a word, as they'd been instructed. One of the larger, more intimidating of the deputies had been babysitting them, and they weren't about to move.

The detective didn't just walk on over, he had a kind of rock-star strut. Yeah, definitely. He looked to be about six feet, maybe fortysomething, and all muscle, showing through his fitted T-shirt underneath a caramel-colored suede coat and a pair of—well, only one way of putting it—ass huggin' jeans. When he took off his glasses, his eyes were the color of jade, intensely contrasted by his mulatto coloring. He was Lenny Kravitz and Matthew McConaughey all rolled into one. Nikki was sure she heard both of her gay friends gasp. She herself felt a bit winded.

"Miss, gentlemen, I'm Detective Jonah Robinson of the Santa Rosa Sheriff's Department."

No one said anything for a few seconds, as if in awe of the detective. Nikki finally spoke up. "Hello, um, I'm Nikki Sands and this is Marco Contiello and Simon Malveaux. They run the spa here."

"Miss Sands, you found the body?" he asked in a gravelly, low voice.

"Yes. That's correct."

"Okay. Here's what we need to do. Miss Sands, why don't you come with me outside here, and answer some questions." He looked at Goliath, still standing guard. "Deputy, talk with Mr. Malveaux here and I'll have Detective DeVoe in to speak with Mr. Contiello. I'll also need a list of everyone who works at the spa, the names and places where the guests who were here today can be located, and we'll have to get all employees here at the hotel and on the vineyard into the station for interviews. I will walk the grid after I speak with Ms. Sands. Rope off the area outside the room as well as inside the spa."

"I can get you those names," Simon chimed in.

"Good. Was there anyone else in the spa that you know of when the body was discovered?"

"No," Marco replied. "Charlotte, the therapist who ran Mr. Debussey's bath, waited awhile, but finally left when he didn't get out. She said that she had to leave for a prior commitment."

"I'll need her statement," Detective Robinson replied. "Along with all of the other information I mentioned. Miss Sands." He put his sunglasses back on. "Follow me, please."

They stepped outside the spa and walked around the length of the pool. The place that only hours earlier had bustled with guests was empty, no one lingering there.

They walked past the steam room and the cascading waterfall connected to a large water wheel that continually spun around, giving the area a rustic look. Nikki followed him back to the open garden area where guests would normally come to eat breakfast, read a book, or linger over a glass of wine while waiting for their spa treatments. Now, the place was deserted. In the back of Nikki's mind, she couldn't help wondering about what might be going on over at the restaurant. Certainly the police were there as well.

"Have a seat." He motioned to one of the wrought iron chairs next to the outdoor fireplace. She did as he asked. He sat down across from her and crossed his legs, leaning back in his chair, his "all business" demeanor now more relaxed. Maybe this was his game. She knew all about the various tactics cops used, from Aunt Cara. Detective Robinson probably liked to get his "suspects" comfortable by appearing relaxed, nonthreatening. Nikki knew it often worked. Many times Aunt Cara had told her that a perp would screw up just as he got relaxed and tired enough with the chitchat he or she was having with the interviewing cop. Thing was,

Robinson didn't need to make Nikki comfortable. She'd only found Georges, not murdered him. "I've heard about you," Robinson said.

Now, that was a new and different tactic. It almost sounded like a pickup line. "Really? And, why is that?"

"You're the lady they call Napa's Nancy Drew."

"Funny." She crossed her arms.

"Right. You know, since I've heard of you and know all about your little hobby, I'm gonna ask you to mind your business on this one. I'm not a small-town cop, Miss Sands. I worked the streets in Houston and I don't want you getting involved in playing your sleuthing game. You might wind up in some serious trouble if you start messing behind the scenes with my case."

"Excuse me?" Wait, wait. Shouldn't he be asking questions about the murder instead of giving her grief? Hell, how did he know she *didn't* do it—Mr. Big Time Cop, from Houston. "Is that a threat? What do you mean, wind up in serious trouble? I didn't do a damn thing."

"Take it as this: you've been warned. Now, why don't you go on and tell me how you found Mr. Debussey and what you know about the vic. I know you know the lingo, 'cause like I said, I know about you."

A shiver didn't just slither down her spine but crept like a spider ready to bite. She shifted in her chair. Had this pompous ass of a detective threatened her?

He took off his sunglasses and stared at her with those icy eyes—no longer the color of jade—until she started talking. She told him everything she knew. How she discovered Georges. How she'd been to see him earlier in the day to discuss the wine list, and how she thought Georges Debussey was a decent guy if a bit eccentric, even a hothead at times.

"Nothing else you can tell me then?" Detective Robinson asked for the sixth time. "About his friends, who his lovers might have been, his business partners? Come on, you said that you dealt with him, you must know something more about the man. Obviously Derek Malveaux had gone into business with him by bringing him here to open his restaurant. Did they get along?"

"Who doesn't Derek get along with? Of course they did." She tightened her arms around herself. She didn't tell Robinson about the book Derek and Georges worked on together, or for that matter, her part in writing the notes and putting them in order. If he was such a big-time detective, let him figure it out. It wasn't as if it would have anything to do with the murder anyway. "As far as I knew, the partnership between them was smooth sailing. Derek gave Georges carte blanche with the restaurant. Basically, Derek fronted the money to have the restaurant and the rest of the resort area built. Georges paid rent on the restaurant and used his name for promotion. I know that Simon and Marco also have the same arrangement with Derek in regard to the hotel and spa. Derek runs the winery and vineyard. He stays involved, but he knows that the people working for him, like Georges, were . . . are competent. I never heard of any hassles between them."

"Uh-huh. And, what about Simon Malveaux and his friend, Marco Contiello?" He uncrossed his legs and leaned in, as if ready to force some hard information.

Nikki wished he'd put his glasses back on. Those eyes had gone from mesmerizing to disconcerting. "They didn't have much contact with Georges. I mean, the restaurant, as you've seen, is a separate entity from the hotel and spa. Georges did his thing. Simon and Marco theirs. Simon runs the spa. Marco oversees the hotel operations. I believe the only contact they have with the restaurant is making reservations for guests."

"How many rooms are in the hotel and also in the spa?" he asked.

"Thirty rooms in the hotel, and ten treatment rooms in the spa, along with a locker room," Nikki replied.

"The hotel is at full capacity this weekend, I assume?"

"Yes. Well, I did hear that one couple didn't make it because they missed their flight and were due in tomorrow, and another couple left because of a family emergency. So there are twenty-eight rooms occupied."

"Are they all couples?"

"I wouldn't know. You'd have to ask Marco. I do know there are no children. That's the policy."

"Gotcha." He winked at her.

Or was that something caught in his eye? Did he actually wink? Nah.

"And as for you? Any problems with Mr. Debussey?"

"No."

He went over all of it again until Nikki wanted to scream at him and pull her hair out.

"All right. I think we're done for now. But I know where to find you, and I know you know the protocol. Stay close to home. We may need to talk again. Soon."

"Sure."

Detective Robinson stood up and started back toward the spa. He turned around before he reached the corner, and put on his glasses. "Remember what I told you. Your name is Nikki, not Nancy. I hope you really told me all that you know."

She smiled at him. A sarcastic smile, to be sure, but a smile. Okay, so maybe there were a few things that slipped her mind when speaking with Detective Robinson. Like the fact that she was wondering about how close Janie and Georges were, and the nature of the relationship between Georges and Lauren—if it really was all just business. Oh, and there was also another small tidbit tucked back in her memory that she hadn't mentioned to Robinson. The designer who'd tried so hard to make the restaurant look like a Tuscan villa and who Nikki thought only a week ago could snap under Georges' pressure. *Had she?* Hey, if Detective Robinson was such a big-city cop and *with* it, then he'd find out all of this info on his own. Nikki would've freely given it up, but one thing a man—any man—should never say to a woman is, mind your own business. *Please. I'll mind my own business like an old woman with new neighbors next door.*

Chapter 5

Nikki walked up her front porch steps to find Andrés seated on her wicker outdoor sofa with Ollie, the vineyard Rhodesian Ridgeback, lying at his feet. Well, in reality Ollie had been Derek's dog, until Nikki had come on board. Now the dog spent his time between master and mistress. The caramel-colored beast thumped his tail at the sight of her, and Andrés stood. He walked over to her and pulled her close. "I heard about what happened. When I tried to come onto the vineyard tonight to meet you for dinner, the police had everything roped off."

"How did you get in then?"

"Derek was down near the entrance with the police and he told them I was okay. They let me in and I've been here waiting for you."

Derek had let him in? She pulled away from Andrés and yawned. "It's been a long day. You shouldn't have waited."

He took her hand and led her to the sofa. She sat down and found a bottle of Pinot Noir on the coffee table in front of her, along with a plate of food. Her stomach growled. Andrés laughed, and she cracked a smile.

"That's why I waited. We had dinner plans, and I had a feeling that you'd be starving when I finally saw you."

She hadn't realized it until now, but she *was* starving. "What is all this?"

"I put together some Thai chicken wraps, a little ceviche, and some Spanish cheeses I had sent to me from friends in Spain. I know it's a strange mix, but it's a warm night, and once I knew what was going on here, I headed back to my place to pick up our supper. I'd been marinating the ceviche for a day, had the chicken and cheeses in my refrigerator, and knew that you of all people would have the lettuce for the wraps. I didn't think you'd mind me getting into the refrigerator."

He was right. Salad didn't stick to the hips like her favorites—bread and cheese—so she made it a practice of stocking the fridge with rabbit food versus fun food. "How did you get in?"

He smiled. "You are not particularly cautious about where you hide your front door key. Come on, I thought for sure it would take me at least five minutes because I know what a smart woman you are. But"—he held a finger up—"in this case, not so smart."

"What?"

"That's right. Under the front doormat? What would your aunt Cara say?"

"I get your point. I'll be sure to put it under a flowerpot next time." They both laughed and the release of tension from the day felt good as it dissipated into the warm, musty air. Nikki could see Derek's lights on across the pond that separated their two cottages. How was he doing? And, Simon and Marco? She'd wanted to call all of them and ask them to come over to be with her. At a time like this a woman needed her pals. Then, she looked at Andrés, his eyes lit by the candlelight from the table as he poured her a glass of the Pinot, and decided that sometimes a woman just needed one man.

They drank their wine and ate the wonderful food Andrés

had made. She told him the horror of the day from pretty much the beginning to the end, sans the gut-wrenching feeling that welled up in her when she'd spotted him and Derek together. But everything else, including Detective Robinson and his weird behavior.

"He does have a point, Nikki," Andrés said. "You do seem to get yourself mixed up in these things and it worries me. Maybe you should listen to the detective."

She set down her dessert, a churro, which Andrés had also brought with him—her favorite dessert. "You're not siding with him, are you?"

He touched the side of her mouth with a finger. "You have some sugar there. And, no, I'm not siding with the detective, but I don't want you to get into this murder case. I think you should let the police handle it. I don't want you getting hurt."

Stubborn hairs stuck up on the back of her neck. "I'm not going to get hurt."

He set his wine glass down next to hers and caressed her face with one hand. That started to melt the freeze that had come over her seconds before, when her defenses had gone up. He then kissed her gently on the corner of her mouth. "You still had some sugar there."

"Mhhm. I did?"

"Yeah, and here, too." He kissed her lips. Her body warmed. "Yummy."

"Yeah," she said almost breathless, when he pulled away.

"I have something to tell you."

She sat up. Uh-oh. "Okay. But wait, weren't we just kissing? Do we have to talk now?" She giggled.

"Yes, but this is on my mind, and especially with what happened here today, I want to talk to you about it now."

Hmmm. "All right. What's this about?"

"You know the business I had in the city today?" he asked.

"Yes."

"I was meeting with my financial advisor, and I've built a bit of cash flow. Quite a bit, and I've invested in a vineyard."

"You have? Wow. That's wonderful. Where is it? Here in Napa, or Sonoma, or wait, did you find something up in Healdsburg? I know you love that area."

He took her hands. "I don't have quite that much to invest, Nikki. My vineyard is back in Spain." His hands tightened around hers.

"Oh. Well, that's great. Spain is your homeland, and I know you still love it, and you know the people there who can grow your grapes and manage the vineyard. I think that's wonderful!"

"*Sí*. I do know the people who can help, but I need to go back for a while, and make sure things are operating smoothly and are underway."

She slumped into the sofa. "Oh." She tucked back a piece of stray hair that had fallen out of the ponytail she'd tied earlier. "For how long are you going back? When?"

"Probably six months. I'd like to see the first planting done, and make certain I have the right people for the job there. I didn't plan to go until next month, but I need to settle some of the transactions with the bank in Spain and I have to be present to do that. I'm leaving Saturday."

"You're what? That's only a week away. What about Spaniard's Crest?"

"I have an excellent assistant. You've met Samuel. He can handle it while I'm gone. And, the staff knows what needs to be done."

"So, you'll be back?" Her heart raced.

"Of course. As I said. I haven't made retirement money. Spaniard's Crest pays well, and when I do go back to Spain I'll have the recognition here in America to promote my wines from Spain. I'm hoping my employers at Spaniard's Crest will want to do a joint effort with the wines."

"Then you plan on eventually moving back to Spain?" Not only was her heart racing, but she could hear the blood flowing through her ears, as if trying to drown out his words. He nodded slowly. "What about Isabel?" Nikki asked, referring to his sister, one of her closest friends, who lived in Yountville a few miles away and owned the five-star restaurant Grapes.

"My sister is independent now. She doesn't always need a big brother hovering over her. You've heard her tell me that over and over. Besides, I won't be leaving for Spain for good for two or more years. You know as well as I do that it takes vines several years to produce wine-making grapes, and it'll take another couple of years to get our first vintage. Sure I'll have to go back and forth to make certain things are running right. But my loyalties for now remain at Spaniard's Crest."

"Oh." It was all she could think of to say.

"Nikki, I want you to come to Spain with me for the next six months."

"What? I can't do that. My job. It's here."

"I know. I spoke with Derek today, this morning before everything happened, and told him I wanted to ask you to come with me, but that I knew what this job meant to you. He said that he felt he could spare you for six months and that you would always have a job here. He won't replace you."

"He told you what? You did *what*? Wait." She stood up and crossed her arms.

"What's the matter? I thought I was doing the right thing. I want you to come with me, and I thought you would want that, and so I spoke to Derek."

"To get his permission, like he's my father? Did either one of you factor me into this? What I might want or think?"

"That's why I'm asking you now." Andrés stood and walked over to her. She moved away from him and turned her back to him. He moved in again and placed a hand on her shoulder. "Nikki, I'm falling in love with you. I am not afraid to tell you that. We have been friends for some time now, and dating for almost three months."

"Two."

"Three."

Had it been that long?

"I want to take our relationship further," he continued.

"No. You want to take me to Spain."

"Yes. I do. I want to show you my culture. Where I'm from. My dreams. I want you to be a part of those dreams. Won't you come with me?"

She turned around to face him. Hot tears burned her eyes. She didn't even quite understand what they were all about. All she could say was, "I don't know."

He shrugged. "At least it's not a no. I'm sorry I went behind your back to talk with Derek. I wanted to surprise you, have everything taken care of."

Her tone softened. "Andrés, I don't need anyone to take care of everything for me. I actually like doing things on my own, for myself. And, talking to Derek about a decision like this would have been one of them." It bothered her that Andrés had done this. What were his motives, really? Were they as simple as he claimed? That he was trying to make it easy? For whom? Himself? Did he feel Derek a threat, and did jealousy come into play? And, what about her boss? Being so willing to let her go for six months? Ugh. Men.

"I know you don't need me to take care of things for you. Maybe I wish you did. I'm sorry. Will you think about my offer?"

"I'll think about it."

He kissed her again, only this time on the cheek. "I know after today you must be tired. Please keep your doors locked, and find a better place to put the key."

"I will. Besides, I have a bed buddy to take care of me."

Andrés raised his brows. Nikki pointed at Ollie.

"Let me clean up for you."

"No." She almost said it too curtly. "I mean. I'm tired and I really kind of want to settle in. There isn't a lot to pick up. We'll talk tomorrow."

He nodded and she watched as he went to his car, his

head low. Maybe she should have been nicer, but dammit if she wasn't peeved at both him and Derek. And, Derek . . . Now really, what was up with that? Saying she could take off for six months. She managed this place. They needed her. Didn't they? Maybe Derek didn't need her after all. And, Spain? Beautiful country. She'd never been there but had heard, and Aunt Cara was on her extended tour through Europe. The tour that was only supposed to last six weeks, but had now lasted two years and a handful of boyfriends. Yes, her aunt was enjoying retirement, and she could see her if she went to Spain. She missed her something terrible.

And, Andrés. Was she falling in love with him? Oh God. Could you fall in love or be in love with one man and still lust after another? Sure you could. What was the saying— you can look at the menu, you just can't order? Hmmm. Her stomach fell as the questions within deepened. But could a woman love two men at once? Maybe. No. No. She didn't think so. Not in her case, anyway.

She took the dirty dishes into the kitchen, Ollie at her heels hoping she'd drop a scrap from dinner. There was nothing left to drop. It had all been so delicious. Andrés could cook, and he was fun, and sweet, and handsome—all of those things. But was he just too much of a good thing, or was he the *good thing* she really wanted? She set the dishes into the sink and turned on her stereo. Bono belted out a line from "Tryin' to Throw Your Arms around the World" about a woman needing a man like a fish needs a bicycle.

Ten minutes later, her head spinning from wine and too many unanswered questions, she got into her favorite jammies—men's boxers and an oversized T-shirt—and plopped down on her couch, still listening to U2. Her feet propped up on her distressed wooden coffee table, a pillow underneath them, Ollie resting his head in her lap, surely wishing he were small enough to climb into it. He always tried and she always had to explain to the giant oaf that it was impossible. He'd have to be content with a headrest.

She closed her eyes and let her tired body and mind drift to sleep. She didn't know how long she'd been like that when Ollie's incessant barking woke her, along with a loud knock at the door. She got up, rubbed her eyes, and with Ollie pacing at the front door, she peered out. Seeing who it was, she opened the door. There stood Janie—Georges' Janie—rolling suitcase at her side. She was a mess, her face tear-stained and smeared with mascara, her eyes puffy and swollen. She didn't look a lot like the golden girl she'd been earlier that day. "Janie?"

She let out a sob. "I'm sorry. I know it's late, but I couldn't reach Trevor. His cell must be dead and I know he had to go to a study group tonight for his final on Monday. He doesn't even know about today. I was with the police until an hour ago, and then I didn't know where to go. I don't want to be in my room. I'm scared and I'm . . . Oh God, I don't know what to do!"

"Come on. Sit down. You're welcome here."

"Thank you." Janie pulled her suitcase in. "I just . . . I don't know what to do. I know she's going to try and frame me. I know it, but I can't tell the police."

"What? Wait a minute. Who's going to try and frame you, Janie?"

"His ex-wife. Georges' ex. Bernadette. She will. You watch. I know she had this done, and it's so insane because she thinks Georges and I were sleeping together. Can you believe that? God, she has no clue. I wasn't sleeping with Georges. That's sick. But no one knows. I mean, I just found out two days ago, but I never even thought of Georges that way, or any way other than as my boss and a good friend and now I know why."

Nikki shook her head, rubbed her tired eyes, and held up her hand. Was she dreaming? "Stop. Okay? Take a breath. You're confusing me, Janie. Why would his ex-wife frame you? And what are you talking about? What did you just find out?"

Janie sniffled and ran her fingers through her long blonde

strands. "Georges. Bernadette thinks we were screwing around." She made a disgusted face. "But I knew. I knew he didn't think of me like that. You know? And, he was so cool about me and Trevor. I knew about the honeymoon and the wedding he wanted to give us. And, I know why. Nikki, you can't tell anyone this. I'm so scared of what the police will think or do. But I have to tell someone and I can't even tell my husband. Not until I see him. I was waiting until he came out here on Monday. He'll totally freak."

"Okay. I promise. What is it?" *Nikki* was about to *freak* herself on the hysterical young woman.

Janie wiped away her tears and closed her eyes. When she opened them she blurted out, "Georges was my dad."

Ceviche and Thai Chicken Wraps with Orogeny Pinot Noir

On a warm summer night with the one you love, or at least think you do—remember the song, "Love the One You're With"—break out a nice bottle of Orogeny Pinot Noir, whip up some Thai chicken wraps, and have a bowl of ceviche. It makes an excellent summer dinner and the wine melds well with the variety of flavors. Orogeny Pinot Noir is a gem of a wine. It has a nice blend of floral flavors, plums, cherries, vanilla, and spice, which works well with the spice added in these two recipes. The finish on the wine is full and clean.

Ceviche is fish pickled in lime juice. There are many ways of making it; some let the fish marinate in the lime juice before adding the other ingredients, some marinate the lot together. Fresh yellowtail and tuna are both delicious prepared this way, and sole, sea bass, and red snapper are other common choices. You can also use shrimp or scallops.

CEVICHE

2 lbs fresh fish
2 large onions
3 medium-sized, fully ripe tomatoes
5 Serrano chilies (optional)
½ cup cilantro
5 limes
salt and pepper

Cut fish into approximately 10–15mm cubes. Slice the onions into rings; chop the tomatoes, chilies, and cilantro as finely as possible. Squeeze the limes. Mix together, season with salt and pepper to taste, and let stand for at least an hour at room temperature, turning frequently to ensure that the fish is evenly treated by the lime juice, which "cooks" or pickles it. Refrigerate until ready to serve. It will keep overnight with no problem, though 24 hours is probably the limit. Pour off any excess lime juice before serving with tortillas or tostadas, on salty biscuits, in tacos, or with avocados. Enjoy.

THAI CHICKEN WRAPS

CHICKEN FILLING

> 3 (6 oz) chicken breasts
> 1 tbsp soy sauce
> 1 tbsp vegetable oil
> 1 tbsp grill seasoning

Heat a grill pan over high heat. Toss chicken with soy sauce, oil, and grill seasoning and grill 6 minutes on each side.

VEGETABLE FILLING

> ½ seedless cucumber, peeled, halved lengthwise
>   and thinly sliced on an angle
> 2 cups fresh bean sprouts
> 1 cup shredded carrots, available in pouches in
>   produce department
> 3 scallions, sliced on an angle
> 12 leaves basil, chopped or torn
> 3 tbsp (4 sprigs) chopped mint leaves (optional)
> 1 tbsp sesame seeds
> 2 tsp sugar
> 2 tbsp rice wine vinegar or white vinegar
> salt

Combine cucumber, sprouts, carrots, scallions, basil, mint, and sesame seeds with a generous sprinkle of sugar and vinegar. Season salad with salt, to taste.

SPICY PEANUT SAUCE

> ¼ cup room-temperature chunky peanut butter,
>   soften in microwave if it has been refrigerated
> 2 tbsp soy sauce
> 1 tbsp rice wine vinegar or white vinegar
> ¼ tsp cayenne pepper
> 2 tbsp vegetable oil
> 1 head of butter lettuce

Whisk peanut butter, soy sauce, vinegar, and cayenne together. Stream in vegetable oil, continuing to whisk till thoroughly combined.

Slice cooked chicken on an angle. Toss with veggies and herbs.

Tear off leaves of lettuce, wash and dry.

Pile chicken and veggies in lettuce wraps and drizzle liberally with spicy peanut sauce before rolling.

Chapter 6

Nikki had to sit down for this. Ollie followed suit. Janie remained standing until Nikki insisted she have a seat on the chair across from her. "Wait. Um, let me get you something to drink, okay? Water, wine—got lots of that—or, uh, tea?"

"Yes, please. Tea would be nice." Janie sniffled and blinked her eyes several times.

Nikki went into the kitchen, put on the kettle, then thought better of it. No time to wait for hot water. This girl was in her own version of hot water. Nuke it. She put two mugs of water in the microwave and reached for a box of chamomile. Calming right? Yes. Calming was in order. Holy cow, just ten minutes ago she was sleeping off the bad effects of the day and then whammo, the day was apparently not over.

The microwave beeped. Nikki did a quick dunk of tea bags, tossed in a teaspoon of Splenda, and took her place across from Janie after handing her the warmed brew. Nikki took a sip, set her cup down, and grabbed her throw off the back of her sofa, wrapping it around herself. "Okay, now Janie, it has been a grueling day for all of us and I know you and Georges were really close, but I think you may be confused or in shock."

"No." She shook her head vehemently. "I'm not in shock. I swear. I know it sounds totally bizarre and it is, but it's the truth. Georges was my dad and I only found out two days ago."

Nikki bit her lower lip. The young woman seemed to be sober, coherent, upset—yes, but certain about what she was telling her. "Then maybe we need to go back to two days ago."

Janie nodded, her eyes welling up again. Nikki leaned forward and patted her knee. "Have some tea. Kick your shoes off and just breathe for a minute. Here, take the blanket. You look a little cold."

Janie cracked a weak smile as she wrapped the blanket around her shoulders. "Do you have kids?"

"No."

"My mom used to make sure I kept warm." Janie's face lit up. "She always worried so much about me. She was awesome. I could talk to her about anything, you know. She was cool. She took me to my first concert when I was twelve. It was Pearl Jam. I mean, how cool is that? She was really young when she had me. But she didn't give me up for adoption. She did it all by herself. I miss her. You remind me of her. You'd be a good mother."

"Thanks." Wait a minute. Hold on a minute. Nikki looked at Janie. Shit. She could actually be old enough to be Janie's mom. Sure she probably would have been fourteen, but it was possible. "How old are you?"

"Twenty-one."

Oooh. That hurt. That meant Nikki would have been fifteen, nearly sixteen. She shook her head, tossing the thought aside, and focused again on the matter at hand. "Why don't we go back to two days ago, like I said?"

"We might want to go back even further," Janie replied.

Nikki nodded, with no idea where Janie was going, but all of a sudden she knew it was going to be a really long night. Damn. Probably should have made some coffee instead of herbal tea.

Janie took a tissue from her purse and blew her nose. "You can probably guess that my mom is gone. She died last year."

"I'm sorry."

"She had breast cancer. She was thirty-nine. How wrong is that?"

"Very."

"No kidding. But, um, she made me who I am. She had me at nineteen and did it on her own. She always told me that my dad was just some guy she met and hung out with for like a week or two, and you know what, I was okay with that. She said that he didn't want a kid, and who wants a dad who doesn't want a kid? Not me. Now I know that my dad didn't know about me, but I'm cool with that. I'm not mad at my mom. Georges, my dad, was married to his first wife when they screwed around and Mom felt bad, and then we moved to San Diego and life was good for us. We lived at the beach and it was just me and my mom. She had cool friends and I had friends and we had a neat apartment, but after I graduated from high school she wanted to move up here." Janie picked up her tea. With the back of her free hand she wiped her face.

"Why?" Poor kid. That's really all she was, a poor kid. Here she'd lost the only parent she knew and now, *this* . . .

"That was the weird part about it, but now I get it."

"What is that?"

"I always liked cooking. Funny, huh? I guess it's true that some things are inherited from your family, and I didn't get good grades in school, but I always wanted to be a chef. My mom wanted me to come to San Fran and go to Le Cordon Bleu. We moved here and I applied. She was already sick, but she wasn't telling me just how sick.

She got me an interview with Georges, who hired me as his assistant. He didn't know who I was then. My mom told him some line about us needing money and since they were old friends and all, but I think deep down Georges knew. I guess she didn't tell him right away because she felt afraid or pressured. I'm not sure which or why."

"Maybe she wanted to see if Georges was still the man she remembered, see if he was someone worthy of being your dad, before springing it on him." Nikki sat up at the edge of the sofa. Ollie groaned beneath her as her foot brushed against him.

"I think it was something like that."

Nikki shook her head. "Do you want something to eat?"

"No. Thank you. My stomach hurts too bad. I don't think I could eat a thing right now."

"Let me know."

"Okay. Thanks."

"Did your mom stay in touch with Georges over the years?"

"No. I don't think so. I think when she moved us up here though, she planned everything out. She searched out Georges and hoped for the best so that she could die knowing that I still had a parent."

"That must have been hard for her seeing how she raised you by herself. But I can understand her wanting to have you cement a relationship with your dad."

"Uh-huh." She looked away and Nikki thought she might start crying again. She was so fragile, and understandably so, but Nikki needed her to keep talking. Janie knew something about Georges' murder, that much she was certain of.

"How long after he hired you did Georges find out the truth?"

"He told me that he found out only two weeks before my mom died. He said that she came to him and told him she was dying and that I was his child. He didn't believe it at first and asked her why she waited so long. She told him why, and then she told him that she'd wanted the two of us to get to know each other first before letting us learn the truth. That way we wouldn't have the pressure of knowing our tight connection."

Nikki nodded. She could understand Janie's mother's reasons to an extent. The woman had protected her daughter for so long and had been her only parent, but decided going into her last days that everyone deserved to know the truth. "Why didn't they tell you before your mom passed?"

"She was in a lot of pain at the end, and they realized that I couldn't handle the stress. I think both of them had enough sense to let me clear my head before adding any more pressure on me. I mean really, can you see it? Your mom is dying and then this man who is your boss turns around and tells you that he's your dad. I'm glad Georges waited and that my mom agreed to it. I think I would've really freaked." Janie pulled the blanket tighter around her shoulders.

"How did you react when Georges told you?"

"It was weird. You know, we were in the car and he started talking about my mother and how they met twenty-two years ago and all of that, and I knew. I'm the one who blurted it out while on the Bay Bridge, on the way here to the vineyard, that he was my dad."

"How did you feel?"

"Relieved. I really did. No matter what, I always wanted to know who my dad was, and I felt relieved because Georges has been so great to me. I mean, you couldn't ask for a cooler dad. And now . . . now I won't even get to know him that way." She broke out in tears again.

Nikki reached for a tissue box on the corner table, took some, handed them to Janie, and sat down by her. "Here." She rubbed her back.

Janie's cell phone rang with a Green Day song. She sighed and took it out of her purse. "Hello. Hi, baby." She started crying and Nikki figured that it would have to be Janie's husband. She decided to give Janie some privacy. She went into her bedroom and turned on her computer. She wanted to see if there was any information on Bernadette Debussey. She could hear Janie from the other room telling her husband between sobs about what had happened. "No. Don't drive this late. You have to finish your paper and you have your final on Monday morning. Take care of what you need to, please. No. I'll be okay. I think I'm gonna stay with this nice lady here. Nikki Sands. She lives in the guesthouse on the property."

Nikki headed to her closet to pull out some blankets. She couldn't send Janie back to the hotel, not in her state. She took out a pillow and a chenille blanket along with clean sheets. She'd let Janie have her bed and she'd crash on the couch.

She walked back into the family room. Janie was still talking to her husband. "Thanks, baby. Okay. Yeah. I'll see you Monday. No, I mean it. I'm fine. You get your work done. You've worked so hard at school. Good luck with the paper and the final. The police want me to stay around for a few days in case they need to talk to me again." She paused, obviously fielding his questions. "No, I have that suitcase. It was easier to use because of the roller things on them. I'm sorry. My duffel is in our closet. Use it."

Nikki returned to her room and got on the Internet as she heard Janie say, "Okay. I love you, too. Good night."

"Your husband okay?" she called out.

Janie came to her bedroom door. "He's good. Worried about me. He wants to drive out here now, but I told him to finish his stuff for school. He doesn't know about Georges being my dad, and I downplayed it. I mean, to him Georges was just my boss. It's not like there's anything he can do for me right now, and you've been really great. You don't mind if I stay here, do you?"

"Stay. Please. You can have my room. I just wanted to look something up about Georges' ex-wife."

"I can already tell you, she's a real winner." The sarcasm in Janie's voice was evident. "I can sleep on the couch. It's no biggie."

"No. Hang on and I'll be right out. I want to ask you about Bernadette Debussey and why you think she might frame you for Georges' murder."

"That's gonna take awhile."

"I figured. You up to it?"

"Yeah. I need someone to talk to, and like I said, there was no way I was gonna tell that cop today. He kind of scared me."

"Detective Robinson?"

"Yeah. The dude with the green eyes. He's really intimidating."

"Don't let him get to you. It's his job." But Nikki knew that she'd let Jonah Robinson get under her skin, too, and she could certainly see how he could do it to Janie. The girl was smart but definitely lacked sophistication. Knowing how cops worked, she figured that Robinson had probably played upon and preyed on Janie's weaknesses of vulnerability and naiveté, the kind that youth carries with it. This thought made her angry. Jerk. How dare he frighten Janie so much that she felt she couldn't be honest with him. But Nikki hadn't been entirely open either. Her reasoning was different, and it wasn't a lack of honesty. She simply hadn't been completely forthright, and if she'd had any doubts earlier in the day about the way she'd responded to Robinson, she didn't anymore. Janie needed help and she'd come to Nikki for it, plus she'd made Nikki promise to keep her secrets under lock and key. Aunt Cara had always taught her that a promise broken harms the integrity of all involved.

Nikki looked Bernadette Debussey up on Google and immediately several links popped up. She opened the first one and read a story from the *San Francisco Chronicle* dated April 19 of the previous year. Nikki found several more articles from the *Chronicle* dated through August. There weren't any more articles to find after August 27— the date when Bernadette Debussey was sentenced to spend the next two decades in prison.

Chapter 7

The following morning Nikki poured Janie a cup of coffee and then one for herself. She brought over a couple of bowls of oatmeal and a side of bacon, her fat allotment for the day.

"You're really nice to do this and let me stay here. When Trevor comes tomorrow we'll go back to the hotel. I was afraid to stay there last night because, you know, I mean, what if someone knows I'm Georges' daughter and they come after me, too?" Janie said.

Nikki hadn't thought about that but could see why Janie might. But foremost on Nikki's mind was the question that had plagued her all night after reading through the articles on Bernadette. She didn't have a lot of time to get the story straight in her head before heading out to see how Simon and Marco were doing, and Derek, too. She knew they'd all have to pull together to do damage control and manage the guests at the hotel until the police gave the okay for them all to go. There were a few people Nikki wanted to track down today. Baron O'Grady was for sure on her list because he *had* been Georges' partner and friend. Maybe

he would have an idea about who might have wanted to kill
Georges. She also wanted to speak to Charlotte, Georges'
spa therapist yesterday, who had conveniently left before
Nikki had found Georges dead in the water.

"I learned a lot about Bernadette last night." Nikki sat
down and picked up a piece of bacon. Before taking a bite
she pulled the fat off, which didn't leave a whole lot of the
meat. "You helped put her in jail? You didn't tell me that
she was in jail."

Janie poured almost half a carton of cream into her coffee and spooned in several sugars. "Yeah. She deserved it."

"From what I read, she did. Why don't you tell me your
version?" Nikki sat back and took a bite out of the bacon.
Mhhm, nothing like that smoky, salty, fat flavor.

"Well, the chick went ballistic, you know. Here she and
Georges are, sitting pretty in their Pacific Heights mansion,
and after my mom died Georges was cool enough to let me
have the guesthouse until I could figure out what I was
gonna do. It wasn't like I could stay at my mom's place.
Too hard."

"I'm sure."

"I don't even get why Bernadette wigged. I started going out with Trevor about a month after my mom died and
we spent a ton of time together. He's great. You'll love him.
But anyway, one day Bernie—that's what we called her—
comes home, and at first she was way cool with me. We
hung out and everything. She's only five years older than
me, so it was good 'cause I needed a friend and everything.
But then she saw that Georges and I were hanging out more
and more. It wasn't because he wanted into my pants. Duh.
I knew that, too. He was into her. I think Georges was kicking it with me because he wanted to get to know me better.
After all, I was his kid." She looked away, and when she
looked back, her eyes had again filled with tears. "I'm
sorry. It's pretty hard. I liked him. I think I loved him, you
know. I did. I am sorry, but he was my dad. That's a total
reality for me now. Now that he's gone."

"I understand."

Janie wiped her face with a napkin and swallowed some coffee. "Bernie flipped out because she thought Georges and I were messing around. One day when I was at work with him in his new restaurant, she ransacked the guesthouse and she shredded my clothes, and the worst part is, she smashed several paintings that my mom had done. Sure, my mom was no Picasso, but she liked to paint and I liked what she painted. She'd left me those pieces and Bernie ruined them." Janie shook her head. "Unbelievable. I went straight to Georges, who believed me because she'd gone crazy on him, too, that night, accusing him of sleeping with me. Once he found out what she'd done to my stuff, he kicked her out and filed for a divorce the next day. She was so pissed. I mean she signed a prenup, so she was getting nothing."

"That weekend she came back and torched the guesthouse?" Nikki asked.

"Yeah, and all my stuff. The police found her fingerprints and everything. She says she didn't do it, but c'mon, it's so obvious."

"Some people aren't too bright. I'm sorry about your mom's paintings and all that you've lost."

"Me too. Listen, can I stay here today? I don't really want to talk to anyone."

"Sure. I've got to go into the office and see what's going on there and then over to the hotel for some damage control. It might be Sunday, but with what's happened I'm sure my boss will hold a meeting. But before I go, can I ask you, since Bernadette is behind bars, why or how do you think she could have murdered Georges and framed you?"

Janie set her spoon back in her oatmeal and swallowed. "Bernie knows lowlifes, you know what I mean? The rumor I heard was that her brother was in a gang, and bad news. Georges didn't let him come over, and that upset Bernie because she was close to her brother. I never met him. Georges got mad at her one time for bailing him out of jail. I think that maybe she could have had her brother or one of his friends kill Georges."

"That said, how could she frame you, and why?"

"She'd frame me because she blames me for her getting sent to prison. You know, some people can't take responsibility for their actions, and Bernie thinks that it's my fault she's in jail. I even got a letter from her that says so." Janie got up and took her notebook out of her backpack. She brought it over to the table and opened it. It appeared to be an entire schedule from Georges' day—yesterday. It even had the time he was supposed to have met with Nikki to discuss the wine pairings for dinner, and his spa treatment appointment.

Janie took out a letter from a pocket in the notebook. "Read this."

The letter said that if Janie had never come into Georges' life, Bernadette wouldn't be in jail and the reason she'd ruined her clothes and paintings was because Janie was always with Georges, that it was disrespectful to Bernadette. She went on to write that she did not burn the guesthouse down and that Janie should have known her better than that and that Janie's testimony was what put her in jail. She also wrote how betrayed she'd felt by Georges. That part Nikki found really interesting. It sure did sound like Bernadette Debussey needed help.

Nikki handed the letter back to Janie. "She's pretty angry. I see what you mean. Did you tell Detective Robinson any of this?"

"I did. I told him what I thought about Bernadette and what I knew about her brother being a criminal. He said that he'd check into it."

"It may be a good idea to show him this letter. Think about it. You may be right: if Bernadette is as angry as she sounds and if she and her brother are close, who knows." Janie nodded. "By the way, do you know where Baron O'Grady is staying?"

"He's at the hotel. I saw him there. Why?"

"Oh, for some reason when he was late yesterday I assumed he'd come in from the city."

"Well yeah, he had, but then he checked in."

Nikki drank the rest of her coffee. "Baron. Is he a good guy?"

"Totally. He and Georges were best friends. I haven't talked to him, but I'm sure he's devastated."

"I think I'll go by and see him."

"Tell him I'm thinking of him. Okay?"

"Sure. If you need anything else please feel free. There's food in the fridge and you can watch TV or listen to the stereo, go on the Internet. Whatever you need."

"Thanks. You really would make a great mom."

Nikki wondered. Maybe. She showered, then pulled on a pair of khakis and took out a silk shell in a paisley pattern of pinks and reds. Pretty and summery, and she knew that the June day would be hot, probably a tad humid, too. After drying her hair, she pulled it back and dabbed on some blush, a little mascara, eyeliner, and lip gloss. Funny how at almost thirty-seven she was just starting to like the way she looked, even with the slightly noticeable lines around her eyes and on her forehead. She'd spent so many years trying to be glamorous, doing all the tricks with the make-up, applying self tanner to give her that *natural* California glow, but now it all seemed kind of humorous when she thought about it. Maybe inching toward forty wasn't so bad after all. And, maybe Janie was right about her being a good mom. The time clock *was* ticking and she *did* want a family. At least she thought she did. Andrés' face flashed into her mind, and then the thought of Spain, and of going there with him. Could she do it? *Should* she do it?

Nikki didn't have any answers to her questions. She slid into her sandals and finished getting ready, then said a quick good-bye to Janie. She did the half-mile hike to the winery's business offices and, as she suspected, found Derek there.

She stood in the doorway to his office. He looked as

tired as she felt, and an urge to comfort him came over her.
If she could only let go of those urges. Why did this guy
have a hold on her? It was maddening. "Hi," she said.

He looked up from some paperwork. "Hey. How are
you?" He stood up as she came in. "I wanted to call you or
stop by and see you last night. Simon and Marco told me
that you were the one who found Georges. I'm sorry. I got
caught up with the police, and I knew that Andrés was with
you."

Sigh. A little stab in the heart. Stupid, yes, but still there.
"No worries. Thanks though. I'm fine. I guess shaken
some, but you know it's not the first dead body I've dealt
with." Okay, that was a pretty dumb thing to say. This man
could tongue-tie her faster than a rattlesnake could strike
its victim.

"Right. Sit down. Want some coffee?" he asked.

"No, I've had my caffeine quota for the day. Any more
and I'll be buzzing around here like a bee on steroids."
Dammit. Stupid metaphor. Think of something smart to
say. "How about Simon and Marco, are they okay?"

"Not bad, relatively speaking. I know my brother is
stressed about how this will affect our hotel and spa business. Marco keeps reminding him of their guru's famous
sayings and how neither one of them can afford to delve
into that negative energy. I couldn't take it. I had to leave
and come into the office. I had coffee with them and we discussed how to handle some of the issues that might arise
from this."

Wait a minute. Wasn't she a part of this place, too? She
was Derek's assistant and the winery manager the last time
she checked. Her shoulders and neck tightened along with
her stomach. "You three met? And discussed damage control?"

"It might sound crass, considering poor Georges, I
know, but Nikki, we have a business to run. We had to work
some things out." He leaned back in his chair and took off
his reading glasses. "You look upset. I know that you liked

Georges. We all did, but you do understand why I had to speak with Simon and Marco about all of this and devise a plan, don't you?"

That was *so* Derek. Calm, cool, collected. Yep. Mr. Rational. "Oh sure." Her voice had risen an entire octave. "Business *is* business." And then, Nikki did what she did in these rational situations. She became irrational. "But, can I ask you if you planned on including me in your damage control plan? Am I not supposed to be your right-hand woman? Oh, but wait a minute, maybe this is like you not asking my opinion about whether I might be interested in going to Spain with Andrés. You just, what? Figured I'd be dying to go, and that you'd be generous enough to give me a six-month leave of absence, as if I'm not needed here? Maybe that's it. Maybe you don't need me here."

"Hold on a second. Stop. Where did that come from?"

"Andrés sprung his Spain plan on me and told me that you gave *him* the okay for me to go, and that you would hold my job."

"Back up. First of all before you go into another tailspin, let me assure you that I did plan on talking with you this morning about Georges' murder and how we can handle what has happened on both a human level and a business one. This was a man's life, I'm well aware of that. And, my first priority is to make certain that everyone is emotionally okay. Especially you. You found the man. I know that Detective Robinson had you cornered for some time yesterday and he can be rather unpleasant, as I also had the *privilege* of spending time with him. Honestly, Nikki, I wanted to give you a day or two to take time out. What's happened here is difficult at best. You *are* my right hand and I *do* need you here. Simon called me this morning and had me over for coffee. He was losing it and Marco begged me to come and talk to him. Once I calmed him down, we discussed a few things and then agreed that we should all get together tomorrow, once the police have pretty much cleared out of here. They've told me that their

CSI team should be finished by then and all of the interviews with the guests will be completed. You were not excluded nor did I intend for you to be."

Insert foot now. Could she feel any worse? Probably not. *Schmuck.* "I'm sorry." It was all she could muster.

He sighed and rubbed the back of his neck, then twisted it. She heard it crack. "As for this thing with Andrés, yes, he talked to me and yes, I did tell him I was fine with you going to Spain for a few months. You've put some great marketing plans into play, things are running smoothly, or they were until yesterday, so I thought that maybe it would be a good time for you to go. Besides, I have some interest in Spanish wines and thought you could do some scouting for me, or perhaps explore the possibility that I could go into business with Andrés."

"You two talked about doing that?" She was floored. Just great. Perfect.

"We mentioned it, and as you are my assistant, you could see how he plans to run things and if it might be a profitable venture for Malveaux to get in on. And, I know that the two of you have gotten quite close. Basically, what I'm saying to you is that you're valued here, but Nikki, you don't have much of a life. You work your tail off, go running in the evening, and then hole yourself up in your cottage. It's been good for you, I think, to date Andrés, and he seems to really care about you. Maybe you should explore that further."

Was he for real? Telling her to get a life? She never saw him with anyone, and if he ever went out, it was to a town council meeting. Maybe not, though. Maybe she knew less than she thought about her boss. If he hadn't given her the brush-off before, he sure had now. All she could manage to say was, "Uh-huh."

"Are you going to go? To Spain? With Andrés?"

"You know, I actually do think I need a day off to chill. You're okay with that, right?" She decided not to answer his question, she was so angry.

"Sure. I told you so. Take two days. Why don't we plan on meeting on Tuesday morning? Around ten. Here in my office? I'll let Simon and Marco know."

"Yeah. Ten it is. Thanks for the time off and for everything." She tried hard not to sound sarcastic. He looked at her quizzically, but she escaped before he could question her.

She started to walk back to her place, but first decided to take a detour and go through the spa. If the cops were about finished maybe she could come to her own conclusions about how the killer got inside the spa. She couldn't directly ask Robinson any questions, but she assumed that either Georges had been shot with a gun that had a silencer on it, or that pile of towels she had spotted by the French doors had been used to muffle the sound of the shot.

The police were still doing their thing and Nikki didn't want any part of it. If Robinson was around, she certainly didn't want to run into him. A thought struck her, something Simon said about not knowing if the French doors had been opened yesterday, and that the only way anyone could tell was if they stood on the hill several hundred yards away. The binocular part had been a slight exaggeration, which of course Simon never did—exaggerate.

Nikki went back to her cottage and got her tennis shoes off the front porch. Ollie was lying there doing his thing— napping. She decided not to go into her place, not wanting to get involved in another conversation with Janie. She wanted to see how far she would have to go to be able to see the doors outside of the bath treatment room.

She invited Ollie to take a walk with her. He thumped his tail, raised his head, and set it back down in answer to her invitation. However, after a couple of minutes, although she'd already told him to forget it and that she was leaving his lazy ass on the porch, he padded along next to her up the hill.

She walked through a section of Cabernet Sauvignon grapes until she reached the crest. On the other side of the hill a new section of grapes had been sectioned off. They were old Zinfandel vines—Nikki's personal favorite. She loved the intense jammy flavors that red zins had. She stood at the top of the crest among the vines and looked back toward the spa and hotel. Ollie plopped down at her side. "Tired already? We only walked this time, we didn't run! I think you need some more exercise, old boy."

Nikki brought her hand up over her brow to shield her eyes. It looked as though the CSI team was packing up. She squinted. "Grrr," she said. Ollie looked up at her. "Oh it's nothing, just that rotten detective." She'd spotted Robinson. What was he doing? Walking over to stop and talk to one of the CSI guys. The investigator looked to be pointing to an area over by the spa building. Robinson shook the investigator's hand and walked around the building. A few minutes later he reappeared with a ladder under his arm and carried it over to his truck, placing it in the back. That must be how they think the killer got into the room. Ladders were a dime a dozen on a vineyard and the Malveaux Estate certainly had no shortage of them. Interesting.

If the killer used one of the ladders, had he posed as one of the workers at the vineyard? For that matter, was he one of the workers? It wouldn't be hard to blend in, especially yesterday. There had been a lot of people celebrating the day, and employees were on hand, even pickers. Most people didn't even go by the bath treatment room, as it was on the far end of the spa, as well as the far end of the property, and butted up to more vines. Maybe the killer didn't have to pose at all. He or she could have looked like a maintenance person for that matter, trimming the trellis. But how would the killer have known that Georges was at the spa, unless of course he'd been followed, or it was someone who knew where he'd be. Janie knew. She had it written in the schedule. Baron knew because Georges told him, and maybe even Lauren Trump knew.

Nikki continued to watch Robinson. He got into his truck and started to head out of the drive. Nikki turned toward the other end of the parking lot. That was odd. There was a man standing there beside a white Lexus coupe. He put his head down when one of the investigators walked by. He then looked in several directions, almost as if he were nervous. Was the guy a cop? Nikki walked in a bit where she could still see the area without losing the man by the Lexus. As Robinson pulled by him, the man waved him down and walked over to the driver's side window. Who was it? What was he doing? They looked to be talking. Nikki got even closer. A couple of minutes later Robinson drove away and the man turned back around. Nikki finally got a decent look at the man—Rick Moran, Georges' accountant and financial advisor. What was he snooping around for? And, why was he acting so nervous? Obviously he had some interest in speaking with Robinson. Was it in regard to the ladder? Nikki didn't know, but she was determined to find out, and she put herself into a jog on her way back down the hill. Reaching the bottom, she saw Moran get into his Lexus. *Crap!* She sprinted to her Camry and quickly got behind the wheel. She had a feeling Moran was up to something, and she was going to follow him. Maybe he'd lead her to some answers about who killed Georges.

Chapter 8

Nikki jammed her car into reverse; dust kicked up behind her as she made tracks. Moran was probably about a mile ahead of her by now. In her rearview mirror she saw Ollie through the haze of dust, looking forlorn and confused. They'd run at full speed down the hill. She was certain he'd expected to go on this ride with her. "Sorry, boy, you're better off lying under an olive tree than chasing after suspicious financial advisors."

Ah, there was the white Lexus up ahead, just around the bend. Nikki backed off on the accelerator. She'd have to keep a decent distance for him not to notice, plus speeding through wine country was highly inadvisable. She'd watched him head toward Oak Knoll Avenue off the Silverado Trail. They turned right onto Trancas Street and then left onto Soscol Avenue, which would turn into the Napa Vallejo Highway. Before long the Lexus was turning onto California 29 and heading south, turning into Sonoma Boulevard. As she watched him make the sharp left turn on Marine World Parkway off Sonoma Boulevard and then take the I-80 exit toward San Francisco, she figured that's where they were headed. She decided to put the car on cruise control, maintain her distance, and turn on the stereo, while wondering where Moran was taking them. Her gut told her he was up to no good, and as they drove into the city her feeling was confirmed as the Castro District came into view. What was he doing here? A few minutes later Moran pulled in front of a rundown building on Ninth and Market—not the best part of town by any stretch of the imagination. It certainly wasn't anywhere one would want to be at night, and the daytime was iffy as well! What kind of business did Moran have going on in the rundown tenement? Yep, he was up to no good, of that much Nikki was sure. She drove past him as he got out of his car. Thank God for her inconspicuous Camry. She went around the block and searched for a place to park. She didn't want to get out of her car, not in this 'hood.

Was Moran down here buying drugs? Maybe that was it. He'd appeared nervous this morning when he was speaking to Robinson, at least from what she could tell from up on the hill. Nothing was fitting at the moment. Nerves were one thing, but Moran smoking crack? Anything was possible, and if he was a drug addict, did he grow angry with Georges and kill him while in a drug-induced stupor?

Nikki couldn't find a parking space, so she continued to circle the block, in a way relieved, as she really did not want to go into that building. As luck would have it, she looked in her rearview mirror, while turning right to make another run around the block, and saw Moran jog out of the building and hurriedly get back behind the wheel of the Lexus, a brown bag in his hand. Must be drugs. Had to be.

Nikki peeled around the corner quickly, hoping that he would not notice her. He did seem awfully distracted. He was hiding something. "Bad boy, bad boy, what'cha gonna do?" she sang.

She followed him as he made a right on Fifth and a left onto I-280 south toward San Jose, then onto the U.S. 101 south. At one point she got wedged between a couple of semis and thought he might've exited. She swerved around one of the truckers, who gave her a blast from his air horn. She waved. "I know. I know. Sorry." Moran picked up speed. Had he spotted her? Hopefully not.

A few minutes later they were headed into the domestic terminal at San Francisco International. Either the accountant was taking off for faraway places or else he was picking someone up, but if so he'd have turned into the arrivals terminal. If he was leaving town, was it because he needed to make a run for it? If that were the case, the international departures might make more sense.

Moran found a parking space in one of the structures. Nikki pulled on ahead and as luck would have it she found one on the next level. She took the stairs at a rapid clip, not wanting to catch the elevator just in case she got on with Moran. If he'd spotted her, then he'd know for sure she was following him. If he'd only seen her car, it was doubtful that he knew the car belonged to her. She was sure she'd kept enough distance from him that he wouldn't have been able to spot her.

She waited outside the terminal at the bottom of the stairs, until she heard the elevator doors open. She figured she had beaten him down, because if he was taking off for someplace, he'd surely have luggage, and getting out of the car would have taken time.

She ducked behind a Suburban. There he was, getting off the elevator with another man dressed in a business suit and a woman with a baby and two toddlers, struggling to keep it together.

Nikki kept her distance behind them. There were enough people inside the airport to blend in, and Moran appeared intent on moving out quickly rather than looking over his shoulder. He glanced behind him one time and Nikki turned her face away. The thing was, if he was getting on a plane she'd have to let this wild goose chase go at security. He did have a suitcase. She doubted she could get a ticket agent to tell her where he was going.

He veered away from the ticket counters. Where was he going now? A few minutes later he came to the airport travel agency, where he checked his bag into what Nikki knew to be the storage area. Since 9/11, lockers were no longer available at SFO. The protocol now was to check anything anyone wanted to be stored at the travel agency. Damn. What was he up to? He took the ticket. She continued to follow him until he was back out the door and onto the elevator leading up to his car. That's where she decided to end tagging along after Moran. She had a feeling that whatever answers she might find that could connect Moran to Georges' murder would be located in that suitcase. She aimed to find out what was in it.

Several minutes later she stood in front of a bored-looking, acne-scarred young man of about twenty-three. She'd already staked him out for about a minute before heading off to the ladies' room and stooping about as low as she could to get information—undoing the top two buttons of her blouse, fluffing her hair, and applying fresh lipstick. She wasn't Pam Anderson by any stretch of the imagination, but she was gonna have to work the assets she did have to the best of her ability.

She found her Southern accent when she opened her mouth to the man at the front desk. "Hi. My name is Sally Anne Moran, and my husband was just up here about fifteen minutes ago checking in a bag." She went on to describe what Rick Moran looked like. She leaned across the counter and watched as the scrawny, dark-haired kid turned his gaze to her cleavage. "And, you're not going to believe this, but he forgot to give me the ticket to retrieve the bag. See the thing is, he had to leave on a business trip to New York and I was scheduled to go to Tennessee to visit my family, and well, he grabbed the wrong bag when he left home this morning because he had to go into work first. Well, I got a hold of him on his way to the airport while I was also drivin' here. He said that he didn't want to have to drag my heavy suitcase all over while he waited for me to come and get it, because he still needed to get in line to get his ticket and all."

Either all the B.S. coming out of Nikki's mouth had the kid bored or else he was mesmerized by the boobs, because he hadn't even looked at her face during this diatribe.

"Anyway, silly man has already checked himself through and is ready to board the plane. He can be so absent minded. Can you believe that he forgot to meet me in the bar to give me the ticket to get *my* luggage?"

The guy didn't say anything.

"Can you believe that?" Nikki asked and ran her finger across his nametag. "Martin."

"Huh? Oh no. That's a bummer." He finally looked up at her. She batted her lashes and smiled.

"I know, but I am sure you can help me out. As I said, the last name is Moran. Do you think you could go and get the bag for me?"

"Oh no. I need to get a manager."

Nikki crossed her arms under her breasts, trying to lift them as much as possible. "Manager? I don't have time for that. You can make decisions on your own. You look like a *competent* man. I'm a good judge of character."

Martin took a step back and eyed her.

"You know, Martin, my husband travels quite a bit. I'm always dropping him off here. Maybe we could meet for a drink sometime. A woman can get quite lonely when she's left on her own."

Martin rubbed his chin, either thinking over her proposition or wondering if she was as full of crap as she sounded. "Okay. I guess I can get your bag. Um, but do you have any ID?"

Damn. He was smarter than he looked. "Of course I do, honey, but crazy thing is, it's in that beige suitcase of mine. As soon as you get it, I'll *show* you the goods."

"I could get in trouble for this."

"Tell you what, I'll make it worth your trouble."

Martin left her standing there as he went through a door behind him. Nikki breathed out a woosh of air. How in the hell was she going to get out of this one? Quickly.

Martin came back with the khaki suitcase. Nikki reached into the side pocket. "Hmmm. I thought that was where my ID was. Hang on, I'll just open it." She lifted it onto the counter, Martin watching her intently. She undid the zipper and cracked open the suitcase, not wanting Martin to see what was inside, because she had no idea herself as to what she might find, and she was already breaking several laws. If Moran had stored weapons or something else illegal in there, she didn't think that Martin could continue to be bought off by a pair of jugs. She almost gasped when she saw what was in the bag. But instead, kept her composure and closed it. She sighed. "Uh, Martin, this is not my bag."

"What do you mean? This is the Moran bag and I checked it with the guy, your husband. This is it."

She shook her head. "No, no it's not. I do not wear polyester and extra large size grandma panties. That bag is filled with it."

"Lady, I don't know what kind of game you're playing, but I think I'm going to go and get my manager."

"You know what, you do that. In fact, I would like to speak to him myself." Martin grabbed the suitcase off the counter and headed for the door. "Hurry up, and bring me back the correct suitcase. I'm sure your manager would love to hear how you botched this up," she said after him. As soon as the door was closed behind him, Nikki turned around and sprinted back through the airport and down to her car.

Her heart didn't stop racing until she was twenty minutes out of the airport. If Martin reported her, there could be big trouble, but then the kid appeared bright enough to want to keep his job. If he'd taken a minute to think about it, Nikki was pretty sure he would have just put the suitcase back and let it go. At least she hoped so.

But what was troubling Nikki even more was the fact that when she'd opened Moran's suitcase, it was filled with stacks of hundred dollar bills, and if she had to guesstimate how much money there was, she'd figure at least a hundred grand. The questions that remained on her drive back to Napa were, where did Moran get that kind of cash, why did he have it, and furthermore, why was he storing it at the San Francisco International airport? She should probably tell Robinson. But, then again, telling Robinson would raise the red flag she didn't want raised, alerting him to the fact that she was indeed snooping. No, she wasn't going to give him that satisfaction. Besides, the cash inside Moran's bag could have been completely legitimate. Right? Anything is possible. For now, she'd let the money stay where it was at the airport without going to the police, until she'd checked out a few more things, because although Moran did look guilty as sin, there were a few other people who needed some checking out in conjunction with Georges' murder, and she was not a woman to leave any stone unturned.

Chapter 9

Driving back to Napa, Nikki decided to exit in Yountville, stop off at Grapes, and get an early dinner to go. She hadn't eaten since breakfast and the day had now started to come to an end; it was after four o'clock. She also secretly hoped she'd run into Andrés. With Isabel in New York, Nikki knew that her friend's big brother was keeping tabs on the place. Passing by St. Joan of Arc Catholic Church on Washington, she put her car visor down to keep the sun out of her eyes. As she did, something caught her eye. Was that Baron O'Grady going into the church? She pulled into the parking lot as she watched the chubby man open the front door. Yep. That was Baron, all right. Nikki read the church bulletin board in the parking lot. No mass right now—but wait a minute. Confession. Confession? It started in five minutes. Okay, now maybe Baron was simply a devout Catholic who went to confession on a regular basis. Maybe. Or maybe he had something horrible to confess. Like murder. Weren't priests bound to confidentiality? The best friend and business partner. Too obvious? He appeared to be so tight with Georges. Maybe he was going in to light a candle for his friend. But what if he did have secrets to hide? The deadly kind? Nikki didn't know, but was determined to find out as she parked her car and walked toward the church.

She made the sign of the cross as she entered, knowing that was what she was supposed to do. But wait a minute, she wasn't Catholic. She'd grown up a Protestant and now had spread her wings spiritually, even studying some of the Buddhist philosophies. Uh-oh. Was she being sacrilegious? She hoped not. Hell was not a place she desired to visit.

She sat down in one of the last rows. There were a handful of people scattered throughout the pews and a few more lighting candles in the front, but no Baron. Then she saw him coming from the other side of the church. She bowed her head as if in prayer and watched as he slipped behind a pair of velvet curtains. Confession. What was he confessing? She wished she could hear. About fifteen minutes later she saw him emerge, then go over and light a candle. He then turned and came down the aisle. He spotted her and their eyes connected. She nodded and stood. He did not smile. She squeezed out of the row. "Hello, Baron. I was here reflecting."

"I see. Yes, well, tis a good place to do that. I had some reflections of me own to tend to." He palmed his hand through his thick head of dark hair and lowered his voice. "I best be going. Nice to see ye, Ms. Sands."

"I'm going, too. I'll walk out with you."

Baron didn't say anything and Nikki had to walk briskly to keep up with him. He moved like he needed to get the heck out of church in the worst way, or away from her. Nikki wasn't sure which.

They opened the doors. Nikki broke the silence. "I'm terribly sorry about Georges. I know you two were quite close."

"We were." She followed him to his truck. "Can I ask ye what ye want of me? I'm not in the mood to talk and want to get back. I'm making plans to go home."

"To San Francisco?"

"No. Ireland. I'm not happy here and now with Georges gone, I don't want to stay. We had a dream together to build these restaurants, but home is where I want to be."

"I'm sorry to bother you, but can I ask you, since you were so close, who might want to see Georges dead?"

He sighed and stopped to face her. Nikki caught a whiff of Old Spice and sweet tobacco. "I can't say that I know. He could be a difficult person, but in his heart he was a good man. Not always honest. Did some things that I did not approve of, and now he will have to take that up with his maker." Baron looked skyward.

"What kind of things did Georges do that troubled you?" Nikki pressed.

"Ye know, Ms. Sands, that is all private business and I like to leave the past where it belongs. I need to be moving along now. Once the police clear me of any wrongdoing, which I believe should be soon, then I have to get on a plane and make me way home."

He climbed in his truck and shut the door before she had a chance to ask him anything further. Wow. Really a different man from the one she'd spoken with yesterday, who'd been jovial and charming. Okay, so he had lost his pal, but did he have to be so rude to her? There was something behind his confession and there was something behind his curtness with her. Nikki felt certain that Baron O'Grady was hiding something.

Chapter 10

After she left the church, Nikki was disappointed to find that Andrés wasn't at Grapes. She placed an order for a filet with a walnut, caramelized onion, and gorgonzola sauce. She wanted something substantial after her day and she knew she had a terrific bottle of Merlot that would go with it. Then, she remembered her house guest and placed a second order, for Janie.

Janie was in the shower when Nikki returned to the cottage. With all the running around during the day, chasing financial advisors carrying copious amounts of cash, flashing her not-so-hefty cleavage at a pock-faced kid, and then winding up in church, where she really could have confessed quite a bit of her own sins of the day, she'd forgotten to make the one phone call she'd meant to.

It was after hours but she placed the call anyway to the Central California Women's Facility in Chowchilla. Since it was also Sunday, she had to go through a whole rigmarole of voice mail, until she finally found the person she thought she'd need. She left a message, but figured that to get what she wanted, which was to visit Bernadette Debussey, she'd probably have to call back in the morning.

Janie came out of the shower looking a bit better than the night before. Nikki needed some downtime from thinking about Georges and she figured that Janie would appreciate that, too. They decided to eat dinner, share the wine, and watch sitcoms until about nine o'clock when both of them started to drift off to sleep. Nikki covered Janie up on the sofa and headed into her room. As she crawled into bed, she couldn't help wondering why she hadn't heard from Andrés. She truly missed him. They hadn't spoken all day and that was unusual, but in a way she felt relieved, because if they did she knew that the topic of Spain would come up, and she wasn't prepared to give him an answer yet. These thoughts running through her mind along with the itinerary of her day finally put her into a fitful sleep.

The following morning, Nikki, still irritated over Derek's reaction to Andrés wanting to take her to Spain, decided to take another day off and continue seeing what she could find out about Georges' murder.

At a little after nine she headed to the spa. Janie was still asleep, and Nikki figured that was the best thing for her. She would have to do some more follow-up on Rick Moran today, but there were a few other things she wanted to check out.

She really needed to get the personnel files at the spa, which she was sure the cops already had. She didn't want to go back to the office to access anything via the computer.

Even though she knew she'd get grief for going about it this way, she decided to ask Simon for the information she needed. He answered his cell right away. "Halooo, Goldilocks. I could see on my caller ID that it was you. What's shakin', bacon?"

"Cute. I need something."

"You do? Why do I have a feeling this isn't good?"

"I don't know. It's not a big deal. I need Charlotte's address and phone number." There was silence on the other end of the phone. "Simon?"

"I heard you. You mean Charlotte, the therapist who ran the Syrah bath splash for Georges?"

"Yes, that's exactly who I'm talking about."

"No."

"What do you mean, no?" Nikki asked. "I need it. I want to talk to her about a facial."

"You can't lie to me. I so know you. And, no. I know what you're up to. Charlotte didn't take out Georges. She didn't even know him."

"That's what you say."

"Nikki, for once let the cops do their job. I'm sure they've already been to see her, and honestly I don't want you bothering her. She's a good therapist and aesthetician. I don't want her quitting on me because you think it's your job to be a vigilante."

Nikki sighed. New tactic must be taken. "Simon, you should know me." She switched the phone to her other ear as she made it to her car. "I won't bother her. Besides, if that Detective Robinson has been to see her she might already want to quit on you. I can smooth out his rough edges. Let her know that we as a company support her and know that she would not in any way have been involved in this." No reply. "I'll buy you dinner."

"Dinner in the city?"

"Yes, in the city."

"A night at the W?"

"What? I don't make that kind of cash! And you know if you don't give me what I want, I will find a way."

"Oh okay, fine. But you be careful, dammit. You always go and get in these messes and then Marco and I have to come to the rescue."

Please. "Yes, I know. I promise, I'll be careful."

She clicked off her phone after writing down Charlotte's address on a piece of paper.

As she drove to Charlotte's place she made two more calls. One to Janie, who told her what she needed to know about the interior decorator, and then to the interior decorator herself. The woman, a Ms. Redmond, was in and agreed to see her that afternoon.

Nikki pulled into the apartments where Charlotte lived on F Street. They were nice and looked pretty new. Granted they weren't five-star, but Nikki had lived in some dumps while "acting," and this place beat them hands down.

She found number 23 and rapped on the door. A young woman with red hair pulled back in a long ponytail opened it. She wore workout clothes. "Hey," she said.

"Hi. Charlotte?" Nikki asked. She didn't recognize her, and didn't know if she would anyway. She hadn't met all of the aestheticians at the spa yet.

"No. I'm Monica. I'm her roommate. Can I help you?"

"Maybe. I'm Nikki Sands. I work at the Malveaux Estate. Charlotte works there at the spa."

"Not anymore," Monica said.

"What do you mean?"

"Not after what happened on Saturday with that murder out there."

Nikki took a step back. "Have the police been by?"

"Oh yeah, and they had poor Charlotte in tears. She's pretty sensitive. Some cop named Robinson was here late Saturday night when Charlotte got home from her other job."

"Other job?" Nikki asked.

"Yeah. She works at Auberge du Soleil in St. Helena."

"I know the place. Nice." Real nice. Simon, Marco, and Nikki had taken a trip up there when the spa was being built. It was a *Lifestyles of the Rich and Famous* hangout all the way. But not exactly what they wanted at Malveaux. They wanted something a bit quainter, plus the kind of cash it took to run Auberge was far more money than even the Malveauxs had. "Well if she's working there, then what about Malveaux?"

"I don't know, but she was freaked about what happened. Said there was some weird stuff with that guy who was killed. I think she told the cops about it, but I don't know." Monica glanced at her watch. "I gotta go. I have a class to teach at the gym in fifteen."

"Right. Sorry. Do you know if Charlotte is working at Auberge today?"

The woman shrugged. "Don't know. She's my roommate, not my kid. It's not like I keep tabs on her."

Nikki backed away as Monica came out and locked the front door. Well, she had to go to St. Helena anyway. The interior decorator's place was up there. Hopefully she'd kill two birds with one stone. She called Auberge and discovered that Charlotte was working. Nikki asked if she had any openings. It turned out that they'd just received a cancellation, so Nikki took it, knowing that getting a facial might be the only way to get to speak Charlotte. She then called Stacey Redmond back and asked the interior decorator if she'd join her for lunch at Auberge. Nikki appeased her by adding that she so much liked the decorating she'd done at the spa, hotel, and restaurant, that she was interested in having her do some work on her place. Hey, whatever it might take to get the answers she needed. Ms. Redmond agreed to the lunch date.

Half an hour later she made it to Rutherford Hill, where the gorgeous hotel and spa were located. The place had a French influence to it, but with a California flair as it sat atop the hill with amazing views of the valley below. The cottages were done in earth tones, all with French doors leading out onto terraces. It looked like a wonderful place to stay, but at five hundred a night for the least expensive room, Nikki figured it might be some time before she soaked up the luxury between the sheets at Auberge. She'd take the more rustic, homey feel of the Malveaux spa and hotel any day, even though they weren't in her price range either. The rooms at Malveaux started at three hundred. Lucky for her, she had an in.

She recognized Stacey Redmond waiting for her at the hostess area. Today Stacey didn't have any red blotches on her face from crying over Georges' demands. No one would be crying over Georges' demands ever again. Stacey looked calm, even vibrant. She smiled when she spotted Nikki, her hazel eyes reflecting a genuine happiness to see her. She tucked her shoulder-length blonde hair back behind her ears. She reminded Nikki of one of the good girls. The kind guys cheated off of during tests in school, the kind who used Noxzema, and wore Izods and Top-Siders. Not exactly square, but smart and just a good girl whose mom surely bragged about her.

Nikki smiled back and approached her. "Hi. How are you?"

"Good, good." They made small talk before being seated.

Once at the table, it was Stacey who first opened up the conversation about Georges. Nikki noticed that her manicured hands trembled. She fiddled with the large diamond on her ring finger. "I heard about Georges. I read it in the paper this morning. It's terrible."

"It is." Nikki did not tell her that she was the one who found him.

A waiter came over and set down glasses of water. Once he left, Stacey quickly changed the subject. "You said that you wanted some decorating done?"

Nikki nodded and took a sip from her glass. She wanted to get back on the subject of Georges, but could tell by Stacey's nervous behavior that she'd have to make her comfortable first. "Would you like some wine?"

"Oh no. I'm pregnant."

"You are? That's wonderful."

"Thank you," Stacey replied. "Damon and I are very excited. It's taken quite some time for us to get pregnant again."

"Good for you. And your little boy? Is he okay? I remember the other day when you were so upset, you said that he was sick."

"He's much better, thank you. We should look at the menu." She smiled, but her hands still shook when she lifted her water glass.

Nikki glanced over the menu and ordered the yellowfin tuna with roasted beets, radish, and lemon oil. Since her lunch partner wasn't imbibing she decided to have iced tea with her lunch. Stacey ordered the scallops, then directed the conversation back to decorating, and Nikki decided she'd appease her, maybe get her to open up. "My room is so feminine right now, which I love. It's pink and black toile, but I think I'd really like a change. I like the colors you used at the restaurant. They are perfect for a vineyard. Did you choose those colors or did Georges?"

"I did. But of course, he didn't like the colors." She looked away.

"I think the colors are fantastic and so does Derek."

"Thank you. I tried really hard to please Georges, but he was kind of difficult to work for."

"Yeah, he seemed to be pretty hard on the people who worked for him."

"Hard to please. Very. But I'm sorry he's gone. I am. No one deserves to be murdered."

The waiter brought their orders, and throughout lunch Nikki felt like there was something more that Stacey wanted to tell her. She asked her questions about her son, her husband, and her pregnancy.

"I'm three months along," Stacey said, and she smiled wide. "It's great. We finally started telling our friends and family. We had a couple of miscarriages after Jacob and I started to think it wouldn't happen again. But now, I'm past the real scary zone and with some prayer we'll make it all the way."

"That must have been difficult for you," Nikki said. "How have you been able to work?"

"It is hard, but Damon is starting a new business. He left the architect firm he worked for and went out on his own recently, and my business is growing, and we really need that dual income." She stabbed a scallop and took a bite.

"Working with someone like Georges must have been very stressful."

Stacey set her fork down. "You know what, it was. And, can I ask you something?"

"Sure?"

"You're not really here to ask me about decorating tips, are you? You keep bringing the conversation back to Georges. I know you saw me upset last week and I was, and for good reason. Georges was not easy to work with. But if you're thinking what I think you are, then you're wrong. I had nothing to do with Georges' murder. I'm not a killer, Ms. Sands. An emotional, pregnant woman who would like to *stay* pregnant, if you know what I mean."

Nikki shook her head. "Not exactly."

"Fine. I'll spell it out." Suddenly Stacey Redmond turned into a lioness. "You were the only one to see me break down last week. I fell apart in front of you because I was so frustrated with Georges' demands and you happened to be there at the time. I'm sorry about that now. I went home and told my husband about the way Georges treated me, but only he and you know. In other words, Damon and I have wanted another baby for a long time now, and it looks like we're finally going to have one. The police have no idea I had a falling out with Georges and they don't need to, because I didn't kill him."

"Okay. I'm sure you have an alibi."

Stacey shook her head. "No. No, I don't. I read in the paper what time they thought the murder occurred, and I happened to be on the road at that time. Here's what I'm trying to tell you: I don't need the stress of the police coming around my home or my business and questioning me. I don't need your questions. I am a mom and an interior decorator. I didn't murder Georges, but it would send up red flags if someone told them that I had a problem with Georges and found him difficult to work for." She lowered her gaze and twisted her napkin around her fingers. "Please, Nikki, keep what I told you between us. I don't need the stress and neither does my family. I have to go." She set down a twenty. Nikki tried to give it back. Stacey refused and left.

Nikki sat there dumbfounded, not knowing exactly what to do. Stacey Redmond had motive and opportunity to murder Georges. The man stressed her out and she wanted to keep that baby. Nikki couldn't blame her. But would she go so far as to kill him? Nikki didn't know that either, and because she didn't, she decided to keep Stacey Redmond's secret. For now.

Sautéed Diver Scallops with Cauliflower, Capers, and Almonds with Robert Mondavi Private Selection Pinot Grigio

There are quite a few places that Nikki would recommend you visit while in the wine country, and one of them would be Auberge du Soleil. It is divine in every sense of the word. However, if you don't have a chance to do so, you can create your own Sunshine Inn. You and your loved one can make a wonderful dinner together. Choose from one of these recipes, compliments of the restaurant. The diver scallops pair wonderfully with a glass of Robert Mondavi Private Selection Pinot Grigio. A dry, fresh fruit-flavored wine combined with mineral and spice notes, which make it a wine to be paired with many different foods.

½ cup balsamic vinegar (reduced)
2 cups cauliflower florets
¼ cup cream
1 tbsp extra virgin olive oil
8 fresh scallops (dayboat, if available) 2–3 oz each
salt and pepper
1½ tbsp unsalted butter
2 tbsp capers
2 tbsp slivered almonds (toasted)
2 tbsp golden raisins
1 tbsp chopped parsley

In a small saucepan, bring vinegar to a boil, reduce by half, and reserve.

Bring 2 quarts of water to a boil and season with salt to taste. Add the cauliflower florets. (Break apart one head of cauliflower into equal pieces. Reserve 1 cup of the better looking florets for garnish.) Cook until tender (about 60 seconds). Drain and plunge florets in ice bath to stop the cooking process. In a saucepan, cover the other cup with the cream and cook for 8 minutes. Purée and put through a fine mesh sieve. Keep warm.

Warm two 7-inch (small) sauté pans. Add olive oil to one pan. Season the scallops with salt and pepper. When the pan just starts to smoke, add the scallops. Cook for about 1 minute on each side, depending on the thickness of the scallop. When scallop shows a little color, turn. In the other pan, add butter and cook the butter until it begins to brown. Add the florets and cook for 1 minute. Season with salt and pepper. Add the capers, almonds, raisins, and parsley.

On warmed plates, put a small circle of the cauliflower purée in the middle. Add the raisin-caper ragout to the middle. Top with the scallops (they should be medium-rare). Drizzle the balsamic reduction and the extra virgin olive oil around the plate to garnish. Serves 2.

Marinated Yellowfin Tuna with Roasted Beets, Radish, and Lemon Oil with Robert Sinskey Vin Gris of Pinot Noir

Pair this recipe with Robert Sinskey Vin Gris of Pinot Noir. The grapes are delicately whole-cluster pressed and the juice is fermented off the skins. The wine is a gorgeous copper blush hue. This is a terrific rosé to drink with tuna.

1 bunch gold baby beets
1 bunch red baby beets
1 bunch chioggia baby beets
extra virgin olive oil
salt and pepper
½ lb sushi-grade tuna loin
4 oz Agrumato Lemon Extra Virgin Olive Oil
1 small shallot, finely diced
1 bunch chives, cut crosswise
½ cup lemon vinaigrette
5 French breakfast radishes, washed
1 bunch cilantro, washed, leaves picked and cut
    into chiffonade

LEMON VINAIGRETTE

¼ cup fresh lemon juice
¼–½ cup extra virgin olive oil
salt and pepper

Whisk lemon juice and olive oil together in a bowl. Season with salt and pepper. Reserve.

Trim beets of tops. Toss beets with salt, pepper, and olive oil. Place in a shallow roasting pan, cover in aluminum foil, and roast in a 325° oven. Roast until knife tender. Cool slightly. Peel while still warm. Cut into quarters. Reserve.

Have a fish purveyor slice tuna into 2-ounce pieces. Place tuna on a sheet of plastic wrap.

Moisten with extra virgin olive oil. Place another sheet of plastic wrap on top of tuna. Pound gently with a meat tenderizing mallet until evenly flattened. Repeat with all tuna.

Remove 1 layer of plastic wrap from tuna. Invert on a cold 12-inch plate. Season tuna with salt and fresh ground pepper. Drizzle lightly with lemon oil (½ to 1 oz per piece).

Dress beets with diced shallots, chives, salt, pepper, and lemon vinaigrette. Spoon onto tuna in little piles.

Slice radish thinly on a mandolin or with a sharp knife. Drop onto beets. Drizzle a little lemon vinaigrette (⅛ oz) over tuna. Finish with chives and cilantro chiffonade. Serves 4.

Optional: make tiny croutons. Dice white or sourdough bread into ⅛-inch squares. Toss with olive oil, salt, and pepper. Bake in 350° oven until golden. Sprinkle over finished tuna dish.

Chapter 11

Nikki didn't suspect that Charlotte was a killer, not really. She wanted to speak to the aesthetician because in all likelihood, other than the killer, she'd been the last person to see Georges alive.

She had scheduled an olive oil and lemon verbena facial with Charlotte. The Malveaux Spa didn't have anything similar, so she thought she'd not only gather what information she could from Charlotte, but also see if the olive oil and lemon verbena facial should be an item added to the Malveaux line. Problem was, she really didn't feel like having a facial at all, especially after the lunch with Stacey that had taken such a bizarre twist.

The woman at the front desk showed her to a changing area, where she stripped except for her underwear and donned a plush terrycloth robe. Nice. She then slid her feet into a pair of thong-type sandals and headed out. Charlotte was waiting for her outside the changing area and introduced herself, then seemed to study Nikki for a moment, as if trying to place her. Nikki had seen her around the hotel and spa a few times. Charlotte was someone most people would definitely notice, even women. She was tall, striking in an Angelina Jolie way, with the lips that posed the question: collagen injections? Her hair was wavy, long and auburn and almost the color of her eyes. Sexy or hot were surely the words men used in describing Charlotte. Be-atch was probably the word—and said just that way— that many women used in regard to Charlotte. Nikki thought, *Now there's a girl I don't want hanging around my boyfriend.* And, which boyfriend would that be? The charming one ready to start a new life in Spain or the one with the aloof attitude and utterly to-die-for blue eyes?

Nikki followed Charlotte to the treatment room, and Charlotte waited outside while Nikki disrobed and got under the sheet. Charlotte came back in after a moment and tucked Nikki's hair into a towel. "Do I know you?" Charlotte asked. "You look familiar."

Nikki felt awkward addressing this while on the aesthetician table, but had no choice. "Actually you do kind of know me, or at least you've probably seen me around. I work at Malveaux. I'm the winery manager."

"Oh." Charlotte's eyes widened. "I see. Okay, then can I ask you why you're here? Are you really here for a facial?"

Oh good, at least Charlotte cut right to the chase. There'd be no trying to figure out the meaning behind nervous gestures or trembling hands. "Actually, a facial is something I need. I'm getting a few laugh lines." She made an attempt to laugh. Charlotte kept on looking at her, which was really odd in a way, too, because she was leaning over Nikki, who was having to look back up at her. Oooh, she'd better *not* be a killer. Bad position to be in if that was the case.

"If you're here about Saturday, I already talked to the police, and I e-mailed Simon this morning about my job at the spa. I can't work there now."

"Oh. Um, actually I'm kind of here to tell you that we know you had nothing to do with Saturday's events and we value you as an employee."

"You do?" Nikki nodded. "That's very nice and I appreciate it, but I've been working here for a while and I started at Malveaux to kind of try someplace new and see how it worked. I've decided that Auberge is a better fit for me." She took a steamy towel that smelled like eucalyptus and placed it over Nikki's face.

Nikki breathed it in and for a second the thought that the woman might suffocate her crossed her mind, but then Charlotte removed the towel and began wiping off her face, then followed that with a cleanser, thoroughly washing her face. Then on to a scrub. This might not be so awful after all. "It is nice here," Nikki replied.

"I think so, and no one was ever killed here."

"Right. So, you said that the police came to talk to you?"

"A Detective Robinson. He asked me a lot of questions. I told him what I knew."

"What's that? I'm only asking because I knew Georges and I feel awful about his murder and I figure you had to have been the last person to see him alive." Nikki didn't know how Charlotte would react or if she would even respond.

"I took Mr. Debussey into the treatment room and explained the treatment to him. He asked for the Syrah splash, and basically, my only job was to fill the bath, explain the benefits, and be available when he was finished to get him water or tea. It's a simple treatment for me."

"And that's what you did?"

"Exactly." She mixed together in her hands oil from small vials and gently massaged them into Nikki's face.

"Do you remember if you opened the French doors leading out to the balcony before leaving the room?" Nikki asked.

"I did open them."

"Did you open them before Mr. Debussey came in for his bath or while he was already in the room?"

"Mr. Debussey had been there a few times before and so I did as he usually requested, which was to open them. I did so before he came inside."

So, the killer had either already been on the balcony waiting, or had climbed up to the balcony somehow while Georges was in the bath. Nikki knew she'd have to go back to the treatment room and see if there was an area in which someone could have been hiding. If that was the case, then whoever killed Georges was aware of his schedule.

The aromatherapy oils of lemon and neroli mixed with olive oil smelled great. Yeah, this definitely wasn't the worst thing a gal had to go through. Granted it could be a bit more relaxing if the talk weren't focused on murder, or for that matter if there were no discussion at all. "But you left early, before Mr. Debussey was finished with the bath."

Charlotte stopped massaging her face briefly, as if grappling with an answer. She began rubbing again as she spoke. "There is a timer that chimes when the bath is finished. So, the timer chimed, Mr. Debussey didn't come out. I knocked. I waited. I left. I had to come to work here. Mr. Debussey was a bit of a pain, so I didn't care all that much if he even left me a tip. I know that he was your friend, so I'm sorry to say that."

Nikki opened her eyes. "It's quite all right. But, how was he a pain, if all you had to do was what you explained to me? You know, to basically just run the bath."

Charlotte wiped off the oil on Nikki's face, again with the steamy towel. She dried it and covered Nikki's eyes with cotton patches and turned on a bright light. Immediately Nikki felt a pinch on her face. Ow. And another one. Ouch. She squirmed on the table. "I'm doing extractions, cleaning out your pores. You have some buildup there."

Now this part of the treatment was far from relaxing. Nikki had to wonder if Charlotte was actually a sadist and getting a thrill out of torturing her, one pore at a time.

"Once Mr. Debussey was prepared to get into the tub, I of course left the room. However, I don't know if you've had that treatment there or not, but if the client needs the therapist at any time they can buzz us with a dealy-bob thing, you know, like a buzzer on the side of the tub, and the therapist carries around one of those things like you get at a restaurant when it's your turn to be seated."

"A remote vibrator?" Nikki asked, sounding strange as Charlotte continued to torture the left side of her nose, making it difficult to breathe.

"Yes."

Nikki thought her entire face might come through one little pore. How much buildup could there be? Yikes. "Did he buzz you for some reason?"

"He did."

"What did he want?" Thank God Charlotte moved from her nose on to her chin. At least that was tolerable, and there must not have been the same amount of buildup, because she finished quickly and turned the overhead light on. The next thing she did was put a mask on Nikki's face. It was cool and smelled a little like bananas.

"First he wanted me to change the candles in the room. He said that he didn't like lavender, that he wanted vanilla scented candles, so I went to get those for him. Then, he wanted a phone, of all things."

"Vanilla scented candles? Were the doors to the balcony still open?

"Yep."

"Then he wanted a phone?"

"Yeah. He said that his cell phone was back at the restaurant, so I offered him the spa remote phone."

"Did he say who he was calling?"

"Nope."

"Did you hear any of the conversation?" Nikki asked.

"He asked me to pour him another glass of wine, and the bottle was out of his reach from the tub, so I did. While I got his wine, he called someone and I heard him tell whoever it was that if it hadn't been for the moronic agent, the first cookbook deal with the publisher would have been a better one, and that whoever he was talking to needed to do a better job with investments. He didn't like losing money."

Rick Moran. He had to have been talking to Moran. "Did you tell the police about this?"

"Of course I did. I got the feeling the detective was looking at me as if I might have been involved, but I took off after the phone thing and the other thing that happened."

The mask was cool on Nikki's face, probably refreshing if she could let herself relax, which was not likely going to happen, especially after Charlotte's pinching fingers from hell. "What other thing that happened?"

"I don't know if I should tell you this, it's not like you're a detective, and you *were* the man's friend. You might not like it."

Nikki removed the cotton patches from her eyes and opened them to look at Charlotte. "Okay, let me level with you. I knew Georges and I liked him, but I have more than gossip-type interest in this thing. I know someone who was close to him who could really be affected by this, and I am really concerned for this person." Janie's face flashed through Nikki's mind as she realized the real reason she wanted to find Georges' killer. Sure, it did have something to do with showing up Detective Robinson, but more than that, Nikki felt a connection to the young woman. There were similarities between the two of them, both losing parents at a young age, and also the fact that there was this protective instinct that had come over her the night Janie had shown up on her doorstep, her face tear stained.

Charlotte stared back at her as though determining if going on and relating this story to her was truly in her best interest. "I already told the detective, so I suppose it can't hurt to tell you. After I gave Mr. Debussey the phone and wine, and let myself out, he asked if I could find some more candles. I went back into the supply area to see about getting him the candles, and a few minutes later when I came back to his room, I heard some noises through the door coming from in there, like moaning and splashing. I figured he was getting kinky in there and I really didn't want to be a part of it. I was sort of feeling weird going in and out of his room anyway, and honestly, he wouldn't be the first client to try and make a move on me."

"Oh my God! Do you realize that you probably heard the killer in there with him, or maybe you heard him taking his last breaths?" Nikki watched as a horrified expression came over Charlotte's face.

"I never thought of that! The police didn't say anything like that to me."

Nikki felt bad because she could see that what she'd said had really affected Charlotte, but what else could the woman have thought she'd heard, after the fact? "What did you think was going on in there?"

"You know, like I said, something kinky."

"Oh. But he was the only one in there."

"You got it, and it freaked me out. Here this big time chef is in the spa tub, well you know, playing . . ."

"Yeah, I get it."

"I thought maybe he wanted the phone to call one of those places. The sex hotlines."

Nikki didn't reply. Charlotte had a point. It could be a possibility, but more likely the killer had either just left and Georges was on his way to the afterlife, or the killer was still in there with him, finishing him off.

"I'm going to leave this mask on for ten minutes and I'll let you relax. I'll be back."

But Nikki knew what she really wanted to do was get this mask off and find out who this agent person was that Georges insisted was a moron. She figured he'd been talking to Moran.

She didn't bother waiting for Charlotte to come back. She was convinced that she had nothing to do with Georges' death and that her mind was surely made up about not returning to work at Malveaux. It was likely Charlotte had told her everything she knew about what had taken place in the spa yesterday. No more time for masks, relaxation, and extractions; it was time for her to get back on the trail of a killer.

Chapter 12

It was two o'clock before Nikki got back on the road again. So, Georges called someone and they spoke about his moronic agent? Who had he called? Presumably Moran. And what agent? He *was* a chef. Not a TV personality. She smacked herself on the forehead in disgust. Shoot, had all those pore extractions caused her brain to seep out? Of course, *agent*—a literary one. Georges had written a couple of cookbooks and had just finished the project with Derek. He would know the name of the literary agent, wouldn't he? Whoever it was had to have brokered the deal, if that's what they called it. Now, how to get that information out of Derek, who hated the fact that she enjoyed being a snoop? And, once she got it out of him, what would she or could she do with that information? Was there another way of finding out this stuff?

She smacked herself on the forehead again. Wait. Could it be as easy as looking in the acknowledgement page of one of his cookbooks? Hadn't she recalled seeing in some of the books she'd read that authors often thanked their agents? It was worth a shot. She drove to the St. Helena library on Library Lane.

She found both of Georges' cookbooks on the shelves. The most recent one only acknowledged Bernadette—obviously before she'd burned down the guesthouse and he'd sent her packing—and his editor, Renee Rothschild. No "thank you" to his agent. Ah, but in the first book Georges didn't just thank his agent, a Henry Bloomenfeld, but everyone under the sun as well. Nikki read the list and had no clue who they were, but was thankful that he'd put in there the one name that she needed.

She walked back to the circulation desk and asked the librarian about a book that might include the names and addresses of agents and publishers. The librarian led her to a volume called the LMP, the *Literary Marketplace*. "You can't check it out, but you're welcome to copy any of the addresses in there," the librarian explained.

Nikki thanked her and started thumbing through it. She found Rothschild Publishers, which she already knew was located in San Francisco. But she did not find Henry Bloomenfeld's name. She went back to the librarian. "I'm looking for a specific name. Is it possible I might find it elsewhere?"

"You could look at some of the older LMPs."

Nikki decided to try that and struck pay dirt. She found Henry Bloomenfeld's name and address in an LMP from a couple of years back. Did that mean he was now out of business? He was also located in San Francisco, but the address given was a post office box. However, there was a phone number listed. From past experience Nikki knew that it was possible to use the Internet to type in the phone number and get an address. Moving to the library's computer, she entered the phone number—and it worked. Ten minutes later she was out the door, back in the car, and heading toward San Francisco. She really did not want to go back to the vineyard, not yet. She was focused now and a drive to the Bay Area might be exactly what she needed.

Nikki was surprised at Henry Bloomenfeld's address—really surprised. It was the same building that Moran had gone into the day before and had come out of with the bag. It didn't make a lot of sense. If this tenement really housed Henry Bloomenfeld's agency, it didn't connect for her. Here he was with a famous client like Georges Debussey, but his office was stuck down here on Market Street.

There was no elevator in the building, so Nikki hiked the five flights of stairs. The hall leading to Bloomenfeld's door stunk like tobacco and age; stains soiled the carpet, which she figured might have at one time been red. Not too sure though, as it looked like mud with bloodstains interspersed throughout. Oh God, hopefully those weren't *real* bloodstains. Someone was playing AC/DC behind one of the thin doors. Dust particles hung in the air, sunlight hitting them from a small window at the end of the hall. Nikki's chest tightened.

She rapped on the office door. Hopefully this was the correct Henry Bloomenfeld. The sign on the door *did* read "Literary Agent/Publicist." Nikki rapped again. This time louder. Was "You Shook Me All Night Long" coming from behind Bloomenfeld's door or the one next to him?

The door swung open. The music accosted her along with a buxom blonde, a cigarette hanging from her mouth, holding a glass of what appeared to be scotch in her left hand. Her blue eyes were heavily made up with false lashes and garish shadow, her lips done in bubble gum pink. A black silk robe was draped over her shoulders, exposing a matching black negligee that didn't leave much to the imagination. She looked Nikki up and down. Run, run—fast! "Wow, baby, you gotta get a load of this. What agency did you call?"

"Hang on, baby, I'll turn the stereo down." Seconds later a man who came up to Nikki's breasts and then stared at them appeared from around the corner—skinny, curly haired, pale, fiftyish, wearing what Nikki knew had to be a designer suit—maybe even an Armani. "Oh yeah. Classy.

Nice. Okay, come on in. Let's get started. Your wardrobe is in the bathroom and the film crew will be along soon."

Nikki held up a hand. "Whoa, ho, ho. I think I'm at the wrong place."

"Oh no, you're not, baby. You're exactly what we ordered," the blonde said.

"No. I'm a writer, a journalist to be exact." Lying to this element came so much easier, and she didn't think it would be a good idea to mention Moran yet. "And, I was looking for Georges Debussey's agent. I think this has to be the wrong place."

The man cleared his throat. "I worked with Georges." He stuck out his hand. "Who did you say you were?"

Nikki crossed her arms in front of her. No way was she shaking his hand. Besides, she still had her doubts about him. Good thing she had some Mace in her purse, and she'd use it, dammit, if she needed to. "I didn't. My name is Cara Sands."

"What paper are you with?"

"I'm not." She looked Blondie and Slimy up and down as they continued to do to her. "I'm writing a book, actually."

"Hmmm," he said. He shook a finger at her. "You obviously know that I'm a literary agent. Most people who approach me in this way, I don't usually help. But you, I might be able to work with. You really didn't have to come here and use the Georges Debussey story on me." Bloomenfeld winked at her. "I might also be able to get you work in Hollywood."

"No thanks." Been there, done that, and hadn't quite made the scene like say, oh, Nicole Kidman, for example. "I'm not looking for an agent."

"You're not?" he raised the unibrow below his forehead that needed some serious waxing. He had a faint New Yorker accent that hung on the end of his words.

"No. I'm here to talk to you about Mr. Debussey's life; and now murder, of course."

Henry took a step back. "Georges was murdered?" He

took another step back and reached for a leather sofa that sat in the middle of the office.

Blondie came to his side. "Hanky? Are you okay, baby? What is it?"

"Get me a scotch, Marsha." Marsha batted her eyelashes at him and looked as stupid as Nikki assumed she was. "Now!" he bellowed.

Marsha scurried away.

"What do you mean, Georges was murdered? When did this happen?" he asked, falling onto the sofa.

Nikki studied him for a moment. Was he for real? Or was this an act? Moran surely must have told him. Or had Moran even known about it? She assumed he did, even assumed he was in on it, but he hadn't been around that evening after the murder. Maybe the fact that Moran had come to this same building the day before had been mere coincidence. It would be quite a coincidence, though, knowing that both men had an affiliation with Georges. Nonetheless, weirder things had happened. Maybe she was on the wrong track here. Or what about the cops? Detective Robinson had put two and two together by now after talking to Charlotte. If Nikki had figured it out, Mr. Highfalutin Detective from Houston would have buzzed by Bloomenfeld's already. Unless Nikki had beaten him to the punch. It was still only Monday afternoon, less than forty-eight hours after the killing. Maybe it hadn't crossed anyone's mind, but news like murder traveled fast, even if it had only occurred less than two days earlier. And with Georges gaining notoriety, Nikki found it fascinating that Henry, the agent, had no clue, even if the police had not paid him a visit. "You hadn't heard?"

He shook his head. "No. When did this happen?"

"Saturday."

He looked up at her and now he was the one studying *her.* "Saturday? And now you're in my office claiming to be writing a book about him? What gives? What's your real deal, Ms. Sands?"

Nikki bit her lower lip. Marsha brought the scotch to Henry, who took a major gulp and then went back to staring hard at Nikki after shooing Marsha away.

"My initial plan for the book had nothing to do with Georges being murdered. It was all about his life and how he pursued the dream of becoming a world class chef and becoming owner and operator of gourmet restaurants here in the city and out in Napa. I happened to be in the city and traced your address, taking a chance you might be here." Nikki got the feeling that Henry didn't only do his business out of the dump, but also lived there.

Henry took another large swallow of the amber-colored contents in his glass. "Uh-huh."

"He didn't tell you about this? With the new book coming out, we thought it would be a good idea to do another book in conjunction, something like a 'here's your life' type thing. You know, a biography."

"Uh-huh." He continued with the scrutiny. "And how did you meet Georges?"

"At the vineyard, actually. At Malveaux Estate." Now that was the honest-to-God truth. "I work there, and we got to be friends and talked about this idea. I was kind of ghosting it for him, that's why I figured he would've talked to you about it, because he talked about you all the time. You know he liked doing the cookbook thing, but sitting down and doing a huge manuscript, you know, that wasn't his thing."

"He talked about me all the time, huh?"

She nodded. This statement bugged him. She could see it all over his face. Why? Had she said something to tip him off that she was pretty much full of it?

"Where was he murdered?" Henry asked.

"At the vineyard. At the new spa there." She knew that he would read it in the paper or hear it on the news, because if he truly hadn't heard about Georges' death yet, he would now go looking to follow up on her story.

"Let me get this straight then. Now you want to play

detective and write a book about his life and murder and you're looking for answers?"

Now we're talking. Okay, it was easy to stay closer to the truth when the guy had just basically spelled it out for her. "Exactly."

"Don't you think you might want to let the cops do that job? Write the book later."

Why, oh why, did every man she talked to tell her the same thing? *Let the cops do the job.* She smiled sheepishly. "Listen, you know, being an agent and all . . ." Which she still couldn't wrap her brain around, looking at his place; regardless of his expensive suit and the decadent furniture inside, something did not ring kosher with Henry Bloomenfeld. "I don't want to sound callous here, but I do have ambition and I could use a buck or two, and since I was already working with Georges and got to know him, I'd like to strike while the iron is hot. See what I can find out."

"Fancy yourself as quite the sleuth, huh?"

She shrugged.

He patted the seat on the sofa next to him. "Sit down, Ms. Sands. I won't bite. Let's talk. Maybe I can give you some answers. Maybe not, and maybe I could represent you, if the story winds up being any good."

She pegged him—total slimeball. "I think I'll stand. Thanks. I think better that way."

Blondie called out from another room. The place was spacious. "Baby, are we gonna do this thing, or what?"

"Not now, Marsha. Go relax."

He held a finger up to Nikki. "I've got to make a call." He walked out of the front reception area and back into another room. Nikki could make out only a few words and they were muffled at that. "Believe. No. Not now. Later. Meet me, five thirty." Nikki didn't catch who he was calling or where they would meet, but she thought that it had something to do with Georges' murder and she had the growing feeling that she should get the hell out of there, because until she looked a little further into Henry Bloomenfeld's past, she didn't know whether or not she was waiting inside the office of a killer. When she heard him yell for Marsha to make him another drink, she slipped out. She'd started walking quickly down the hall when he opened his door and yelled, "Wait, Ms. Sands. We need to talk. Wait." Nikki turned back to see him stepping into the hallway. She'd started to pick up speed when she ran into a full-figured redhead.

Henry yelled at Red to stop her. The woman reached out to grab her, but being agile, Nikki spun away from her and raced off. She didn't slow down until she was a block away. The man was creepy, shady, and possibly a murderer. She didn't entirely buy his grief act.

Dammit, and she'd given him her actual last name and the fact that she worked at Malveaux. Boy, had she chosen the wrong place, time, and person to tell the truth to. What if he was the killer, and tracked her down? She spotted a smoothie place and ducked inside, just in case, but she doubted the waifish man could have kept up with her. Not that he needed to, because he *did* know where to find her.

She looked at her watch. Three forty-five. There was only one thing to do—kill some time, because she was going to follow Slimeball Bloomenfeld and see who it was he planned to meet. Maybe she would find some answers there. Good thing she'd just paid off her Visa, 'cause she was going shopping. Bloomenfeld knew what she looked like and she'd need some sort of disguise. Ah! Finally a logical reason to head on over to Nordstrom. For all she knew it was the one time when new clothes and accessories could mean life or death.

Chapter 13

Forty minutes later, Nikki was dressed in a black skirt tighter and shorter than she would normally wear, along with a red scoop neck sweater—very, um . . . call girl chic. With her other clothes in the bag, she found a wig shop and made herself over with a wavy blonde one. She looked in the mirror. Maybe she should go back to blonde. It did make her look younger, and although being taken seriously in her career was a good thing, the idea of having more fun, especially at that moment, was quite appealing. She bought the wig and got into her car where she put on a dark red lipstick from her bag—not her usual color, but this was an unusual circumstance. She applied eye makeup and blush—all in new colors, as she didn't normally carry much makeup with her—with a heavier hand than usual, and then took out the pair of sunglasses that she'd purchased and grabbed the eyeglasses she'd also bought just in case she had to follow Bloomenfeld and the mystery guest into a restaurant or something. She hoped she'd get that lucky, rather than their going into some apartment building. She did look "the part" for the neighborhood, which was what she was shooting for—wanting to blend in.

She drove back to Bloomenfeld's office and parked across the street and down a half block, grateful to finally find parking after being flipped off by an old man that she'd cut off in her pursuit of the perfect spot. She could see the front door and anyone coming in or out. She saw on the dashboard clock that it was almost fifteen minutes before meet time. She crossed her fingers that he hadn't already left. What if he'd gone straight out and ignored the redhead she'd passed and nearly fallen over in the hallway? What if she'd put him on alert because he was the killer and he had to do something to cover his tracks? Had Detective Jonah Robinson questioned him yet? She still had no read on Henry Bloomenfeld.

Twenty minutes later, feeling groggy from sitting and waiting, her patience wore out. She must've missed him. She could never do the real cop thing. How they ever did stakeouts—who knew? Nope, her first stakeout would have been a bust if she'd had to wait much longer. Patience was not one of her better virtues.

Luckily for her, the stakeout was up, because out walked a disheveled and almost frantic looking Bloomenfeld. Behind him were Blondie and the redhead, who went off in the opposite direction. They looked to be giggling and counting a wad of cash. Nikki could hear, from her open car window, Blondie yell out, "Bye, lover. Thank you."

The redhead said, "Mucho gusto."

Bloomenfeld didn't look back or say anything—a man with a mission. Guess Nikki hadn't shaken him too badly. He'd still had his, ah, *priorities* straight.

She laughed at this thought and turned the key. Her trustworthy Camry started up. She waited to see if he was going to get into a car. He didn't. Not part of the plan, but okay. She rolled up the window, turned off the engine, and got out. Hopefully no one would break into her car.

She footed it behind him, keeping him in sight. He

walked three blocks up and two blocks over. Nikki stopped. *No, no, no.* She shook her head, looking down in defeat. Now what to do? Bloomenfeld had just walked into a strip joint. Sure, she was hoping for a public venue to get a good look at his partner, but a strip bar? Not exactly her choice. Her stomach turned over. Think this one through. She really wanted to know who Bloomenfeld was meeting with inside the seedy place. God. Couldn't this guy take a reprieve? Was he some type of sex addict? Duh! Maybe that's where he spent his wad. Why couldn't he have just opted for a cup of java at Starbucks?

There *was* one thing going for her in this situation: she realized that when she was at his office, he'd had a drink going and then followed up with another. She'd place a bet on it that he hadn't stopped the boozing with her exit, and now inside the bar, he'd surely have another. A man who didn't weigh much more than she did would probably be halfway to blursville by now. She decided to give it half an hour and see if Bloomenfeld and his mystery guest came out, and if not then hopefully he'd be *plenty* sedated and it would be *plenty* dim inside so that he wouldn't take notice of her.

After some time she made her way across the street and toward the bar. That sinking feeling in her stomach came back; well, it wasn't like it had ever left, it just grew worse.

A big dude—and that was the only way to refer to him, *dude*—stood at the aluminum front door. The guy had to be six foot five and two fifty. Linebacker material. He wore a chest-tight T-shirt, jeans just as tight, and a cowboy hat, which he tipped at her when she walked up to the door. "Howdy, little filly. They've been looking for you. You better get on in there."

"Oh no, I don't work here."

"Sure." He winked and opened the door.

Oh, no. She walked in. The John Wayne–type pervert smacked her on the ass. She grimaced but entered anyway. She found herself in the darkened bar, her eyes slowly adjusting. As they did, she realized that almost facing her

from one of the booths was Bloomenfeld. His pal had his
back to her and was wearing a baseball cap. The stage was
to the left and she made it a point not to look at whoever
was dancing to Prince's "Darling Nikki." Great. Just super.

Another man approached her and took her by the shoulder. When she tried to pull away from him, he squeezed
even tighter. He wasn't as big as the cowboy, but almost.

He took her to a side door. Why hadn't she thought to
take out her Mace? Who was this bozo, and why was he
dragging her to the side, and now to a door? Uh-oh. She
was in big trouble. He opened the door, and inside were a
half dozen barely clad women sitting on locker room–type
benches, putting their makeup on by looking at compact
mirrors. One of them—a pretty, dark-haired girl, maybe
twenty-two, tops—glanced up at her. The rest didn't even
notice.

"Here's the new girl. Make sure she's got something
decent to wear."

"Or not," a leggy blonde remarked and they all laughed.
"I thought you said that she was a redhead."

"Redhead, blonde. I don't know. Gary hired her. Go on.
You go on in three songs, baby."

John Wayne number two also smacked her on the butt
and walked out. What was it with these idiots and their ass
smacking? *Jerks!* With wide eyes she looked around. Jeesh,
twice now she'd been mistaken for an adult entertainer.
Not a good day. She couldn't wait to get back into one of
her sweater sets and a pair of jeans. She moved toward
the back of the room, hoping to find an exit. At this point,
she didn't give a rat's ass who the mystery guest was. All
she wanted to do was return to the safe haven of her car
and get on the freeway headed back to the pastorally calm
vineyard where no one brutishly smacked your rear. What
in hell was she doing? She should've listened to Detective
Robinson and every other Joe Schmoe telling her to let the
cops do their job. She was no cop, by any means, and now
she got the feeling she was in a heap of trouble because

there was no exit door in the small dressing room. She made her way to the back.

The attractive dark-haired girl came up to her and said, "I'm Alyssa. You're not a dancer, are you?"

Nikki shook her head.

"Are you vice?"

"No," she whispered.

"Who are you?"

The redhead looked over at them. "Shut up, Alyssa. Always trying to make buddies here. If you want a pal go to Girl Scout camp. Leave the new chick alone."

"You shut up. I can talk to whoever I want."

The redhead shot her a dirty look, got up, and walked out.

"So, what's your deal?" Alyssa asked, her brown eyes shining. Either she was on something or totally fascinated by the newcomer.

"There's a man out there."

"Uh, yeah. A few."

"Right. Well, I don't think this guy is on the up-and-up."

"Okay," she said sarcastically. "There's a surprise."

Cut to the chase. "I think he could be involved in a murder of someone I know—I mean knew—and I'm trying to get some information so I followed him here."

Alyssa put a hand on her hip. "Really? No bull? Yeah, there's a lot of crap that goes down here, but murder?"

"No bull."

"You want some help?" Alyssa asked.

Nikki nodded.

"It'll come with a price."

Nikki took out her wallet and handed Alyssa a hundred dollar bill.

"You're on, sister. What do you need to know and where can I find you?"

"I need the name of the man he's with, and see if you can find out the gist of what they're talking about." Nikki described Henry to Alyssa.

"I know that geek. I can't stand him. I'll help you, for sure." She shook a finger at her. "You know what, I gotta tell ya, he is a bozo I could see hiring someone to do a dirty job like murder for him. He hires some of these chicks to do *movies* that he puts out on the Internet."

"I thought he was a literary agent."

"I don't know about that. He approached me once to have some pictures taken, but I'm not into that. I'm not even into this. I'm putting myself through school. It's a shitty job, but the pay is good. Hey, you better get out of here. Tell you what, let me do the talking to get you back out the door. My shift actually ends in an hour. I work the day shift and go to school at night. There's a coffee shop about a mile up on Market in the 1800 block called It's Tops. Meet me there."

Nikki nodded. Alyssa took her hand. They looked around and didn't see either one of the cowboys. Alyssa got her to the front door, where the cowboy still waited to hold the door for the elite patrons.

"Where's she going?" he asked.

"She's sick. She puked all over me. I just cleaned it up. She's high on something. Get her out of here." Alyssa shoved her.

"Gary ain't gonna like this."

"Yeah well, Gary don't like his girls on coke either. Get out of here, honey. Sober up." Alyssa shook her head and muttered, "White trash."

Ouch. That really hurt. Not the first time she'd heard those words. She thought about growing up trailer-park poor back in Tennessee, speechless over Alyssa's ploy of getting her out the door. Alyssa winked at her, turned, and went back into the bar. Nikki hiked back to her car, not sure if her ego was more wounded at the idea that Alyssa had reminded her of the roots she'd long forgotten— purposely—or if it was because the girl had just pulled off a star performance. Damn if Alyssa didn't make a better actress than she had.

She licked her wounds and got into her car. A thought struck her. Bloomenfeld was at the bar and not in his office. Maybe she should do some snooping while he wasn't there. No. Bad idea. Well, when did she ever listen to logic?

It wasn't too difficult breaking into Bloomenfeld's office. She had her handy-dandy Swiss Army knife and had used it in other similar situations—a trick her ex-detective Aunt Cara had taught her many moons ago.

She wanted to make a brief sweep and get the hell out. She started with his desk and found some files. Nothing important. She went back into the other room and found an unmade bed and some more file cabinets. She started going through them. There was a file on Georges. She pulled it out and read over it. There was the initial contract that Georges had signed. An agency agreement. Then, there was a letter of termination written by Georges, dated about six months earlier, stating that Bloomenfeld was unethical, had stolen money from him, and that Georges intended to pursue legal action if he didn't cease and desist in his actions. Holy cow.

Now, Nikki knew why Henry had looked at her the way he had when she'd come into his office claiming that Georges always talked about him. He knew she was lying because Georges had fired him six months earlier and had threatened to sue him.

Nikki put the file back and left quickly. More and more, Henry Bloomenfeld looked to have a motive to want to see Georges six feet under. She would have to find out. But first she'd have to meet Alyssa at the coffeehouse.

She waited at the old diner-style coffee shop almost half an hour past the time Alyssa was supposed to show, and started to figure the Benjamin she'd given Alyssa had been in vain, when the girl came in dressed like a college student in a navy turtleneck and blue jeans. Nikki's heart went out to her. Why was she dancing at The Busy Beaver?

"Sorry I'm late. The boss got pissed after you left and made me stay and do two more dances—on the house."

"Isn't there anything else you can do? Someplace else that you can work?"

"Like what? I've got a two-year-old with a heart problem, no insurance, and I got to get through school so I can get a decent job and take care of him."

"I'm sorry."

"Thank you. It'll pass, right?"

Nikki reached into her purse and thought, what the hell. She handed Alyssa the other hundred dollar bill she had in her wallet. "Take it."

Alyssa hesitated, then reached across and timidly took the cash. Nikki could see a look of vulnerability and shame. She knew it well. "Thanks. Maybe I *will* try to find a different job."

Nikki smiled at her, hoping to give her some encouragement.

The waitress came over and Alyssa ordered a sandwich and a soda. The waitress gone, she looked back at Nikki. "I got a name for you."

"You do? Who? Who was the man with Henry?"

"His name is Rick Moran."

Chapter 14

"You know him?" Alyssa asked. The waitress set down her soda and Alyssa stuck a straw in it, swirling the crushed ice.

Nikki nodded. "I've met him."

"Can I ask you something?"

"Sure." She tried to wrap her mind around the idea that Moran and Bloomenfeld were hanging at a strip bar right after she'd told Bloomenfeld about Georges' murder. What were those two up to? With Bloomenfeld's reaction to hearing about Georges' murder, she had to wonder again if Moran had even heard the news about Georges. He'd left the restaurant right after Nikki had sat down with Janie yesterday to go over the wines. Hadn't he? Could Bloomenfeld and Moran simply be associates or friends who met through Georges? Just because Georges broke off his relationship with Bloomenfeld didn't mean that if Moran had cultivated one with the, uh, *literary agent* that he would necessarily sever ties. But none of it boded well for either man, and more and more Nikki was becoming convinced that the two of them had something to do with the murder.

"Who are you? You're not a cop or you would've questioned those guys on your own. Are you a private detective?" Alyssa asked, breaking Nikki's thoughts.

She shook her head. Funny as it was, she decided to tell Alyssa the truth. The woman deserved it. She'd gone out on a limb for her. Granted, she'd tossed her some cash, but Alyssa did seem to want to help, and Nikki didn't exactly enjoy the white lies she'd told. From beginning to end, she told her how she knew Georges, where she worked, and how she'd found him murdered, plus who Henry Broomenfeld was in relation to Georges, as well as Rick Moran. She also told her about Janie and then being questioned herself by the police.

Alyssa studied her. "You're doing this because that cop Jonah Robinson challenged you?"

Nikki laughed. "No. Not really." Then she came close to pinching her thumb and index finger together. "Maybe a little."

Alyssa smiled. "I like you. You're cool. I can't stand those chicks I work with. But you are very cool."

"Thanks." Nikki took a sip of her water. It was late and she knew she should be getting back home. She knew—as much as she didn't want to—that she and Andrés needed to talk about *things*. "Plus, I think it's even more than that for me. It's . . . I don't know. I liked the man. Georges, I mean. He was a character and he didn't deserve what he got. I'm nosy, too, and this thing stinks real bad. Now with Janie coming to me . . ." Oops. Nikki had not told Alyssa about Janie's DNA. Even though she didn't think Alyssa would pass that info on, she'd kept it to herself. It was a promise she made to Janie. And who knew, now that Georges had started becoming a household name in the vein of Emeril, Alyssa here, desperate for money, just might find herself on the phone with a journalist from the *National Enquirer*.

"Janie? The assistant, right? What do you mean she came to you?"

"She's scared because they worked so closely together

that the cops might target her. And, she's young, kind of naive. I feel for her, you know, so I guess she's one of the reasons I want to look into this."

Alyssa set down her sandwich and in mid chew said, "How do you know this girl is as naive as you think? Couldn't it be possible that she killed her boss over some sort of grievance? Hell, God knows I wouldn't mind taking out the idiots I work for."

Alyssa had a point. Nikki knew damn good and well that people weren't always what they seemed. However, Janie *was* Georges' daughter. She really believed that. Why kill the man she'd recently found out was her dad? A thought hit her, something she'd avoided because Janie was so believable. What if Janie had lied to her about her parentage and that's why she made Nikki promise not to say anything? Or, what if the fact that Georges had kept this information from his *daughter* had angered her to the point of seeking revenge? Could Janie be a sociopath? She knew from experience and studying Aunt Cara's criminal profile books that sociopaths were the best liars of all, and completely without conscience. "You know, I guess I don't know. I've been lied to before."

"Haven't we all?" Alyssa checked her watch. "Hang on a minute." She took out her cell phone and called what Nikki assumed to be her child's caregiver. "Hi Lilia. How is Peter? Good. Okay. Thank you. Yes, my study group goes until nine tonight. Can I say good night to him?" She paused and held a finger up to Nikki, who finished off her water and decided the hell with it and ordered a tuna melt along with a Coke, realizing she was hungry as her stomach rumbled. "Hi buggaboo. I know, Mommy misses you, too. I'm sorry. I'll be home tonight. Yes. I'll come in and kiss you and snuggle, but you better be in bed. Okay. Take all of your medicine for Lilia, okay? I love you, boo. Bye-bye." She hung up her phone and stashed it back in her bag. "Sorry. I had to tell him good night."

"Don't be sorry. It's fine."

"I need to get to my study group, but, Nikki, look, I don't meet a lot of quality people and I don't have many friends. I don't have time. Peter takes up my time after work and school and I don't put myself out there at school because if people found out what I did, they'd ostracize me. I'm doing this study group because I'm having a tough time with this business class I'm taking."

Nikki sat back in the booth.

"I guess what I'm trying to say is that I felt a connection with you. That might sound weird, but you look like someone who *gets* people and you've been nice to me, and well, I want to help you with this . . . this murder thing. That dude. That Henry. He comes into the bar almost daily and he's up to no good. I can't stand him. He's always totally disrespectful. He's slimy, you know."

Did she ever. "I don't want you getting involved in this. I'm grateful you got me the info that you did, but you have a child and a lot going on. The last thing you need to do is help me snoop around to find the killer of a man you didn't even know." The waitress set down Nikki's tuna melt and soda.

"No. I know I have a lot going on in my life, but I want to help. I know how to handle myself. Let me see if I can't work him for more information. I'll be careful, and it's not about you giving me any money. Really. I can't stand that guy, and if he killed someone, I want to see him get nailed for it."

Nikki squeezed a lemon into her soda and took a sip of the Coke. Refreshing. She sighed. She could use the help of someone in the city, because it wasn't like she could be here regularly. She still had a job back at the winery and Henry was here and up to something and after running away from him the way she had, she didn't think she could get close enough again to garner any more information. But she hated the idea of putting Alyssa in any danger.

"I can do this, Nikki. Funny thing is, I've been taking some criminology psych classes thinking maybe I want to go into law enforcement. I know, sounds crazy since I'm a stripper."

"You're not just a stripper."

"I know. But there is the stigma. Anyway, I've been going to school taking general classes working toward a BA, but kind of floundering, figuring out who I want to be when I grow up, and I don't have that kind of time. I gotta figure it out now, for my little boy. Maybe I should be a private dick." She laughed at her choice of words and Nikki joined in. "C'mon, let me try this, see if I'm any good. Think of it as on-the-job training."

Nikki looked at her. The woman was bright and maybe all she needed was a break. "Tell you what. See what you can find out. But please be careful."

Alyssa beamed. "Thanks." She took a pen and notepad out of her backpack and jotted her information down. "Here's my number."

Nikki fished out her business card and wrote her home number and cell down on the back of it. Standing up to leave, Alyssa said, "I'll call you, but call me first if you need anything."

"You got it."

Nikki watched her walk out of the café and crossed her fingers she was doing the right thing by involving her. Nice woman. Maybe by doing this she'd find a start toward a new beginning. Nikki hoped so. She finished her dinner and headed out. Before long she was crossing the Bay Bridge and driving back to Napa with a gazillion thoughts traveling through her mind.

All of them about Georges and the people he knew. Henry Bloomenfeld, of course, the literary agent who didn't know the definition of ethics; then there was Rick Moran, the accountant Georges did not seem to care for, and who was obviously slumming it up with Henry . . . and for what reason? She could not overlook the fact that Janie could have had a reason to see her father dead. How could

Nikki find out if Georges was really the young woman's
dad? Had Georges included Janie in his will and stated in it
that he was her father? Even the seemingly happy-go-lucky
Baron O'Grady appeared to have something to hide, or at
least confess in church last night. And, what about Lauren
Trump? She'd gone to the spa, according to Baron O'-
Grady. Lauren and Georges. Were those two simply carrying on a business relationship, or were they carrying on?
And if so, or even if not, could Ms. Trump have a reason to
want to see Georges in the grave? Could Charlotte have
been right about the possibility of hearing something other
than murder going on in the treatment room? In fact, now
that Nikki thought about it, she had not seen Lauren Trump
anywhere after the murder. There were a lot of people
around and Nikki had had other things to deal with, including that overbearing detective Robinson, but Lauren
Trump was a hard woman not to notice. Could she have
gunned Georges down at the spa? If the two of them were
having a fling, he would have let her into the treatment
room most likely without a second thought. Maybe the
killer hadn't been on the balcony as Nikki had thought.
Maybe Lauren had walked through the spa and into the
treatment room. She would have gone unnoticed if she'd
already been having a treatment of her own.

And, don't forget the pregnant interior decorator,
Stacey Redwall. Could the poor woman have feared that
Georges' pressure on her would cause her to lose the baby
she so desperately wanted?

A lot of possibilities and theories hung in the air, and
Nikki knew that one by one she'd have to begin clearing
them away.

Upon her return home, she found Janie gone. Her things
were still there. She must have gone out for dinner, or her
husband had arrived and they were spending time together.

Ollie was also nowhere in sight. He was probably at
Derek's.

She played her messages. Two were from Andrés saying that he was worried and wanted to talk to her. She wasn't up to it. Not now. Maybe after a bath and some time to think about their situation instead of Georges' murder, she'd call him back and they could talk. There was a message from Derek, too, saying he also needed to talk to her. *When it rains it pours*. Then both Simon and Marco left messages, along with Detective Jonah Jerko. "Miss Sands, I have a few more questions for you. I've tried to reach you several times today. However, your cell phone was not on. Call me."

It's still a free country, buddy. "I don't have to have my cell phone on," she muttered.

She did find a note from Janie on her bed saying that Trevor had to stay in the city for one more night because of something work related and that she had to get out. She'd apparently gone out for dinner. Nikki hoped she was okay, but there was still the thought in the back of her mind about whether or not Janie was indeed the innocent she appeared to be.

Nikki opened her front door. Derek's lights weren't on. He must've been either up at the main house or out to dinner himself. She closed the door and sighed. She took a long bath and sipped a glass of Pinot Gris, then climbed into bed, staring at the phone.

She closed her eyes and thought about Andrés, his proposition—Spain. What did she want out of life? Was it him? Were his dreams hers, too? A family. Hmmm. That *would* be nice. Before long she drifted off to sleep and her dream consisted of Andrés, Spain, and babies, and then while holding the dream child in her arms, Derek entered the room. Andrés was also in the room. Was the baby hers? Who was the father? Who did she want to be the father? A candle flickered on a nearby table. Andrés blew it out. Smoke. That faint smell of smoke after a candle gets blown out. *Stronger now*. Someone screaming her name.

Her eyes shot open and out of her dream, Nikki came to the horrid reality that her cottage was on fire. *Flames everywhere*. Again, someone screamed her name. "Nikki! Nikki!" It was Janie.

Coughing and gagging, she remembered the duck-and-crawl rule as she saw bright orange flames flickering from her family room, spreading toward her bedroom. No time to save anything. *Get out! Get out!* Where was Janie? Nikki looked over at her French doors, where she could see Janie pounding on them outside her bedroom. The smoke filled her room. *Losing air*. She made it to the doors and pulled herself up in a coughing fit. She unlocked the doors and opened them, collapsing outside on her deck. Janie grabbed her and dragged her away from the burning cottage. Sirens echoed through the valley from a distance as she lay in the grass where Janie had pulled her, watching her place go up in flames.

Chapter 15

Nikki, tucked into the corner of Derek's mocha-colored leather sofa, sat in stunned disbelief, grateful to be safely in his home. Looking up, she managed to smile her thanks as he offered her a cup of tea. Her eyes hurt from the tears she'd shed the last couple of hours as she realized all that she'd lost in the little cottage. Clothes she could replace, furniture, knick-knacks, but not photos with memories attached to them. Vacations with Aunt Cara, her first real acting gig, being on the set, move-in day at the cottage, birthdays with friends, all of it—up in smoke. How had this happened? She'd drifted off to sleep after the grueling day and the next thing she knew, she'd heard Janie yelling her name and then the smell of smoke, and then the flames. Thank God Janie had been there. She was outside now, talking with an arson investigator, who Nikki knew would be in soon to speak with her. The paramedics had shown up and, after giving her oxygen, had recommended that she go to the hospital, which she had refused to do.

Thank God Ollie hadn't been in the house with her, or Janie for that matter. If they'd been inside and hadn't noticed anything, then they both could have . . . *That* thought was too horrific to think about.

Derek came in from the kitchen with a plate of sliced apples and cheese. He set it down on the coffee table and took a seat across from her, a look of concern on his face. "I thought you might want to nibble on something."

"Thanks. I don't know if I could eat anything right now, though."

"I understand. Nikki, I was wondering when the last time was that you changed the batteries in your smoke detectors. They should have worked."

She nodded. The thought had already crossed her mind. She usually stayed on top of things like that, and if her memory served, it had been about four months ago that she'd changed them. She'd done it in the midst of some cleaning. Hadn't she? Damn, her mind was fuzzy right now. "I *think* the batteries were fine."

He frowned. She had to remember that the cottage was his home, too. He *did* own it. Her stay there was a part of the arrangement they'd made because she was the winery manager, and when she'd moved to Napa, Derek seemed more than eager to have her close by. What had occurred to change that? The flirting stopped, the mixed signals were no longer mixed but almost always simply business, and that was before she and Andrés had become . . . whatever it was they were. Nikki didn't have a clue, and here she sat in his family room drinking tea while he appeared to want to comfort her, and yet the standoffish attitude still remained. Did he blame her for the fire?

"I'm glad you weren't trapped in there," he said.

"Me, too."

"I called Andrés. I thought you might want to go and stay with him." Derek sank back into his chair.

Her head snapped up. She did not need this right now. "What? Why would you think that?"

"You *are* together. You're dating, a thing, an item, you know."

"No, Derek, *you* don't know. For one thing, yes Andrés and I are dating and we like each other and he's my friend, but for God's sake, you and he make me crazy with this control thing about me, like I'm some doll you can toss back and forth."

He looked at her incredulously, his eyes wide.

"I'm not a rag doll, and you don't know our situation. We're not even sleeping together." Oops. Now, why had she gone and said that? It really wasn't any of his business. And, it wasn't like he even cared. That much was obvious. "But, good. Fine. I'm glad you called him."

Derek's face reddened. "If you'd like, you could take a room at the hotel."

She sighed. "Right now, I don't know what I want. I'll have to weigh my options and see how *I* feel."

There was a knock at Derek's door. He answered it and there stood the fire marshall along with Detective Robinson. Oh God, as if things couldn't get any worse. Janie stood behind them. The detective asked her to wait outside. The girl looked injured and tried to peer around him. She waved at Nikki, who tried to smile back at her. The detective shut the door in Janie's face. Nikki watched Robinson cruise in, and had to wonder: was he only an ass to her, or was it with women in general? Nah, it was her. She could tell by the smirk on his face. Ah, she was not gonna get any sympathy here. He already looked suspicious of her. *Great.*

The fire marshall had that family man look about him—the opposite of Detective Cool—clean shaven, trim hair, silvering around the sideburns and he smelled of smoke and oddly enough, musk. Probably bathed daily in his cologne to get the smoke smell off of him. The look in his eyes seemed to be sympathetic, and he smiled kindly at Derek and Nikki. "I'm terribly sorry for the loss of your home."

Derek nodded. Nikki didn't say anything. What was there to say?

"I'm afraid I have some bad news," he continued. "The fire was not accidental."

"Arson?" Derek asked. "Someone deliberately started that fire?"

"Yes. Afraid so."

Derek sat back down, collapsing in his chair. He looked like Nikki felt—like he'd just been punched in the stomach.

"Who? Why? What in the hell?" Derek asked.

"That's what we're here to find out," the detective said. "It's possible that this fire could be connected to Mr. Debussey's murder."

"Excuse me?" Nikki asked, finally finding her voice. "I don't understand. I was in my home. Are you saying that someone could have been trying to murder me, too? It's not like I had a strong connection to Georges. We knew each other, but why would anyone kill him and then me?"

"I didn't say that," Robinson replied. "There could be a few scenarios we need to look at, if the fire is connected in any way with Mr. Debussey's murder."

The fire marshall excused himself, explaining he had more work to do at the scene.

"What type of scenarios are you talking about?" Derek asked.

Robinson didn't answer right away, almost as if he was trying to decide if he wanted to let them in on his thoughts. "Maybe there was evidence in Ms. Sands' home that someone was trying to hide."

Nikki gasped. "I resent that. Are you accusing me of something, Detective?"

"No, Ms. Sands, I'm not. Should I be?"

Derek shot him a dirty look. "Nikki had no reason to kill Georges, and furthermore, she was inside her house when it burned down and was nearly trapped inside. I hardly think that qualifies as someone wanting to get rid of evidence."

"Unless things got out of hand before she could get out, and she didn't realize it until it was too late. Ms. Sands *was* an actress, from what I understand."

"Yeah, I was. So? You know what, Detective, this conversation is ridiculous and over. Unless you have some kind of evidence pointing at me and you want to charge me with a crime, I'd suggest you leave." Nikki stood up. "I don't get you. What is your problem with me?"

"You put your nose where it doesn't belong. You have no respect for law enforcement. I've heard the stories and if I'm right, I've got a feeling you've already involved yourself in this case. It's possible you may be involved in Mr. Debussey's murder, but more than that, I think you're poking around where you shouldn't be."

"I am not involved in any way with this situation. And, you, Detective are bordering on harassment. As for my not having any respect for law enforcement, that's the biggest crock I've ever heard. I was raised by a Los Angeles homicide detective. I have a ton of respect for your job, but you know what, I don't have any respect for you, because from what I can see you've got it in for me so bad, you can't point your own nose in the direction it should be going on this case."

"Really now? And, what direction might that be?" The detective shifted his weight from one foot to the other.

She shrugged. Derek stood watching them, obviously not knowing what to say.

"Funny thing is, I got the feeling you *do* know where I should be looking."

"You're the cop, you figure it out," she replied.

"I've got questions for you, Ms. Sands. Lots of them."

"Yeah, well, I know my rights as a citizen, and if you want to ask me any more questions, you need to speak with my attorney."

The detective spun on his heels and walked toward the door. Upon reaching it, he turned back around and pointed a finger at her. "I'll be watching you."

"Guess what? I'll be watching you, too." She turned away as well and walked into Derek's bathroom, not able to take another second of having to deal with Detective

Robinson. She splashed cold water on her face. Of all the
nerve. When she was done, she looked up to see Derek
standing in the doorway. He came over to her and placed a
hand on her shoulder. They stood like that for a moment,
looking at each other in the mirror. Him with his wavy
blond hair, etched cheekbones, and golden skin, her with
her light brown hair, green eyes, and far less golden looking skin—cream-colored, maybe. She closed her eyes
and turned into him, the tears coming. He held her there,
pulling her into his chest. She cried like that for several
minutes.

Her sobs quieted. "Are you snooping like he says?"
Derek asked.

She pulled away from him. She wasn't going to lie to
him. "A little."

"Nikki."

"I know. I can't stand him, and I don't trust him. You see
the way he is with me. I don't know what his beef is."

"I think he said what it is, pretty plain and clear. He
wants you to let the police do their job, and yeah, he isn't
exactly 'couth' about it, but he does have a point. Have you
ever thought the man is looking out for your safety, too? I
don't want you snooping anymore, either. You could have
been killed tonight, and what if his theory is right? What
if the fire at the cottage is tied into Georges' murder?
What if someone for some reason wants you dead, too?
You could have died tonight, Nikki, and I don't know
what I would . . ."

Another knock on the door pulled him away from her
before he could finish his sentence. This time it was Andrés.
He ran to her and took her in his arms. They felt as good as
Derek's. Dammit. Damn Detective Jonah Robinson. Damn
killers. Damn men, especially ones who smelled good, with
strong arms. Damn, damn, damn.

Andrés held her out at arm's length. "I came as soon as
I heard. Derek called." He glanced at Derek. "Thank you."

"No problem," Derek mumbled.

Andrés pulled her close again and kissed the top of her head, which rested under his chin. "Thank God. Thank God you are all right." He took her face in his hands. "*Dios mio.* The thought of losing you . . ." His eyes welled with tears.

It hit her hard. This man was in love with her. Her stomach swirled into a hard knot at first and then into a fluttery feeling. It was possible that her body had entered an entirely different dimension. Surreal, like she was outside of herself. She looked at Derek, who stood there—watching, hands in his pockets. What was that expression on his face? Sadness, anger, confusion? *What*?

"Maybe the timing really *is* good for you two to head off to Spain. The cottage will have to be rebuilt and after all of this, I'm sure Nikki could use time away," Derek said.

Andrés nodded, his eyes boring into her, and she didn't know how to respond. She heard herself say, "Yes, maybe so." Again outside her body.

"Why don't you come and stay with me?" Andrés asked.

She shook her head, and snapped back into the present. "No. I, um, thank you, I think I want to be alone for right now. I think I'll stay at the hotel if the offer still stands." She looked at Derek.

"Of course. I'll call over there and let them know you'll be taking a room." He placed a quick call to the front desk at the hotel. Marco was off for the evening, but Derek settled everything for her.

Andrés looked wounded but said that he understood.

"What about Janie?" Nikki asked, suddenly remembering her houseguest. "She was outside when the detective was here. It looked like she wanted to see me."

Derek peered out his window. "She's still there. Someone's with her on the porch." He opened his front door. "Hi, Janie. Why don't you two come on in?"

Janie and a young man entered. Janie rushed over to Nikki. "Are you okay? I'm so sorry."

Nikki hadn't seen Janie much after she'd pulled her away from her burning house, because the paramedics and emergency vehicles started arriving shortly thereafter. "I'm fine. How are you?"

Janie nodded. "Okay, I guess. Worried about you."

The man next to Janie took her hand. He was slight, only a little taller than the petite girl, not exactly handsome, but not ugly either. He had soft blue eyes, the kind that were so delicate, Nikki knew he had to squint in the sunlight. Even though, by the looks of him, he was in his midtwenties, he already had a crease between his eyes that indicated the sun got to him, or he thought an awful lot—maybe both. He was light complexioned, his hair blondish brown, more on the brown side—okay, dishwater blond. He looked like a nice guy.

"This is my husband, Trevor," Janie said. "Thank God I got a hold of him while you were with the paramedics and he rushed out here."

Trevor put his hand out, taking Nikki's. "Gosh, I am so sorry Miss Sands."

"You can call me Nikki."

"It's terrible. I wish I could have been here earlier, but I got held up studying for finals and working on my thesis. I'm glad I had my cell on. She caught me in the library and usually I turn it off in there. Thank you for taking care of Janie. She told me how great you've been."

"No problem. She saved my life."

"Maybe we should all be going now," Andrés interrupted. "It's getting late. I'll help you get settled at the hotel."

Nikki agreed. "We're staying there, too," Janie said. "Trevor went over and checked us in. That detective wants to talk to me again tomorrow. He is so not nice."

Trevor rubbed Janie's arm. "I'll be there with you tomorrow."

Janie smiled at him. "Trevor is a law student. He's gonna make an awesome lawyer. He's so smart. He clerks for a huge firm in the city right now."

"Come on, baby. We should let these folks head out, and I know you're tired, too."

They all went to the front door and Derek said good night. Andrés left to go for his car, which he had parked at the front gate to avoid getting in the way of the emergency vehicles.

She waited on Derek's porch for Andrés to drive her to the hotel, grateful she didn't have to walk. Besides, Andrés clearly wanted to be there for her in any way possible.

She turned around, hearing a porch floorboard creak, and saw Derek behind her. "Nikki, I really am sorry. We'll have the place rebuilt. It'll be better than before."

"Maybe you shouldn't. Maybe I should find another place."

He didn't say anything. Andrés pulled his car around the corner onto the dirt drive.

"Nikki, maybe it *would* be a good time to take off, go to Spain, let the cops solve this thing."

She nodded. "Maybe you're right."

Chapter 16

Andrés made sure she settled into her room at the hotel. All she had were the clothes on her back, and the "disguise" she'd worn in the city tucked away in a bag in her car. Almost as if he'd predicted that she'd need something—and he always seemed to know her needs—he'd packed a small bag for her with a couple of his T-shirts, a sweatshirt, and some sweats.

"They're too large, I know. I wanted to go by Isabel's and get you some of her clothes, but I also wanted to get here as soon as possible."

"This is wonderful. No, I'm glad you came as soon as you could. You didn't tell Isabel about this, did you?" Nikki asked.

Her dear friend Isabel, a fabulous chef, had left a few days earlier for New York to be honored by *Dining Magazine* as one of the best upcoming chefs. She'd invited both Andrés and Nikki to come with her; however, Nikki's weekend was committed to the formal opening of the hotel and spa. Andrés was caught up in business of his own and couldn't get away from his work, either. Besides, Isabel had started long-distance dating another chef who lived in Vegas, and the two of them had met in New York. Nikki hadn't wanted to get in the way of that.

"No, with the time difference back east, and knowing my sister, she's probably been asleep for hours. It's almost ten here."

Doubtful that Isabel was sleeping. After all, she was in New York City with a man she liked. They were more likely dancing the night away, but Nikki wasn't about to say that to big brother. Instead she responded with, "Good. Please don't tell her. She'll worry and want to come back and this should be a special week for her. I want her to enjoy herself. I don't want what's happened here to interfere with that."

He poured her a glass of water. The room was extraordinary. Granted, Nikki had gone through the new hotel rooms when they were being finished and had taken people around during the tours, but as she sat down in one of the oversized velvet plush chairs that faced a fireplace, she sighed, taking it all in. Under other circumstances the luxury and romance of the room would have lifted her spirits and drawn her away from any looming problems. But nothing was ordinary at the moment. Even the two dozen roses, standard in all the rooms, and the golden hues on the walls, the candles scented with gardenia, and the king-sized bed covered in a luxurious down comforter could not ease the aches and pains in her body and her heart. Escaping from her home as it burned and the mental image of it going up in flames had seared her soul. Everything that she'd owned, everything that made up who she was, had been destroyed as the fire consumed the cottage. She sighed and choked back the tears, knowing that if she started crying again, Andrés would insist on staying with her. And tonight she really needed to be alone.

He sat down in the chair across from her, facing the fireplace. "Do you want me to light the fire for you?"

"No. I think it'll be some time before I want to take in fire as a beautiful thing."

"I understand." He took a sip from his water. "Nikki, I know you need time and I know that this is difficult, but I do want you to think about going to Spain with me. Things always happen for a reason, and as hard as it may be to come to terms with your situation, maybe this is a sign that you need to be away from here for now. I won't pressure you anymore about it, and even if you want to come along only as a friend, I won't press you to make more of a commitment than that. I want to do what's right for you. I love you, Nikki. Your happiness is what I want."

"Thank you. I will think about it when my head and my heart are clearer, and I'll let you know as soon as I'm able to decide."

He lifted a chenille throw from the end of the bed and covered her as she curled up into the oversized chair. He kissed her good night. "You call me when you're ready."

She nodded and thanked him for his concern, and as he closed the door behind him, she could no longer hold back the tears. Not only for the loss of her home, but also because she didn't know what the right thing to do might be. With his last words, she knew that Andrés was basically telling her that it was time to shit or get off the pot. Sure, he'd said no pressure, but it laid over her like a dense fog, because she knew by letting him go to Spain without her she could lose him and whatever they might be able to build together, and he was a special and wonderful man. Then, Derek's face flashed through her mind and caused her to grow angry with his words, telling her to go. But what was it about him that kept her there?

She tossed the blanket off and decided to crawl into bed. The scent of freshly laundered sheets floated into the air as she slid under the blankets.

But she couldn't sleep, and there was no television in the room to help distract her. When designing the hotel, everyone had agreed that the rooms were far more romantic without televisions. Instead, there was a stereo in each room with a selection of CDs. She decided to put in Bebel Gilberto and her Portuguese bossa nova sounds. That rhythm, that sound, and Bebel's voice could usually help loosen tensions.

The day came back to her in a whirl. What a day— from her travels into St. Helena and meeting first with Stacey Redwall, the preggers designer who was, at the least, nervous about their conversation, then Charlotte, who may have raised the point that Georges could have been more than just taking a bath when he died in the spa. Did he have a lover in there with him, or had Charlotte heard the killer?

Then there was the meeting with Henry Bloomenfeld and *his* meeting with Rick Moran. Those two were probably in cahoots. She'd been stupid enough to reveal to Henry where she worked, but that didn't matter because Rick Moran knew who she was, and he'd tell Henry that she was no writer. Could the two have plotted to kill Georges and now felt threatened by her? Could either have come to the vineyard and watched, waiting for the moment to torch her place? Of course, she could no longer leave out Baron O'Grady. He hadn't been overjoyed to see her at church and had been less than thrilled about answering her questions. Maybe he was the one who felt threatened by her and wanted her out of the picture.

Clearly, someone knew she was searching for answers, Detective Jonah Robinson included, and they didn't want her to continue. She didn't know who'd murdered Georges, but she was sure that when she found out why he was killed, she'd also find out who'd done it.

She closed her eyes and thought again about Andrés and

his proposition. She believed in signs, always had. Should she just go and leave this whole mess behind? But she knew she couldn't do that until justice was served, until Georges' killer was caught. Until whoever burned down her home and tried to send her to her own grave was behind bars. Because now this thing was *personal*, and Nikki wanted revenge. She'd get to the bottom of this, and until then, her guy problems and what she should do with her life would be put on hold. She knew she had to right the wrongs that had been done to Georges, and now her. Satisfied with this fact, she finally fell asleep and slept peacefully through the night.

Only to be awakened by the ringing of her cell phone the next morning. She'd set it on the nightstand when she'd gone to bed. She answered it at half past nine. Wow, she'd been really tired. Nine-thirty for her was seriously sleeping in.

"Hello, Miss Sands, this is Lauren Trump. We met the other day at the restaurant. I am, or I was Georges' publicist. I heard about your home. I am so sorry. How horrible for you. I hope I didn't wake you, but can we meet? I have something to discuss with you."

"Sure." She made a late lunch appointment at Grapes and hung up the phone, curious about the request, but nonetheless anxious to talk to her. Nikki had planned to think up an excuse to call her anyway and question her about Georges, as well as about Rick Moran. Now, she wouldn't have to. The woman had called her.

But wait a minute, was that too easy? What did Lauren Trump want with her? And how had she heard about her place burning down so soon? It had been less than twelve hours. What if *she* was the killer and had tried to take Nikki out the night before? What if Baron had somehow made it known that Nikki had asked him questions about her and she'd been the one to want to get rid of her? What if upon learning through the *grapevine*, which traveled fast in these

parts, that Nikki was alive and kicking, she decided to take
another shot at her? Thank God they'd chosen a public place
to meet.

She got out of bed and put on a pair of Andrés' sweats and
a sweatshirt. One thing was for sure: shopping was in order
before she met Lauren. But she really wasn't up to it. Maybe
after a cup of java and some breakfast she'd feel like herself
again.

Marco was in the kitchen fixing huevos rancheros, pink
grapefruit with caramelized brown sugar on top, and an av-
ocado and mandarin orange salad. He'd become quite the
chef since the concept of the spa had come to fruition.
Breakfast was the only meal served at the hotel and spa. All
of the other meals could be eaten at Georges' or the many
restaurants throughout the wine country. Nikki couldn't
help wondering if anyone would get the chance to eat at
Georges' at the Vineyard. Would it be considered tainted?
Murder was a hard thing to get past. How could it not cross
patrons' minds as they sat eating a gourmet meal at the new
restaurant?

Nikki sat down next to the fireplace inside the small
eatery. She could see Marco back there swaying to Diana
Krall's voice. There were a few couples inside and others
on the patio having breakfast. Simon ran around pouring
coffee and bringing mimosas or champagne for those guests
who desired to indulge.

"Hi, Goldilocks," Simon said, coming over to her table,
coffee carafe in hand. He set the carafe down on the white
linen tablecloth. "You poor doll. How are you? Marco and
I were out late last night. We just needed to get away and go
see a movie, take our mind off the tragedy of Georges, and
then we come home to see what's happened to the cottage."
He placed a hand on his chest. "All I could think about
was you, and if you were safe. We immediately went to
my brother's place and he told us that he'd gotten you into
a room here. Thank God. How are you?" His eyes were

sympathetic and even before her caffeine fix, she was actually happy to see him. He wasn't like nails on a chalkboard this morning.

She started to reach for the carafe.

"Oh, jeesh, I am so sorry. Here, let me do that." He took the carafe and poured her coffee. "Do you want something stronger? Champagne, mimosa, mixed drink, how about a shot?"

She smiled. "No. Coffee is fine. I've got a lot of things to take care of today. Thank you, though. Maybe tonight, if I feel like coming over to the happy hour."

The breakfast area also served as the wine bar and happy hour hot spot from five to seven.

"Of course. Of course. Well, I've got to tell you that the guests are a bit edgy, as you can imagine. That mean cop called this morning."

"Detective Robinson?"

Simon nodded. "What is his problem? He is so cute, but so nasty."

"Tell me about it. I'm on his list."

"You and everyone else. He gave me the okay to tell the guests who were checked in during the *murder*"—he lowered his voice when he said murder—"that they can all go home today. Supposedly, he's cleared them of any wrongdoing. I don't know. I think this is going to set us back. We are going to need some great marketing to get this thing going again, so it's not tainted. We let everyone stay for free, and that's seemed to help."

Nikki took a sip from her coffee and set it down. "It'll be okay. Teamwork, right? We'll all do it together." Maybe one of the reasons Robinson hadn't linked Moran or Bloomenfeld to the murder was because he'd been busy looking into the hotel guests. She hadn't focused on the guests, figuring most of them probably didn't even know Georges. She understood though, why the police would have had to look into each separate guest, especially since they were all probably antsy to get home, as Simon suggested.

He took her hand. "Who do you think did this? Do you think the same person who killed Georges started the fire at the cottage?"

"I don't know, but I have my suspicions."

"You're looking into this, aren't you?"

She shrugged. "A girl's gotta do what a girl's gotta do."

"You be careful."

"Do you know anything about Lauren Trump?"

"The publicist? Georges' publicist?"

"Yeah. Her."

"Not a lot. She was supposed to come in for a treatment the day he was killed. We had her on the books, but she called like ten minutes before and said that she had to go back to her hotel room and finish up some business before opening night."

"Did you believe her?"

Simon leaned in closer to Nikki. "Why? You don't suspect her, do you? I know that Detective Robinson asked her some questions. That's about all I know. Well . . ."

"Well, what? What else do you know?"

He waved a hand at her. "It's gossip. That's all, and you know I can't stand gossip. The Guru Sansibaba says that idle talk of others' affairs is simply a reflection of the anger, jealousy, and pure boredom coming from within. It's the sign of an empty soul."

"Simon." Nikki raised an eyebrow. "This is not gossip. If you know something that could pertain to Georges' murder, you need to tell me. What would the Guru say about keeping information? He's not a priest."

Simon sighed, leaned in even closer, and started dishing. Like hell he didn't enjoy gossiping. "Okay, well the word from one of the housekeeping staff, and the only reason I know this is because Marco speaks Spanish, sort of, as they do, because he's Italian and they all talk to him and then he talks to me."

"Simon, get to the point."

"Right. So, one of the housekeeping staff went to clean Georges' room the morning before he was murdered, and well, it wasn't like the privacy sign was up. Poor girl got an eyeful."

"Was it Lauren Trump?"

"She didn't know who it was, because she only saw the woman's back when she rolled over as soon as the girl walked in, but she said that the lady had short, silver hair and was very tan."

Nikki snapped, "It had to be Lauren."

Simon nodded. "I think so, too, but you know people make things up and I'm not going to get all involved. You know who Lauren Trump was married to?"

"No."

"Anthony Tortelli."

"The defense attorney for Joseph Cordova?"

"The one."

Nikki sat back in her chair and sighed. Joseph Cordova was from a huge Mafia family in the Bay Area and had recently been arraigned on drug trafficking charges and for plotting the murder of the city's attorney. He was bad, bad news, and if Lauren Trump had any ties with that element . . . Was it possible that Georges' murder had been a Mafia hit? Did Detective Robinson know all of this? He had to. What if Lauren's ex-husband knew that she and Georges were carrying on and, even being an ex, didn't care for it? And, as a favor for his attorney, Cordova gave the word and Georges was taken out by the mob? If that was the case then this thing would likely never be solved. Mafia hits were the least likely to ever be seen all the way through the justice system, and it wasn't like Lauren was going to admit to her affair with Georges. Especially not to the cops, and the housekeeper who supposedly saw them had probably already been warned by her friends in the know to keep quiet.

With those thoughts crossing her mind, Nikki realized that none of these theories could answer why anyone would burn down her cottage—especially if it was somehow tied to Georges' murder. Then again, maybe it wasn't all tied together. Maybe the cottage being torched by an arsonist was an entirely separate thing. But why?

"Simon," Marco yelled out.

Simon reached across the table and touched her hand. "Keep this mum. If it's true, you know how *those* kinds of people can be—dangerous. I better get in the kitchen and finish serving. Do you want a full breakfast?"

"Amazingly I do. I'm famished."

Simon scurried away and Nikki was once again left with her thoughts. If the incidents were separate, then she'd have two cases to work on. She didn't have the energy for that. And now, with the word "mob" thrown in the mix she couldn't help but think twice. Simon didn't mince words. She liked to figure these puzzles out, but if the mob was involved, she didn't think she wanted to tangle with that. Maybe she'd get some more answers from Lauren Trump herself. Interesting that Lauren didn't use her married name. Probably guilt by association.

Nikki ate quickly, went back to her room, showered, and headed out to buy some clothes to wear. By the time she bought several tees, some jeans, and a sweater set as well as some flats, she had just enough time to head back to her room, change, and put on a dash of makeup. Good thing she'd splurged on that disguise yesterday, because she hadn't had time for the cosmetics counter. She'd have to get back into the city soon to see about some work clothes, plus she wanted to check on Alyssa.

She made it to Grapes in under ten minutes, and although she was only five minutes late, she found Lauren Trump on the back patio with a bottle of Chardonnay nearly polished off, her eyes bloodshot and her face splotchy, which Nikki assumed was from crying.

Nikki sat down across from her. "Lauren?"

Lauren hurriedly wiped her eyes and put her sunglasses on.

"Are you okay?"

Lauren burst out in tears. "No. No, I'm not. I've done a horrible thing."

Huevos Rancheros
and Caramelized Grapefruit
with Schramsberg's Blanc de Blancs

This brunch is not only delicious and elegant but easy, too. Serve it with Schramsberg Chardonnay-based, vintage-dated sparkling wine. Blanc de Blancs blends citrus with tropical fruit notes and contains a soft vanilla flavor on the back palate.

HUEVOS RANCHEROS

6 6-inch corn or flour tortillas
vegetable oil
½ cup onion, chopped
1 clove garlic, minced
1⅔ cups (14 oz) canned tomatoes, chopped
8–10 green chiles, chopped (substitute: 2 4 oz cans green chile)
¾ tsp salt
6 eggs
⅛ tsp pepper
1 cup shredded cheddar cheese
¼ cup butter, melted

Fry tortillas in oil until crispy. As you fry try to form a small well in each tortilla. Place tortillas in a baking dish. You may require two dishes depending on size.

Sauté onion and garlic in 2 tbsp of oil until tender. Stir in tomatoes, green chile, and ½ teaspoon salt. Pour equal amounts of tomato mixture over each tortilla.

Preheat oven to 350°.

Carefully break eggs, one on top of each tortilla. Sprinkle remaining salt, pepper, and cheese over eggs. Drizzle butter over; cover. Bake for 15 minutes. Serve immediately. Serves 6.

CARAMELIZED GRAPEFRUIT

    1 grapefruit
    2 tbsp brown sugar
    2 tbsp port wine
    2 tbsp butter

Cut your grapefruit in half and pour 1 tbsp each of brown sugar, port wine, and butter on each half. Bake at 350° for 10 minutes; serve hot. Serves 2.

Chapter 17

"Lauren, what are you talking about?"

Lauren shook her head and sobbed. A waiter approached and set down a plate of salmon in a black bean sauce and an extra plate.

"Sorry, I took the liberty," Lauren said and sniffled. "Have some." She took the bottle of Chardonnay from the ice bowl and held it out for Nikki.

"No. I think I'll just have water. Thank you, though."

Lauren poured the rest of the bottle into her glass. "I didn't call you here to go into this. I called you to talk about marketing. I know you do some of that for Malveaux and I felt the need to get with you and make a plan, and I'm going back to the city in a few days, so I thought we should talk now and start putting one together. I believe Georges would not want the winery or restaurant to suffer. You know, the vineyard restaurant was the ultimate dream for Georges."

"No, I didn't realize that."

"Well, it was and we have to see it succeed for his sake and for his honor. God, I'm rambling, I'm really upset and

I had one glass of wine because I got here early and now look, I've about finished off the bottle." She held it up again in the afternoon sun and laughed a bit. "Looks like I didn't actually *about* finish it off."

Nikki sliced off a couple pieces of bread and scooped up a serving of the salmon for each of them. "Lauren, I agree with you about the marketing, but that can wait. You're obviously very upset. What do you mean that you've done something really terrible?"

"Can I get some more wine first?"

"Do you think that's a good idea?"

"I won't drive, I promise. And right now I can't think of a better idea."

"Maybe you should try and eat something first."

"Nikki, I was sleeping with both Georges and Baron."

"Waiter!" Nikki hollered. The waiter came over and she ordered them *both* another glass of the Chardonnay, along with the mussels in a garlic, ancho butter sauce, and the paella. After a blow like the one Lauren had just delivered, she'd have wine with lunch, too, and plenty of lunch— comfort food, Latin fusion style. After the waiter took their order, Nikki said, "Can you repeat that?"

"I was having sex with both Georges and his best friend."

"Holy cow."

"You said it. I don't know why I'm telling you this. I'm drunk, sad, and confused, and God knows I have no idea who I can talk to."

Nikki knew from past experience, Janie included, that she could have made a decent living as a psychologist. Maybe it was because Aunt Cara had always taught her to keep a good game face on and always, always listen. She'd told Nikki, "Don't let anyone know too much of what you're thinking 'cause then they'll tell you what you need or want to know, and think that you're on their side whether you are or not."

"Um, can I ask you something?"

"What? Like what was I thinking?"

"That, too, but aren't you married?" Nikki pointed to her ring finger.

Lauren laughed. "Oh, no! You've heard the stories, too. I tell you, that Detective Robinson had me holed up in his office for hours yesterday quizzing me about it. I sure in hell hope he doesn't bring Anthony in on this, but no doubt he will. Anthony will have a shit fit, but there's not a great deal he can do."

"What are you talking about?" The waiter approached, opened the bottle, and handed to cork to Nikki. She looked up at him. "No time for formalities, friend. If it's skunky, I'll let you know. Just pour." Who had time to sniff, swirl, taste, and approve when she knew she was on the verge of some hot and heavy info? The waiter poured her a glass. She took a major sip. Full bodied.

"Yeah, yeah, I'm married to Anthony Tortelli, attorney to the Cordova family, but we're going through a divorce."

Was Lauren delusional? Did she think that would stop the mob from seeking retribution for their attorney? No wonder Baron had been at the church last night. Poor man was probably praying for his soul for more than one reason.

"Anthony has that job with the Cordovas only because my best friend from childhood is old man Cordova's mistress, and I arranged a meeting for Anthony with the Cordovas and it all went from there. Anthony is an excellent attorney, and the Cordovas know it, but none of the family would have done this. Anthony left me. He's after one of the Cordova cousins and that's better business for them anyway. It's fine with me. I'd lost interest in him." She slurred her words. "It's not like it didn't hurt my ego though. Anthony's new girlfriend, the cousin, is something like twenty-three." She picked up a knife and feigned stabbing it in her heart. "I guess you could say my ego needed a boost."

"Georges and Baron?" Nikki asked. Wow. Who would've guessed?

"Georges and Baron." She half laughed again and drank some more wine.

The waiter came back with their entrées. Nikki had already eaten her salmon. It looked as though Lauren was going to stick with the liquid lunch. "Do you want some? It's great. My friend Isabel owns this place. You should eat."

"Oh, maybe a little." She put some of the food on her own plate and picked at it.

"Why did you do this? I can understand the ego thing, I really can." Nikki had a fleeting thought of Derek and Andrés. "But Georges and Baron were best friends and partners."

Lauren started to cry again. "I know. I'm horrible, aren't I?"

Well, yeah. Nikki wasn't going to tell her that, though. Silence was the best policy. Just listen and let her think there are no judgment calls.

"I couldn't help it. I met Georges over a year ago when his second cookbook came out. I went to his book signing and had dinner at his place in the city. We got to talking and when I told him what I did, he complained to me about how his publisher really hadn't helped him much with the marketing and that he didn't want to remain a regional-type chef. He aspired to be the next Emeril. I told him that I could help him with that. Then the whole Bernadette fiasco came about right before things started to really happen for Georges, right around the time the connection with your boss, Derek, and that whole deal transpired."

Nikki acted like she didn't have a clue about Bernadette, Georges' ex-wife. She wanted to hear Lauren's version. "What are you talking about? What Bernadette fiasco?"

Lauren smiled. "I did my job. See, you don't know about the fiasco."

Mum is the word.

Lauren proceeded to tell her about the fire, about Janie

moving into the house, Bernadette's suspicions, and then being prosecuted for arson. "Funny thing is I knew that Janie wasn't screwing Georges because I was. Bernadette is an idiot. Way too low class for Georges. I don't know what he ever saw in her. He was into the Bohemian thing or something when she came along and did *she* have a jealousy issue! Janie is a sweet kid and her mom had just died, and well, Georges wanted to help her. I loved him for that. And Janie is crazy in love with that kid she married, Trevor. Bernadette's suspicions were pointed in the wrong direction."

"And you kept all of that from going huge with the media?"

"I did. Anthony was doing his thing with the Cordova cousin by then, so I made a deal with the Cordovas and Anthony. He could have the cousin and I would be way more than fair and civil in a divorce if they would help me keep things about Bernadette and Georges hush-hush. They have some media holdings. Sure there were tidbit stories, but no media circus. It helps having my friend Anne being old man Cordova's side dish."

"I guess," Nikki replied.

"They agreed to help and things stayed quiet. Georges was able to pursue his dream and I was able to market and publicize for him."

"What about Baron? It sounds like you two adored Georges." Nikki took a bite of the paella, one of her favorite dishes at Grapes, with the shrimp, chorizo, and chicken mixed in with the Arborio rice. It blended well with the Chardonnay, and the wine helped this huge story go down a whole lot better than if she were listening with a Coke in hand.

"Oh, Baron. He's sweet. He's funny with his Irish idioms and he's been lonely here in the states and he wants to go home to his family, but he felt a loyalty to Georges for getting him started in the industry. He does, or did adore Georges, like a brother. He's devastated over this."

Obviously not that loyal. "I still don't get it. Sure he's a nice man, but . . ."

"I know, I know. I already told you that I'm terrible. I felt sorry for him, and one ~~night while~~ Georges was out ~~here in~~ Napa working on details with the interior designer—that Stacey Redwall—for the restaurant, I went into the restaurant in the city. It was a slow night. Baron and I shared some wine and then we shared some more and later at my place, things just happened. You know how that goes."

Not really. "So, it was a one night stand?"

"No." Lauren twirled her wine glass in the light, the color a pale gold. She set the wine down and whispered, "Here's the thing about Baron. Not only is he sweet, nice, and funny but, oh my gosh, he is, well . . ." She held her pointer fingers up, several inches apart.

"Gotcha," Nikki said.

"You can't give up a lover like that. I figured, what was the harm? I had Georges and Baron and neither one wanted a commitment and neither one wanted to go public. It was all fun and games."

"Did they think so?" Nikki asked.

"Georges and Baron? Oh, no. They didn't know."

Nikki set her fork down after taking another mussel from the shell and savoring the flavor. She followed up with a little more wine. "Neither one knew that you were sleeping with the other?"

"No. Why would I do that?"

"Wait a minute though, Baron and Georges were friends, Georges had to have told Baron about you."

Lauren tilted her face toward the sun. "I sort of used the fact that I was married to Anthony at the time to my bene-fit in that case. I really didn't want Georges telling people about our affair. I was helping him build his career, and a famous chef carrying on with his publicist sounds so seedy."

Because it is.

"I told Georges not to tell a soul. Made him promise, which he did."

"And you don't think he told Baron?" Nikki asked.

"No. Baron is so Irish Catholic that every time we slept together he'd go to confession. He felt so ashamed but he couldn't help himself. We were compatible in that way. He would have never told Georges because he was completely ashamed, which I found charming."

At first Nikki had thought she liked this woman, but now she saw her for what she was—sick and twisted. The last thing she would want to do was plan a marketing campaign with her.

"How do you know that Baron didn't find this out, about you and Georges? How do you know that Baron didn't kill him because he really did know that the two of you were sleeping together?" Was Baron at the church to confess more than just sleeping with an almost-divorced woman, for having sex out of wedlock, for adultery? Or, was he there to confess to murdering his best friend?

Lauren polished off her wine, took off her glasses, and looked Nikki straight in the eye. "Because, Nikki, Baron and I were in bed together that afternoon."

Salmon with Black Bean Sauce with Beaulieu Carneros Chardonnay

The wine to pair with salmon in black bean sauce would be Beaulieu Carneros Chardonnay. This wine contains subtle flavors of green apple, pear, citrus, and hazelnut. It's not a huge, oaky chardonnay, which allows the fruit to linger on the palate. Chardonnay can be a hard wine to pair with foods, but Nikki finds this one pairs well with seafood, mild cheeses, or a chicken salad.

    2 tbsp soy sauce
    2 tsp sugar
    2 tbsp olive oil (divided)
    2 tbsp cornstarch
    1½ cups chicken stock
    4 salmon fillets (6 oz each, 1 inch thick)
    2 garlic cloves, minced
    1 tbsp peeled, minced fresh ginger
    2 tbsp jarred black bean sauce (available at grocery
        stores or Asian markets)
    2 tsp rice wine vinegar

In a large bowl, combine soy sauce, sugar, and 1 tablespoon of the oil. In a small bowl, combine cornstarch and chicken stock.

Make three slashes on skin side of each salmon fillet, cutting halfway into fish. Place salmon in shallow dish and pour soy-sauce marinade over it. Cover and refrigerate 30 to 60 minutes.

In a medium saucepan, heat remaining tablespoon of oil and add garlic, ginger, and black bean sauce. Cook 1 to 2 minutes or until garlic is golden. Add vinegar and the cornstarch mixture. Bring to boil, then reduce to simmer. Cook 10 minutes, remove from heat, and keep warm.

Remove fish from marinade and place on foil-lined broiler pan, about 3 inches from heat. Broil 4 to 6 minutes per side, or until cooked through. Serve salmon over rice topped with sauce. Serves 4.

Mussels in Ancho Chile Butter Sauce with Château de la Ragotiere Muscadet de Sevre et Maine Cuvee M

The wine to drink with this appetizer is Château de la Ragotiere Muscadet de Sevre et Maine Cuvee M.

All the wines produced by the Couillaud brothers, Bernard, Francois, and Michel, are among the finest and most complex that the Muscadet appellation has to offer. This rare Cuvee M, however, is in a class by itself. According to AOC law, only wines aged on the lees for two years or less can include "sur lie" on the label. Cuvee M is aged for far longer. It is a rich, stony, mineral-driven wine. It's outstanding with steamed clams or mussels.

2 large dried ancho chiles
2 cloves garlic
½ cup butter
20 fresh, live mussels
1½ cups dry white wine
Note: New Mexico, pasilla, or California chiles can
   be substituted for ancho chiles.

Put chiles in a bowl and cover with boiling water. When they are rehydrated, drain them and put them and garlic cloves in a food processor or blender; process until finely chopped.

In a small saucepan over medium-high heat, melt butter. With machine running, add hot butter to chiles and garlic in a fine stream. Blend until color is homogeneous and mixture is smooth.

Heat a sturdy pot until very hot, and add mussels. Once they start to "spit," add wine, cover pot, and keep at high heat. Reduce to low after a minute or so, and continue to steam for 3 to 5 minutes, until mussels open; discard any that do not open. Serve with ancho chile butter sauce and French bread. Serves 4.

Chapter 18

Two hours later, Nikki drove back to Malveaux after having a cup of coffee and putting Lauren into a cab. The woman was smashed by the time lunch was over. Hell, she'd obviously been halfway there before lunch had started! Nikki pondered Lauren's story. She *could* be telling the truth and nothing but, or everything she said could be a total fabrication, except for the part about who she was playing bed games with.

A thought came to Nikki that churned up the paella digesting in her gut and gave her the willies. Baron saw her the other night at the church. What if those two—Lauren and Baron—were in cahoots on this thing? What if Baron *did* know about Georges? They were good pals, but what if Baron had a lot to benefit from Georges being dead—not just the woman, but something more? Nikki needed to hunt down Georges' wills and trusts attorney and see who the bulk of his estate was going to. Probably Janie, but Georges seemed a generous guy and there was no telling what he was worth. He had a couple of restaurants, a couple of cookbooks garnering royalties, and the release of the new cookbook he'd worked on with Derek—*Georges at the Vineyard Cookbook*. Nikki intended to find out Georges' worth and who was going to benefit from his death. Money and greed were among the primary motivations people killed for, and murder victims were usually killed by someone they knew.

Baron and Lauren liked hooking up, and together could have decided that once Georges was out of the picture, they could get even more than, umm, just mere *satisfaction* from being together—some cash. Maybe the two planned the murder, used each other as an alibi, and now Baron, being the good Irish Catholic—which Nikki found nothing short of amusing—had to absolve himself of his sins behind confessional drapes. Or one could be far more the deceiver and using the other. One of them could stand to inherit a bundle, so the other with this knowledge could have calculated the whole thing, hooked the other into a relationship, did away with Georges, and the other none the wiser. But then that would blow the alibi thing out of the water.

Unless it was all Lauren. Yes, Baron could be in the dark, and Lauren, with her own ties—though they be loose, from what she'd told Nikki—could have really been in bed with Baron at the time of the murder and had someone else do the dirty work. All of Nikki's theories seemed plausible to her. Should she share them with Detective Robinson? Ah, but then the jerk would know he'd been dead-on when he'd accused her of being nosy, and he might even arrest her for . . . For what she didn't know, but she wouldn't put it past him to come up with something. Well, if he found out about the *thing* at the airport she was pretty certain there were at least a couple of laws she'd broken. No, she wasn't going to go tattling to the detective until she spent some more time on the hunt. Because right about now, it was getting good.

She pulled into the vineyard around three and planned to go into the office for a few minutes just to touch base and

check her messages, even though she was still officially off.
The office gave her some sense of normalcy. Sure, Derek
was giving her some time off, but she had obligations to her
job, which was something she truly did love, and to stay involved would help her get through all of the insanity. She
knew that if she slowed down for a minute, she would be
haunted by thoughts of watching her place burn down, and
she couldn't even go there right now.

She pulled up next to the offices, which blended nicely
with the rest of the winery, done up in the same Mediterranean style. Odd that Derek's Range Rover was parked
there, and next to it, a silver blue convertible Beemer.
Nikki's dream car. Visions of cruising down the 101 with
the top down, her hair blowing in the wind . . . Ah well, the
Camry got good gas mileage and if it ever needed any
work it wouldn't cost an arm and a leg. But still, one of
those little Beemers would be nice.

She parked her car and went in. All was quiet. The office slowed down in the late afternoon and probably the
events over the weekend had brought the day-to-day operations to a near standstill. Nikki couldn't help wondering
who Derek was with.

She started to breeze by his office, the door half open,
enough for her to hear a woman laugh. The owner of the
dream car? Nikki picked up her pace. Get in, get messages,
get out. Derek didn't tell her about any meeting he had and
she hadn't seen anything on the schedule. She must be a
friend.

"Nikki? Is that you?"

Nikki stopped, tightened her fists, released them, and
peeked inside his office. His baby blues looked right at her.

"Hey, Nikki, this is Renee Rothschild."

Renee turned around and smiled. Nothing short of
beauty-queen gorgeous with her stupid sea green eyes,
caramel-colored long hair, flawless beige skin—yeah beige,
but the kind that is almost the color of a latte. A suit that
Nikki knew came straight from the BCBG store, because

she'd had to stop and gawk at it in the window when she'd been in the city yesterday preparing for her "deep under-cover" stint. The suit—summery green, with a cream camisole underneath. The skirt—straight, at the knee, with a slit up the back, as Nikki knew. Very businesslike, with the perfect amount of sex appeal. Yep indeedy, Ms. Roth-schild had to be the owner of the blue Beemer, and surely her hair blew in the wind while cruising down the 101 look-ing like Carmen Electra meets Jennifer Aniston, just enough brass with the class to look like a model in a Puff Daddy music video.

Nikki smiled back and stepped in, her hand outstretched. Boy, did she feel meek in her J. Crew tee and jeans! "Nikki Sands. Nice to meet you."

"Ms. Rothschild is, I mean was, Georges' editor at Rothschild Publishing."

"My father is the publisher," Renee said.

Of course. The Beemer, the suit, the fact that Renee looked under thirty and was a senior editor at a publishing house in the city—a job handed to her by good ole dad.

"Renee came out to talk with me about Georges and the book," Derek said.

"Oh," Nikki replied.

"Why don't you have a seat? I think maybe you should be in on this. I know I told you to take some time off, but Renee didn't have a lot of time, and so I agreed to meet with her today." Derek clasped his hands behind his neck and leaned back in his leather swivel chair. "Renee, you want to tell Nikki what you were just telling me? She's my assistant and the winery manager; she may have some thoughts."

Renee nodded all of her caramel tresses in Nikki's di-rection and again flashed her perfect smile. "Sure. I came out because, as you know, Georges' new cookbook that he did in conjunction with Derek on the wines is scheduled to be released next month. Obviously, we have a problem be-cause now with Georges gone we don't—"

Nikki interrupted, "You don't know if you should print it."

"No, that's not it. We're definitely going to print it, but the thing is, we now have issues with the royalties. My assistant, Scotty, was able to get us an appointment with Georges' attorney, Leonard Kingston, in the city for Thursday morning, but I'd really like to have my ducks in a row before we go in and meet with him. See, per our contract with Georges, the royalties in case of death would go to an heir, and I don't know who that would be. I know he doesn't have children, so it all depends on who he's named in his will."

Nikki bit her tongue, not ready or prepared to bring up Janie. "What does this have to do with Malveaux?"

"I needed to come out and meet with Derek to be certain that this is a venture he's willing to go forward with and not break contract." She looked at Derek and winked. "Which I know he wouldn't, but now we have to get with whoever is going to be receiving the royalties and have them made aware of how things will work and so forth."

Nikki shifted in her chair, not really sure why she'd even been asked to join this meeting.

"Did Georges mention anything to you about an heir, Nikki? I know you worked a bit with him on the cookbook," Renee said.

"Actually all I did was dictate notes from Derek, organize them for Georges, and pass them on. We didn't get into anything personal. He didn't say anything to me about an heir." Well, *he* didn't, but *his daughter did*.

"No problem. He didn't say anything to Derek either. I didn't figure that he would, but it was worth a try. I really wanted to drive out and see the place, too. I know what it meant to Georges, and obviously it means a great deal to his coauthor." Renee looked at Derek and uncrossed her long, tan legs. Nikki couldn't help notice Derek glancing at them. "I'm certain when Scotty and I meet with Kingston on Thursday we'll be able to get this all figured out."

"Scotty?" Nikki asked.

"Yeah, as I said, he's my assistant—Scott Nielsen. We go everywhere together. I need someone to keep me organized. He's out sick today. At least that's what he claims. He better be back in by Thursday or I don't know what I'll do. He's the best, but he does this moonlighting thing, you know"—she lowered her voice—"he's a female impersonator."

What was it with this woman? Just 'cause she drove a Beemer, looked like God's gift to men, and her daddy provided her with endless amounts of cash under the guise that she had a *real* job, she couldn't pick up the phone and make inquiries on her own? No. She had to have some poor schmuck named Scott do it.

"I would deal with Leonard Kingston myself but he's a really unpleasant bastard. I've dealt with him over the phone before, in a similar situation with an author's estate. I've never personally met him, and the phone call was enough to turn me off. I want to go into his office with my guns loaded. My weapon of choice is Scotty. He has a way with people. I don't know what it is with gay men, but they all seem to have that schmooze factor. I refuse to go meet Leonard Kingston without him."

Okay, so maybe she was a smart woman after all, or maybe a manipulative one, and she hadn't been anything but nice to Nikki. However—and the pointer finger was raised here—Nikki could not help but notice the white-hot chemistry between Renee Rothschild and Derek.

"You and your assistant go meet with Kingston then, and if there's anything I can do on my end, let me know," Derek said. "Why don't you have Scott give either me or Nikki a call, since she's now been made aware of the situation, and we'll go from there."

"Sure. One other thing," Renee said. "You know, I really liked Georges a lot. He was fun to work with and I'll miss him. Rothschild Publishing specializes in cookbooks and some of these chefs can be difficult, but Georges wasn't. He could be kind of silly if he'd had more than his share to drink, but he was a good man."

"I agree. I think Nikki would, too," Derek replied.

"That said, I know this might be short notice, but he told me how excited he was to be opening the restaurant here and how he wanted to have the book launch here. He was really enthusiastic. I understand that his body is being flown back to France for burial next week and since there won't be an official ceremony here, I was wondering if Friday we could do something in his honor?"

Oh, jeesh. Not only was she pretty, smart, and owned the dream Beemer, she was thoughtful, too.

"That's a great idea. We'll do a dinner in his honor at the restaurant." Derek smiled. "Make it informal, seeing how that's only four days away, but I'm sure he would have liked that."

"Me, too," Nikki said. Brilliant. That sounded brilliant. Here Renee goes on and eloquently discusses a tribute for Georges, Derek follows up with the right kind of input, and Nikki only adds a "me, too." Yep, brilliant. "I can handle the arrangements," Nikki added.

"No. I'll do it," Derek said. "You've got enough things going on right now, and since you'll probably be heading to Spain for a few months, I should get used to taking on some extra work."

"Spain?" Renee turned to her.

"With her boyfriend," Derek answered.

"Sounds terrific. You'll be coming back here though, I take it?" Renee asked.

"Of course," Nikki replied. She could feel embarrassment mixed with maybe a tad of anger stinging her cheeks. "I actually haven't decided yet. I love my job here and don't want to lose it, and Andrés isn't really my . . ."

"Now Nikki, we discussed it; you won't lose your job here. You're a valuable employee to me, and I've already told you that I'd like you to check out the countryside, see if there's a plot for Malveaux over there." Derek shifted in his chair and eyed her.

Renee tossed her hair behind her shoulders. "Sounds like a dream. Not only Spain, but the job. How could you pass something like that up? You have to go."

Nikki stood and smiled. "Yeah, well, I need to check on a few things in my office and then, um, head over to my room."

"Oh, yes. You're staying at the hotel, aren't you? I'm sorry about your place. Derek told me."

"Thanks. Nice to meet you." Nikki said good-bye and left the office, swallowing back the lump that had nearly seized her throat. After she'd calmed down, checked her messages, replied to a few e-mails, typed a memo, and gone over a wine order being sent out the following week to a big-time movie star, she locked up her office and headed back to her car. Passing Derek's office, she could hear Renee and Derek still talking. She couldn't help herself from listening at the door.

"What do you say? You want to go and grab some dinner with me?" Derek asked.

"I'd love to," Renee replied.

Why had Nikki stopped to listen? She closed her eyes and sighed, then walked outside into the early evening. She hadn't realized that she'd been there for over an hour. What could those two have been talking about for that long? Oh, who cared?

She took her cell phone from her purse and called Andrés. He wasn't home. She left a message for him asking if he wanted to meet her for happy hour at the hotel wine bar. The idea of being with him in Spain was suddenly sounding more and more appealing, but right now the idea of just being with him appealed to her and she hoped he'd get her message. But what if he didn't come? Could she blame him? No, not really. She'd been such a dumb ass. That was the only way to put it. Here the man couldn't get enough of

her, gave her space to sort through whatever she needed to
sort through, was always there when she needed him, and
in return, what did she do? Yanked his chain, that's what
she'd done. She was almost as disturbed as Lauren Trump.
Maybe not that bad, but Andrés didn't deserve a game
player. Dammit. No he did not, but . . . But, oh, it was confusing. She loved being with him, cared about him, he
made her laugh, and damn he had one fine bod and a pair
of amazing, mesmerizing eyes, so why, oh why, in the hell
could she not make that commitment?

Chapter 19

Nikki sat down at the wine bar, Marco was behind it. "Ah, *Bellisima,* Simon and I are pleased you are fine. When I saw what happened to the cottage I was frightened for you."

"It's okay. I'm obviously fine."

He frowned. "You do not seem fine. Come and stay with me and Simon."

"No, really I'll be okay. The hotel is amazing and everything is here, and please do not worry."

"Do not worry? *Impossibile. Vino?*"

"Yes. Grazie."

"Vivanda?" he asked.

Nikki knew he was asking her if she wanted food.

"I made *margherita* pizzas with pine nut, smoked mozzarella cheese, and basil. I also have spinach salad with maple bacon and caramelized walnuts. It's my own version."

"Look at you becoming quite the chef. Maybe you should take over at Georges'. I don't know what's going to happen or who will replace him."

"Oh, no, no. I could never be like a Georges Debussey. He was a great *cuoco*, chef as you say here. I am certain that the other *uomo* he worked with, the Irish man, he will do the job. No?"

"I don't know about that. He mentioned something about going back to Ireland," Nikki replied. *Or, maybe to the slammer.*

"I do not know either." Marco shrugged. "A Syrah? Or a Viognier if you want *bianco* tonight," he said, referring to a white wine. "Wait, wait, *uno momento.*" He snapped his fingers. "I have a beautiful Albariño wine tonight with the appetizers. It's from Spain you know." He raised his eyebrows at her.

She was too tired to fall into that trap. As much as she wanted Marco to be a sounding board to her love life, at that moment she simply wanted to enjoy a glass of wine and some good food and keep her fingers crossed a handsome Spaniard would join her. "Sounds nice. Where is Simon?"

"Getting beautiful, like the Spanish wine is. *Bellisima*, like you."

No dice. She wasn't taking the bait. She smiled and continued to act stupid. Marco got the hint.

"He will be here pronto." Marco looked at his watch.

"He better be." He winked at Nikki and went to get her wine.

She twisted around on her chair and spotted Janie and her husband walking in. Janie approached her. "I'm so glad you're here. I've been thinking about you, and I was telling Trevor how worried I was, and how great you were to me and how I confided everything to you."

"She did," Trevor said. "Thank you again for helping my wife."

"Sit down," Nikki said. "No need to thank me. Janie saved my life."

Janie blushed. The young couple sat down on the stools next to her. Marco brought her wine over and took their orders, too.

"Do you know if they saved anything from your house?" Trevor asked.

"I'm not really sure, actually. From the looks of it, I don't think so. The fire got hot really fast and spread quickly. I forgot to ask the fire marshall, and I'm almost afraid to ask Detective Robinson." Nikki tasted her Albariño.

"That's tough. Janie told me that the detective is a real jerk. She said that they also told you that it was arson?" He raised his brows.

Nikki nodded. "That much they told me. Why? I don't know."

He shook his head. "Man. A fire." His eyes went distant for a second and Nikki could have sworn they were glassing over with tears. He shook his head again and looked away. "Sorry. Fire is horrid. I lost my folks in a house fire."

"Oh my God. I'm so sorry. That's really awful."

He nodded.

"Thank goodness for his grandma. My baby wouldn't be here without her," Janie said.

"Did she save you?" Nikki asked.

"Sort of, I suppose," Trevor replied. "The night the fire happened, I was spending the night at my grandmother's house."

Nikki didn't know what to say. Poor man. "Is your grandma still alive?"

"No. She passed away about a year ago. She was living in an assisted living home at the time. She'd grown pretty senile and had diabetes."

"But Trevor went to see her every week before she died," Janie chimed in. "When we first met, he'd come by the restaurant and get takeout for the two of them and then go and see her. I regret never getting to meet her."

Trevor took her hand. "She would've loved you, baby."

Janie smiled at him.

Sweet.

Marco set their wine down along with two platters of pizza and salad for all three of them.

174 Michele Scott

"Andrés may be joining us, too. I'm not sure yet," Nikki told him.

Marco wiggled his eyebrows at her, in a Groucho Marx sort of way.

Nikki waved him away and turned back to Janie and Trevor. "Janie, you said that you told Trevor about confiding in me?"

"I did. I told him last night when he got here about Georges being my dad, and that I'd told you because I needed to talk to someone and you were there for me."

Trevor set his slice of pizza back on his plate. "Crazy, isn't it? Who would have known? I don't know why he couldn't have told her earlier."

"I told you, baby. He said that he wanted to honor my mother's wishes. See how I fared after she died, to see if I could handle any more of a shake-up. He did the right thing, but now, well now . . . I can't ever know him as my dad."

Trevor put his arm around Janie and hugged her. She kissed his cheek.

Ah, young love.

"I know that Georges just revealed all of this to you before his murder, but Janie, did he, also, maybe indicate anything about a will?"

Janie looked truly horrified as her eyes widened. She shook her head, and replied, "No. Not to me. Of course not. Why would he need to do that?"

"Seeing that you're his daughter and he knew this for some time, my guess is that you would be included in the will, and his publisher is trying to track down the heir in order to make certain that person receives the royalties from his cookbooks."

"Oh. No. But, until they find the killer, I don't want anyone to know, and you promised."

"Janie, I think you have to say something and it will likely come out in his will anyway, which I'm certain will be revealed in a matter of days."

"Then that detective will come after me. I mean, it totally looks like I have a motive. Doesn't it?"

"Baby, Ms. Sands is right. You have to tell the police. You didn't kill him and the truth will come out. I'm in law school. They can't arrest you without evidence. The worst they can do is detain you for questioning, and then they have to release you. And that won't happen."

Janie took a sip from her wine and looked up at Trevor with complete trust. Her eyes brimming with tears, she nodded. "Okay, tomorrow we'll go and tell the police."

Nikki thought a second about Detective Robinson and how if he hadn't already uncovered the fact about Janie being connected to Georges, which he obviously hadn't because he'd have been on her faster than a rabid dog, he'd figure it out soon. Nikki thought it a good idea, though, to buy a day or two's time. "Why don't you wait for another day, okay?"

"Why?" Trevor asked. "Like I said, they won't be able to arrest her."

Nikki set her wine down. If the police honed in on Janie because she reported to them about her parentage, then whoever the real killer was—if it wasn't Janie, which Nikki believed—would simply have more time to cover his or her tracks.

"I think that it's a good idea for Janie to give it a day to get her emotions in check, and maybe she should wait until the will is read, because if she's not an inheritor the police won't be able to tie Georges and her together, unless one of us says something."

"I'm sure she's the heir," Trevor replied.

"Maybe, maybe not. Say Georges didn't have a chance to change his will, or was only recently convinced that Janie was his daughter. You have to consider that there is the possibility that she was not included. You do realize that there was no DNA testing?" Nikki asked Trevor. "So there is no real proof."

"I'm his daughter. I know it, especially after he said so.

I know it." Janie wiped her face with the back of her hand. She reminded Nikki so much of a little girl at times, and then other times when she'd been around Georges getting her work done for him she came across as a confident young woman. Maybe that was because Georges boosted her self esteem—something a dad would do, even if he hadn't let the cat out of the bag until recently—sort of like loving his child at arm's length.

Nikki reached for Janie's hand, her stomach sinking. The poor girl didn't have a mom to advise her in these situations, and she glanced at Trevor, who also didn't have parents. However, he appeared to be an intelligent young man—maybe a bit of an idealist, but smart—and he had his wife's best interest at heart. That much was obvious. "I know, Janie. There is still a way to get proof though."

"There is?"

"Yes. Your dad's body will be at the coroner's office for at least a week, I would imagine." Nikki knew from Aunt Cara that it could take a week or two before autopsy reports were complete and the remains released. "Why don't you call an attorney tomorrow and see if you can't have an order drawn up for a DNA sample? Trevor, you probably know someone who can help. Don't you? Janie said that you were clerking for a law firm."

"I was, but with my finals I had to quit, and now I'm doing up résumés and am on the hunt. I flew down to L.A. a couple of weeks ago and interviewed with a firm there. Maybe I can call them."

"I'm sure. What kind of law do they specialize in?"

"They actually deal in wills and trusts."

"Oh. That's a good coincidence. Call them tomorrow and see what Janie can do, if anything, about having a DNA test."

"I'll do that. It's going to be all right, honey." He put his arm around Janie. "Thanks, Ms. Sands."

"Call me Nikki, please. Ms. Sands makes me feel old." Nikki looked up at the clock on the wall. She'd been there an hour now and no Andrés. Maybe he *was* angry at her. She couldn't exactly blame him. She excused herself and told them both to try and relax, enjoy the hotel and spa.

She got up and started for the kitchen. She wanted to see if Simon had shown up yet. An idea had come to her, and it would have to involve Simon.

Marco was putting another pizza in the oven and swaying to the samba music playing over the speakers. "Marco."

He turned from the open wood oven and, after placing the pizza paddle down, he came over to her, grabbed her by the waist with one arm, and placed his right hand on her left, bringing them both up. "Let's dance, *Bellisima*."

She couldn't help but laugh. He twirled around the tight quarters, all the while lifting her spirits.

"Excuse me." Simon walked in and tapped Nikki on the shoulder. "Are you cheating on me?"

"No, I'm not, but he is." She pointed at Marco. They all cracked up. It felt really good to release the tension that had been building over the last few days.

"You finally show up," Marco said.

Simon did a twirl. "I know I'm late, but don't I look hot." He licked his finger and placed it on his hip, making a sizzling sound—so eighties, and *so* Simon. "I ordered this shirt from Saks. It's a Prada, and look at my belt."

"Hmmm, let me guess, the big *G* on the buckle, Gucci maybe," Nikki said. "Two hundo for a belt, what would the Guru Sansibaba say?"

"That's not fair. He'd say, 'Enjoy your wealth and live life to the fullest, but give to others, too,' which I do. Now be nice." Simon walked over to the freezer and took out a bottle of Stoli. "Want a martini?"

"No thanks," Nikki replied. "You know, Simon, since I lost all of my clothes and things in the fire, and you are such the fashionista, I thought you might want to go into the city tomorrow and help me pick out some things."

Simon clapped his hands. "Duh. I am so there."

"Wait a minute, what about the spa?" Marco asked.

Simon frowned. "But poor Nikki. She needs me, and this is our opportunity to get her out of those Doris Day sweater sets she's always sporting. It's a Wednesday, hon, middle of the week, and with the . . . You know, the murder," he whispered. "Well, I don't think we'll be too busy."

"True. How can I say no to either one of you? Go, go, and I will take care of things here."

Nikki gave Marco a kiss on the cheek. "Grazie."

She turned back to Simon. "Early morning, okay? I want to get there when the stores open. Let's leave by eight and we'll grab coffee and croissants at Bouchon first."

"I'll be at your door with bells on."

Nikki went back to her stool in the wine bar and had one more glass of wine, hoping Andrés would show. Trevor and Janie had taken off, and she sat watching Marco and Simon cooking in the kitchen together. Love was a wonderful thing. She felt kind of bad that she'd basically wooed Simon into going into the city under the shopping guise, but she knew if she'd told him the truth about what they were going to do, he'd have flipped out. She probably could have convinced him after he'd had his martini. But who had the energy for that? This way she'd have him in the city before she sprung on him why they were really there.

Margherita Pizza with
Serra de Estrela Spanish Wine

Pizza began as a small savory pie sold by vendors on the streets of Naples. The popular margherita Pizza was named for Queen Margherita of Savoy. As the legend goes, the queen was staying in Naples and was curious about this strange dish. She requested a local chef make her a pizza; he created a tomato, basil, and mozzarella cheese combination in her honor. The preparation of the various ingredients can give each member of your family a special task.

Pair the pizza with a Spanish wine made from Albariño grapes. The one Marco suggests is Serra da Estrela. This wine contains wonderful apricot flavors that are complemented with lemon-lime and a subtle floral accent. It's a classic wine that makes a perfect match for Mediterranean dishes with green olives, garlic, and capers.

¼ cup pesto (recipe follows)
1 large prepared pizza crust
1 cup smoked mozzarella cheese, shredded
1 large tomato, thinly sliced
¼ cup slivered sun-dried tomatoes (recipe follows, too)
¼ cup of kalamata olives
2 tbsp pine nuts

Spread the Pesto on the pizza crust. Top with ½ of the mozzarella cheese. Place the fresh tomato slices evenly over the cheese. Sprinkle with the sun-dried tomatoes, olives, and pine nuts; top with the remaining cheese. Bake at 400° for 10 minutes.

PESTO

    2 cloves of garlic
    1 cup basil, chopped
    ¼ cup parmesan cheese
    ¼ cup olive oil
    1 tbsp pine nuts or walnuts

Place the garlic in a food processor or blender and process until minced. Add all other ingredients to the garlic and process until pureed. Refrigerate, covered, for 2 to 3 days, or freeze until ready to use.

SUN-DRIED TOMATOES

    8 roma tomatoes

Cut the tomatoes in half lengthwise. Place them in a circle on 8 pieces of paper toweling. Dry in the microwave for 45 minutes at 30 percent power. Turn every 10 minutes. Continue to dry at 30 percent power, 10 minutes at a time, until most of the moisture is removed. Store in a cool, dry place in a covered container.

Chapter 20

"You want me to what?" Simon asked. He and Nikki stood outside the building on Montgomery Street, where the offices of The Kingston Law Group were housed. Simon stomped his foot. "I knew it was too good to be true. You take me to lunch at that digi place on Nob Hill, and then buy whatever I suggest at Nordy's—"

Nikki interrupted. "I know, and I love everything you picked, and I promise you I'll wear everything."

Simon placed a hand on his jutted-out hip. "I did do a great job, didn't I? Maybe I should be a personal shopper. Oh, wait a minute, I see what you're doing. No, uh-uh. I don't think so, Goldilocks. You have been so digging up the dirt and that's why someone started that fire at the house and now you want me to go in there and be someone I'm not. Excuse me. Hello!" He waved a hand in front of her. "Where is your common sense, girlfriend? Out the door, that's where."

Nikki let him rant on, knowing that before long he'd wear himself down and then she'd give him the one-two punch, which would send him flying into the offices of Kingston with her.

"This is not a good idea. Not at all. A bad guy killed Georges, now he's after you and he probably knows you're butting in where you shouldn't be. Why do you do these things? God, what you must have been like as a teenager."

Nikki nodded. "Yeah. Um, Simon?" She shifted her weight from one foot to the other. "What would the Guru Sansibaba say about you not being willing to help a friend?"

"Oh, aren't you a tricky one? There you go using my spiritual connection to get me to do something that is just so wrong. I'll tell you what the Guru would not want me to do—lie."

Nikki sighed and took Simon's hand. "But he would also say that truth and justice should be sought, right?" That was the first swing in the punch. "And sometimes to get to the truth, there has to be a little tiny white lie thrown in there, right?" She squeezed his hand.

"It's not a teeny lie."

"Okay, it's not teeny, but it might help me—I mean us—find the killer and see that the truth is uncovered."

His head bobbed and he rolled his eyes at her. "You're difficult."

"I won't wear any more sweater sets, like I promised, and then I'll take you for drinks and a meal at another fine establishment. I know just the place." That was the knock-out jab.

"No more Doris Day, goody-two-shoes crap, huh?"

She crossed her heart with one of her fingers. "Promise."

"Fine." He blew a big breath out and hunched over as if he'd been defeated. "What's my name again?"

Nikki went on to explain that Simon was to go into Kingston's offices with her and they were to play the parts of Renee Rothschild and her assistant Scott Nielsen. She'd been busy that morning, implementing the plan she'd thought of the night before while talking with Janie and Trevor. First off, she phoned Rothschild Publishing that morning to let Scott Neilsen—Renee's assistant—know that it was necessary to reschedule Ms. Rothschild's appointment with Mr. Kingston for the following week as Mr. Kingston had to go out of town. Then, she called Kingston's offices and insisted they had to meet today, as Renee Rothschild was leaving town on Thursday for a family situation and they *had* to meet before she left. It took some teeth pulling, but Kingston's secretary said that he agreed to meet with them. Finally, she'd done as planned and driven into the city with Simon, shopped and dined and afterward spilled it all on Simon, who she knew would need some convincing but would come around. When it came down to it, he loved to play Rock Hudson to her Doris Day.

"Why are we doing this again?" Simon asked.

"Because we have to find out if Janie is really Georges' daughter, and if she isn't his heir, then we need to find out who gets Georges' estate. It may lead us to the killer." Nikki had to tell Simon about Janie. In order to possibly protect the girl, Nikki had to break her promise to her.

"Don't you think that hot-but-surly S.O.B. dick—pardon my French but dick is the correct nickname for detective, especially for that Robinson dick—might have thought of this already and that he's talked with this Kingston?"

"Exactly. I'm sure he has, and therefore, we are wasting time standing here."

"I know the dick is, well, you know, a dick, but Nikki, why do you have it in for him so bad?"

"Let's just say, and be forewarned my friend, that it's never wise to tell a woman to chill, or back off, or to mind her own business."

"Oh, I get it. He told you not to play Nancy Drew. He might be onto something there."

"You're on my side. So, shut up, and come on, let's go.

You can do this. You've got a flair for drama. You know, Simon, you remind me of Rock."

"Hudson?"

She nodded.

"I can see that," Simon replied and stood up straight, hoisting his shoulders back. "All right, Doris, I'm going in with you."

"Follow my lead," Nikki said as they rode the elevator to the tenth floor. When it opened, Nikki took a pair of glasses out of her Louis Vuitton briefcase—an extravagant birthday gift from Aunt Cara purchased while Cara was in Paris. She may not have looked quite as chic as Renee Rothschild, but she knew she cleaned up well when she put some effort into it. At Nordy's she'd changed into one of Simon's picks, a fitted jacket with a corset lace-up back and pencil skirt in a chocolate color with a turquoise silk cami underneath and a pair of slingbacks to match. Nikki thought poor Simon might faint when he first saw her.

She strode up to the receptionist seated behind a large semicircle light wood desk. A stern-looking dark-haired woman with a large face, but no chin to speak of, looked up. "May I help you?" she asked.

Nikki's knees knocked together. What if Scott Nielsen or Renee had called back for some reason? What if the jig was up? They were here now and they needed to go through with it. "We're here to see Mr. Kingston. Renee Rothschild with Rothschild Publishing and Scott Nielsen."

The woman nodded and buzzed Kingston's office, then let them in. A man, presumably Kingston, had his chair back to them and was shouting obscenities into the phone. He spun around. The receptionist closed the door behind them. He motioned for them to sit down. "I'll speak to you about this later. Do not do another goddamn thing until we talk." He slammed the phone down, his face beet red, his blue eyes practically bulging out of his head. "Leonard Kingston. Sit down, please." He stood and stretched out his hand.

Nikki took it and introduced herself as Renee and Simon as Scott. They all sat and Nikki couldn't help wonder if she'd seen him before. His eyes had a distinct look to them that she thought she recognized. No, it likely was the intense way he stared at her. It kind of reminded her of Andrés, who also looked at her as if he could see through her. A bit disconcerting, especially since she and Simon were there to try and pull off one huge lie.

"I know this is about Georges Debussey, and I am very busy, Ms. Rothschild. The will is scheduled to be read next week. I don't know what is so important that it couldn't wait until then." He eyed Nikki. "So, do you want to tell me what it is?" Kingston dabbed his forehead with a handkerchief. He set it down and ran a hand through his thinning gray hair.

"We're here, Mr. Kingston, in regard to Mr. Debussey's estate as you stated," Nikki said.

Kingston shook his head. "I am aware of that. It is terrible, isn't it? Poor Georges. He was a great guy. I still can't believe it. I hope they catch the bastard that did it. But that still doesn't explain what you want from me."

Nikki nodded. Simon opened up a notepad and acted as if he were prepared to take notes. "It is horrible. Do you have any idea who would kill him?" Might as well take a stab at it while she had the chance.

"The only one that comes to mind is his former agent. I'm sure you remember the ass, being Georges' editor."

Did he know they were pulling the wool over his eyes? The way he said "editor" made Nikki wonder. "Oh boy, don't you know. An ass indeed. I can't stand Henry Bloomenfeld."

"He was pretty angry when Georges dumped him. You did receive my letter last month about me taking over the literary affairs for Georges?"

Nikki looked at Simon. She nudged him with her foot. "We did receive that, Mr. Kingston, and I placed it in Georges' file. I'm not certain Ms. Rothschild has had a chance to take a look at it as she's been terribly busy. Thus, the reason I'm here. She gets overwhelmed at times and needs some help."

Nikki kicked him this time.

"Good assistants are hard to find," Mr. Kingston said.

"They are indeed, and I am blessed to have Scotty here." She smiled at Simon. "Anyway, I will take a look at your letter and get back to you on that." She had to take a chance here and hope it paid off. "However, since neither you nor Bloomenfeld worked the last cookbook deal with Rothschild, neither of you is eligible to collect any royalties."

Kingston nodded. "I'm aware of that. Is that what this is about? Georges came to me after discovering that Bloomenfeld was skimming his royalties before sending Georges his paychecks. We thought about suing, as you know through the e-mail correspondence you and I had on the topic. And, thank you for getting me all of those sales numbers so quickly."

"Thank Scotty. Not a problem though. I'm surprised we haven't met before now. It's a shame it has to be under these circumstances." Nikki shifted uneasily in her chair and crossed and uncrossed her legs.

"People are busy, and this was why Ms. Rothschild wanted to meet you now," Simon interjected. "Because business should not be about e-mails and phone calls, but about people. Wouldn't you agree?"

Kingston didn't reply.

"You and Georges didn't go forth with the suit against Bloomenfeld," Nikki stated as if she knew this was the correct answer.

"No. Waste of time and money. Georges thought about it on principle, but in the end it would have cost him more in my fees than what Bloomenfeld stole."

"Right. Mr. Kingston, we're here because we need to know who the beneficiary is of Georges' royalties," Nikki said.

Kingston leaned back in his chair and swiveled it to the side. On the table behind him, against the high-rise window, were some photos. "Beautiful family," Simon said, pointing to an eight by ten of Kingston about fifteen years younger, an attractive blonde woman with early-nineties big hair, and a little boy of about ten.

"Thank you," Kingston replied. "As I've explained already, I will be reading the will and have a copy sent to your office upon release here in the next couple of weeks, as soon as I notify the beneficiaries. What's Rothschild's hurry?"

"As you know, we have the cookbook coming out in a few weeks, and being that Georges coauthored the book with Derek Malveaux, his untimely death complicates matters. We already have the print run and orders in the thousands. We expect the book to hit the bestseller list, at least for cookbooks, and basically we can't go forth without the beneficiary's signature." Nikki knew this was bull, and so would Kingston, but she had another story ready to tell. Simon had his head down and she thought he might pee his pants.

"You can go through with the run. I've seen the contract and there shouldn't be a problem with that as long as the beneficiary receives the royalties," Kingston said, his eyebrows arched high.

"I realize that, but the problem lies with Mr. Malveaux himself. He's a very ethical man, and well, he doesn't feel comfortable with this. You understand."

"And, Mr. Malveaux has agreed that if you can help us out today, he'd like you to represent him with the next book," Simon said.

Nikki was so stunned that she couldn't even kick him this time.

"He did, huh?" Kingston looked at Nikki.

She smiled and nodded. "Yes. He'd like to do a book on the wine-making process, which interests so many people these days. And, I told him since he didn't have an agent he should consider using you. I know that Georges had a lot of faith in you, and I figured since we were meeting today that I would suggest it."

"Why don't I call Malveaux myself then, and we can work this out?"

"We spoke to him this morning again and he was on his way out of town for a couple of days. I believe his aunt is ill," Nikki said. Oh boy, was it getting deep in here or what? And, she was getting the feeling that Kingston wasn't buying it.

Kingston brought his chair in closer to his desk and placed his hands out in front of him. "Georges had a daughter. She is the beneficiary of not only his royalties, but his estate, which is worth twenty million dollars.

Nikki swallowed hard. Holy cow. "He had a daughter?"

"He was worth twenty mil?" Simon asked.

"Yes. The daughter's name is Jane Creswell, and I've been trying to get a hold of her since this morning. Apparently she has a new cell phone number. She used to work for Georges, so I'm sure I'll track her down in a day or two. I figured if she knows by the end of the day, then what does it hurt for Malveaux to know? But, I'd like to get a hold of the girl first. There are some complications involved."

"Complications?" Nikki asked.

"Yes. The girl does not know that she is Georges' daughter, but that's really all I can say for now. I'll be in touch with you or Mr. Malveaux directly in the next couple of days after I reach Ms. Creswell."

"Of course, and thank you for your time and help." Nikki and Simon stood, shook Kingston's hand again, and left his office.

Neither said a word until they got into the elevator, where they let out a relieved sigh. "Wow," Nikki said.

"Wow? Wow? Like I'm sweating like a pig. I so didn't think he was buying it, and then he coughed up like a man having his fingernails being torn off."

"He sure did. He must have bought it. You know what this means, don't you?"

"No, Goldilocks, but something tells me, it ain't good."

"Oh but it is. Maybe Rick Moran and Henry Bloomenfeld were stealing money from Georges. Kingston just told us that Bloomenfeld had been skimming Georges' royalties." She then told Simon about following Moran to the airport and the suitcase filled with cash. "And, I saw Bloomenfeld the other night with Moran." She failed to tell Simon exactly where she saw them. "One of them might have gotten scared, because maybe Georges was on to them? Maybe Moran was moving the money around and hiding it and Bloomenfeld was in on it with him. Bloomenfeld had plenty of reason to be angry at Georges. He fired him just as his career was taking off. Moran might simply be greedy, and Bloomenfeld has been using him as a tool to continue to hang on to the goose with the golden egg."

Simon nodded. "If anyone should have been angry it should have been Georges. Bloomenfeld is a thief. Of course, Georges should have canned him and the jerk should have expected that."

"You're right and rational people get that, Simon. But a criminal like Bloomenfeld does not. To Bloomenfeld, Georges' termination of him gave him a motive to continue stealing through a partnership with the financial advisor. And maybe it also gave him a motive to kill. Moran would have had to help him because he still had access to Georges. They could have been in on it together."

"Nikki, this thing is getting ugly. I think maybe you should tell Dick Robinson."

"Maybe you're right." It was the last thing she wanted to do. Jonah Robinson had it in for her. She took her cell phone from her purse and toyed with the idea of calling the detective. She saw that she had a message and checked it. It was from Alyssa. She flipped shut her phone and looked at Simon. "I'll call the police, really I will. But first we have *one* more stop."

"I don't like the sound of that."

"Relax. It'll be fine. Get my purse."

"Why?"

"There's a handful of dollar bills in my wallet and you're gonna need them."

Chapter 21

"A strip bar? No way. Okay, first I had to play your assistant . . . which, I might add, I should have gotten an Academy Award for."

"Okay, Academy Award, what? Maybe, but what was with telling Kingston that Derek wanted to hire him as his agent?"

"That saved the deal, Goldilocks, and you know it. The old stiff wasn't going to tell us anything, unless I sweetened the deal."

Nikki rolled her eyes.

"No comeback? That's because you know I'm right. And this is the gratitude I get? I take you shopping. I play Hudson to your Day, and honey you are a hell of an actress. I don't know if I'll ever believe a word you say after the performance I just witnessed. But now, you want me to go in there with you and pretend I'm a straight guy and put dollar bills in women's G-strings? You know about my nakedness phobia."

"They wear bikinis. They're not even topless. You can play a straight guy." Nikki winked at him.

"Excuse me? I can play straight about as well as Liberace."

She got out of the car and went to the passenger side. Simon locked it. She pressed her keychain and unlocked it. They played that game for a minute, until she grabbed the door before he could lock it again, took him by the sleeve, and dragged him out of the car. "Okay, deal. You do this with me, we go back to the mall and I buy you the shirt you wanted."

"The cigar shirt? Ooh, I would look so fifties bad boy in that." He yanked his arm from her grasp. "Fine. But couldn't this place at least be in the nice part of town?"

"It's a strip bar, Simon."

Nikki kept her dark glasses on, in case Bloomenfeld or Moran was inside. There were a few men and they all took note of her when she came in with Simon. She leaned in and whispered, "We're dating if anyone asks, and we like to spice things up sometimes. That's why we're here."

Simon gave her a dirty look. They sat down in a cushy, torn, faux velvet booth. Nikki scooted close to Simon. "Put your arm around me." He did. Nikki scanned the place looking for Alyssa. She hadn't spotted her yet.

"Why are we here again?"

"I told you. One of the dancers has some information for me about Bloomenfeld and Moran."

"You know, you're like Nancy Drew gone to seed. It's plain wrong."

"Shut up and order a drink." A waitress came over and Simon ordered an appletini.

The waitress gave him a funny look. Nikki nudged him under the table. "Uh sir, we don't do those here," the waitress said.

Simon waved his hand. Nikki nudged him again. "Fine. I'll have a Cosmopolitan then."

The waitress jotted it down. Nikki ordered beer on tap. She faced Simon. "Hello, you are supposed to be straight."

"Uh hello, I'm not. I am so not. Why don't we pretend you're gay and trolling? You're the one drinking the beer."

"I'm not liking you right now."

"Ditto. Back at you," Simon replied.

"Drink your drink." The waitress had come back and set their drinks down.

Simon picked his up and in two big gulps it was gone. He snapped his fingers and called out to the waitress, "Another one, honey." He turned to Nikki. "There, how was that? I called the striptease waitress honey. Now that's straight."

"No comment."

Duran Duran started playing "Rio" and Alyssa appeared on stage. Simon sucked down another Cosmo as Alyssa gyrated and did her thing. She made eye contact with Nikki once. It was hard to watch the young woman up there, and not because she had any bad feelings for strippers or weird nakedness phobias, but because she knew the woman had great potential and could do a helluva lot more with her life.

"Great music. She's good." Simon pointed at Alyssa. "I wonder how she does that thing with her hips. I've gotta learn that move."

"You do that."

The song ended and a couple of minutes later Alyssa came to the booth and squeezed in with the two of them. "Who's the gay guy?" she asked.

"I am not gay," Simon replied.

"Yeah, and I didn't just take money for dancing for perverts."

"He's harmless, drunk, and a good friend. He's helping me with this thing, too," Nikki replied.

"Hey, I am not drunk either."

Both women ignored him as he finished off his third drink. Simon couldn't hold his liquor, and the way he was sucking down the Cosmos, Nikki knew she'd have to get him out of there soon. One thing she knew about Simon: he was notorious for having a really big mouth when drunk. The kind that usually gets people into trouble.

"You got my message?" Alyssa asked.

"Yeah. What's up?"

"That Henry guy and his buddy . . ."

"Rick Moran?" Nikki asked.

"The same one that was here the other day. Anyway, they were here last night. Henry was plowed and the other dude was on his way to blitzville, so I cozied up to them and Henry said that they were heading to Mexico and asked if I wanted to go."

"Did they say where in Mexico and when they were going?"

"Cozumel, and they're going tonight. They told me and another girl to meet them at the airport bar at seven if we wanted to have some fun. Henry was tossing all sorts of money around, and said that he'd recently come into it. That seemed to make the other guy uncomfortable. He told Henry not to say too much, but Henry told him to shut up."

"They had to have killed Georges," Nikki said. "I'm betting they were stealing money from him, killed him because he found out, knew I was looking into things, and torched my place hoping to get rid of me, too."

"Someone burned your place down?" Alyssa asked.

"Poor girl, but it's not all bad because at least she won't be wearing any more sweater sets," Simon chimed in.

"What?" Alyssa asked.

"Never mind," Nikki said. "I'll tell you when we have time. Right now, we better get to the airport and stop those two from getting on a plane."

"Shouldn't you call the cops?" Alyssa asked.

Nikki sighed and nodded. "I suppose I should."

"I hope I helped," Alyssa said. "Right now I've got to go back on stage. But I have good news. I have a job interview tomorrow. I'm applying for a receptionist job at a private investigative firm. I kind of like this stuff, and you gotta start somewhere, right?"

"Good for you," Nikki replied.

"It won't pay me what I make here, but we'll manage. I know we will."

Simon coughed and Nikki looked over at him. He was tearing up. "I love a happy ending. Good for you, honey. Here, take this." Simon opened his wallet and emptied it, giving her all the cash. "You, honey, are an outstanding dancer. I love that hip thingy you do."

Nikki had no clue how much was in the wallet, but she knew the Guru Sansibaba would be proud and so was she. "Come on Mother Teresa, we better finish the rest of our do-gooding for the day." She gave Alyssa a hug. "You know, since you're looking for another job and I've seen what you're capable of doing . . ." She raised her brows. "What I'm trying to say is that we might have a position for you at Malveaux."

"You mean work at the winery?"

Nikki nodded. "You've got experience in the entertainment business, and we have an opening for a taster. Call me, and I'll set up an interview for you."

Alyssa hugged her back and asked them to wait a minute. When she returned she was fully dressed, her purse draped over her shoulder. "I'm going home. I quit. Let me help you out with him."

The women stood on either side of Simon, his arms draped over them. He kissed them each on the cheek. "As the Guru Sansibaba says, 'Everything happens for a reason.' Thank you, both. I love you. What a beautiful day. Now I know why I had to play Rock Hudson, not just once but twice today."

"What?" Alyssa asked.

"Don't ask." She offered the girl a ride home.

"Nah. I think I'll take the trolley. I like this time of evening and I want a moment alone before I go into mom mode."

Nikki nodded even though she didn't exactly know what *mom mode* felt like, but she knew that, one day, she hoped to find out. They said good-bye.

Once Nikki settled inside her Camry she phoned Detective Robinson and told him all that she'd found out about Moran and Bloomenfeld. He rudely thanked her and said that he'd have SFPD arrest them before they boarded their plane.

"But Ms. Sands, I believe that you and I need to have a chat. I'll be by your place in the morning."

Oh joy. Something to look forward to.

Chapter 22

The next morning Detective Robinson showed up before Nikki had even polished off her first cup of java. She sat waiting for Marco to bring over her breakfast of croissants with applewood bacon, tomatoes, and brie, along with biscuits with rosehip jam, and a bowl of strawberries. Customary champagne was on the morning menu, but she passed. She had work to do.

Marco scolded her for getting Simon drunk and told her that he'd be useless for the day, sleeping off the remnants from the night before. She promised to make it up to him by helping around the spa for the day, covering for Simon. He'd taken her up on the offer.

"Morning," Robinson said as he took the chair across from her. He set down a large plastic bag he was toting.

"Good morning, Detective, would you like some coffee?"

"Never touch the stuff. Call me Jonah. You did, from the sound of it, solve my case. I was on a different wavelength. I suppose I should apologize to you, but you know I was only looking out for your best interest. Citizens should not be out trying to do a cop's job. It's dangerous, Ms. Sands."

"Nikki."

"Nikki," he replied and smiled.

Who knew the guy had it in him? A real honest-to-goodness smile.

"Maybe next time someone turns up dead, you let me do my job and you do yours."

"Hopefully there won't be a next time," she replied.

Jonah smirked.

"I take it the police in San Francisco caught up with Moran and Bloomenfeld?" she asked.

"We caught up with Bloomenfeld," Robinson replied. "Moran . . ." He shook his head.

"What? He wasn't there?" A chill shimmied down Nikki's spine.

"Nope. I spoke with one of the detectives there, and they think maybe Moran got scared and took off. We've got an APB out on him."

"An all points bulletin?" Nikki asked. "What do you think he got scared of?"

"Getting caught for starters, or maybe, Bloomenfeld. I'm not sure who the mastermind was, but we'll get to the bottom of it, and we'll get Moran. Don't worry."

Nikki attempted a weak smile but couldn't even muster that. How could she not worry? If Moran and Bloomenfeld killed Georges and then burned her place down, hoping she was inside, because she was snooping, would Moran not come back to finish the job? She sighed and reasoned that it was her overactive or overreactive imagination at work. Moran wasn't coming back for her. If it had been Bloomenfeld who'd flown the coop, her need to look over her shoulder until he was behind bars would be greater. But Moran appeared to be a wuss. "The other day I was out on a walk at the vineyard," Nikki said, "and I saw you talking to Moran. He waved you down?"

Robinson smiled. "Walking, huh?" She nodded. "Yeah, I saw Moran. Said he was wondering how the investigation was going and if we'd found out anything. I told him no.

Hell, even if we did I wasn't about to tell the guy. My radar went up that he was asking, and for good reason obviously."

"Obviously. Um . . ." She bit her lip and shifted in her chair. "I also saw that you had a ladder in your truck."

"You see a lot when you're out *walking* the vineyard." He put his elbows on the table.

"I do."

"Mhhm. The ladder was taken in for evidence. We didn't get any prints, but we're sure it's how the killer got up to the balcony, either before or after Debussey was in there. I questioned the therapist, Charlotte, and she confirmed that Debussey had requested music. He may not have heard the killer climb up."

"There are also plenty of tall plants up on that balcony to hide behind."

"There are."

"Did anyone see anyone?" Nikki asked.

Robinson shook his head. "No one out of the ordinary. That doesn't surprise me. On a day like last Saturday, as busy as it was here, someone could have posed as a worker and gotten in and out pretty easily."

Nikki agreed; she'd already figured that was the case. "Now what about Bloomenfeld?"

"They'll be transporting him to Santa Rosa some time today so I can have a crack at him. So far, he isn't copping to a thing. Nada. Even though SFPD is doing what they can to jerk his chain."

Nikki tilted her head.

"It means they got something else on Bloomenfeld that they're using to try to get him to talk. Apparently Bloomenfeld had some pirated videos in his possession and they weren't the garden-variety type either."

"I met him. He is a real creep."

"Anyway, he isn't admitting to murder, and he isn't admitting to having any type of partnership with Moran. Claims he has no clue where Moran is. But it'll be a grounder once I get my hands on them. I'm also sure I'll get him to confess to torching your place, or at least tell me Moran did it."

"A grounder?" Nikki asked.

He laughed and shook a finger at her. "See, you're not quite the detective, are you? You can solve a case, but you don't know the lingo. A grounder means an easy case to wrap up. I figured you'd know that."

"Nope. No clue."

Marco came over and set down her breakfast. "You don't have much time. I need you in the spa." He turned on his heels.

Yep. He was pretty mad at her. Not good to be on Marco's bad side. She'd have to sit down with him at happy hour and pretend she was interested in being enlightened by the Guru Sansibaba's words. That would surely get her back on his good side.

"Looks like you better get to work," Robinson said. "There's another thing though. We tracked the cash Moran and Bloomenfeld had gotten their hands on. A couple hundred grand. Stupid though, they had stored it at SFO in the storage area. Moran had taken it out of storage yesterday and deposited the bulk of it into a bank account. He was setting up a transfer into a Cayman account in both his and Bloomenfeld's name. The transfer would have gone through last night if it hadn't been tracked. Then, Moran didn't show up at the airport, which leads us to believe that Bloomenfeld did away with him, too."

"Huh. Interesting," was all Nikki could say.

"Yeah, but the detectives down at SFPD mentioned that after questioning one of the clerks, an interesting story came to light, which makes me wonder if there was another person involved in this."

"Really? Who?"

He smiled. "Yeah, apparently a real attractive brunette worked the clerk to get ahold of the suitcase with the cash and then she must have gotten scared, because she didn't take it with her. She's about five five, maybe 115 pounds, green eyes, brunette, the clerk said she had nice, um . . ."

"I get it." Nikki felt the heat rise to her face.

"I'm sure you do. I told SFPD I had an idea about who the woman is and I'd take care of it. Since, uh, you're so good at figuring things out, do you have any idea who the mystery lady at the airport was?"

She sighed. "What do you want, Robinson?"

He laughed. "Nothing. I just like getting a rise out of you."

Marco walked past them and gave Nikki a sharp look.

"Looks like you better get your ass in gear before the boss man has a fit," Robinson said.

She was thankful he had dropped the airport incident.

"Yeah, I owe him. But first, can I ask you where your thoughts were on this case? You said that you'd been traveling down a different path." She picked up her coffee cup.

"I thought his partner was the one I'd be locking the steel doors on. He had motive, and according to those in the kitchen that day, Mr. O'Grady had taken off after giving a few instructions and had not returned for over an hour, which gave him ample time to kill his partner."

Nikki knew where Baron had been during that time . . . supposedly, anyway: shacking up with Lauren Trump. She wondered if that had become Baron's alibi. "Where did he say he was?"

"He says he was with a woman. He didn't tell me who, so that's why I figured he had done it." Robinson smiled. "Oldest alibi in the book is a woman, but if you can't produce one, what good is she? He told me that she had an ex who had some badass contacts and that he didn't want to get involved with them. I told him what he was up against, but he said that he'd done nothing wrong and that he'd rather take the heat from the cops than deal with his girlfriend's ex."

Maybe Baron *was* leaving the states to get away from Lauren and her Mafia ties. Who could blame a man who'd probably grown up amid the violence in his homeland? "You said that he had a motive. What? Just the fact that he stood to inherit some cash or part of the business?"

"Nah. That would have been a stupid move on Baron's part. He'd have made more in the long run hanging on to Georges. The man, from what I understand, was a cash cow and only getting bigger daily. Baron had more reason than that. He had a five million dollar life insurance policy on Georges."

Nikki's mouth dropped. "He did?"

"Yeah. Get this, too. I went to ask him why he had a life insurance policy on his buddy, and the poor sap shriveled. Said that he knew if anything happened to Georges he couldn't stay here and survive the business. He'd want to go back home and make sure he had enough to live on for him and his mother. He claimed Georges knew about it and therefore didn't leave anything to him in his will, which Baron told him was fine because he never expected Georges to die anyway, and he said that he would have never expected anything be left to him. Said he's not a good businessman. According to my investigation, he's right. He can't manage money worth a damn, but he's an excellent cook and word is that Georges needed him for that reason. Source says that Georges was the brain and a helluva cook, but real traditional-like. Baron was the creative one."

"How did you find out about the policy?" Nikki asked.

Robinson smiled. "I am a cop. I visited Georges' ex-wife in jail."

Nikki had forgotten about Bernadette Debussey. She'd left the voice message on Monday to see if she could visit her and had figured someone would call her back. But now it looked as though that wouldn't be necessary. "Interesting. Baron never told you the identity of the woman he was with?"

"Nope, and now, thanks to you, he can keep his little rendezvous with Miss Trouble nice and tidy."

Jonah Robinson's demeanor toward her had been no

less than horrible, but there was something about him now that softened her. Maybe his quirky sense of humor and way with words, or maybe when it came down to it he had that coolness about him that only a handful of people ever exuded. Sure, lots of folks pretended they had it, but Nikki got the feeling that Jonah never needed to remind himself he was cool. It was a given. When they'd first met, she'd thought it was only his look that fit the category, especially because his behavior had been downright mean, but sitting here talking with him changed her mind. She crossed her legs and shifted in her chair.

"Why are you telling me all this? Doesn't this go against your grain? You know, since I'm so disrespectful to the police."

"Hey, I was only doing my job. Trying to keep you outta trouble." He leaned in and lowered his voice. "You got a friend around here, too, who also asked me to keep an eye on you, make sure you kept your nose clean. But lady, I was too busy and you apparently did not keep it clean. The reason I'm telling you all this is, I figure I owe you an apology and you deserve some explanations. You were the one, after all, who turned me in the right direction."

"Wait a minute, back up. You said that I have a friend who asked you to keep a watch on me. Who?"

Robinson winked. "Now I can't go and reveal that."

"Andrés? Was it Andrés Fernandez?"

"Nope. I'll tell you that much. Listen to you. Don't you have quite the following?" He took out his card and passed it to her. "I'm sure you threw the first one away, so take this one and add me to your list."

"My list?"

"Of admirers. You ever make it into Santa Rosa and want a decent meal, I might know a place or two."

"Are you asking me out, Detective?" Her face grew warm.

"Not my style. Like I said, you ever get on a few miles north, we'll hang out."

This was weird. Flattering, kind of, but so very weird. "Uh, sure." It was all she could think of to say.

He looked at his watch. "I better get on back to the station. SFPD should be transporting Bloomenfeld soon. Here, I figured you might want this. I know we haven't officially closed this case yet, and won't until we find Moran. My ass would be on the line if anyone knew I was doing this, but you know, I was a real shit to you the other day and you were devastated about the loss of your home."

"What are you talking about?" Nikki asked. He was a tough one to follow.

"Here. It's not much, but it's what was recovered from the fire. I wish it were more. Sorry." He reached down and handed her the white trash bag.

"Thanks." She didn't know what to say, or if she even wanted to see the contents. Would they bring back memories from the cottage?

He stood and slid on a pair of sunglasses over his jade green eyes. "See you around, Nikki. Don't worry, we'll catch up with that bastard Moran. As soon as we do, I'll let you know."

"Right. Bye."

She watched Mr. Cool swagger out of the eatery and the patio, almost like he was disappearing into the morning light. She peered down at the bag. Her hands shook and for whatever reason she could not bring herself to open it. Dammit. Why couldn't she do it? What did it mean? Was she freaking out like Simon and Marco with their weird phobia? No. She was not. She'd open the damn bag. No big deal. Memories were good. The ones she'd had in that cottage were all good, for the most part, and she wanted to salvage what she could. She was simply being stupid. Open the bag. But she couldn't. Not yet, anyway. Confronting memories—good or bad— was not something she wanted to do, not now. Maybe later.

Marco came over and slapped both of his hands down on the table. "You done here?" He picked up her coffee cup. "I need your help."

"Wait a minute, I didn't even get to eat my breakfast yet, only coffee."

Marco shrugged. "Not my fault. You should have woken up earlier and eaten earlier and not talked too long to that policeman."

"Marco, I was out helping solve a murder. Aren't you proud of me? Can't you understand that?"

He shook his head. "You had Simon out with you, and both of you could have been hurt. We have done these things before, and the more I learn about you"—he shook a finger at her—"the more I discover you get into dangerous situations." He stopped ranting for a minute.

Both he and Simon were *so* dramatic. They really needed to take their own advice, or their Guru's, and mellow out. Nikki had to bite her lower lip to keep from laughing. Wait a minute. Were those tears in Marco's eyes. "Are you crying?"

"No." He wiped the one side of his face with the back of his hand. "I am mad at you. It is one thing for all of us to go on these crazy adventures with you. But if I am not with you two and something happened . . ."

She got it now. Marco not only loved Simon but he loved her, too. She stood up and hugged him. For the first time in a really long time, Nikki felt like she had a family—a dysfunctional family, but still . . . "I love you, too. Next time—there won't be a next time—I'll be sure and include you."

He stood up straight and gave her a playful shove. "Now go. Get to the spa."

She figured she'd be working the front desk. "Okay, but can you have someone take this bag up to my room. Just have it put in the closet?"

"What is it?"

"Some of my stuff." She didn't want to go into it. She knew if she told Marco about the bag he'd insist she open it and she simply did not want to do that yet. "So, what's on the agenda today?" she asked. "What's my job?"

Marco shifted from one foot to the other and looked

down at the ground. "Two of the girls called in sick, which makes me wonder, and with Simon out, and being completely booked this morning, I need you to go and give a massage."

"Massage? I'm not a masseuse. I don't want to go rub some stranger's back. I wouldn't have the foggiest idea how to even do it. Besides, can't you get in trouble for that?"

"Get in there and do it. You can rub a shoulder or two. You rub my shoulders and are good at it."

"But that's you and you're my friend. I can't do this to some stranger."

Marco sighed. "It's not a stranger anyway."

"What? Who is it then?" Marco mumbled something. Nikki couldn't understand him. "What did you say? I didn't hear you."

"Go, go. I don't have time for this. Look, there are more people coming in to eat."

"Uh-uh. Not until you tell me who it is."

"It's Renee."

"Renee?" Nikki asked.

"Yes. The woman who was here last night with Derek. She said that she met you the other day. Renee Rothschild."

Chapter 23

Nikki took a step back. "Renee Rothschild. She's still here?"

"*Sí.*"

"Why? Where? I mean where did she stay?"

Marco put an arm around her. "I don't know. Maybe the hotel."

"Wouldn't you know if she stayed at the hotel?" Her voice had risen a couple of octaves and the edge in it would be hard for anyone, even those who didn't know her, not to notice.

"I think I would know. *Sí.*" He nodded his head, and looked away from her.

"Of course you would know. That would mean . . ." She didn't want to say it out loud, but Marco knew where she was headed.

He put his arm around her. "I am sorry, *Bellisima.* Derek brought her here for breakfast. They had mimosas and she talked to him about doing a book on the spa and hotel. She said that it would make a nice follow-up to the wine and cookbook."

Boy did Renee Rothschild know how to work fast, and work it good. What better way to a man's heart than through his ego . . . and Derek's, Nikki knew, happened to be this vineyard and winery. Maybe not so much an ego trip for him but a legacy. "You heard all of this?"

He looked chagrined. "I could not help but listen."

Eavesdropping? Wonder what the Sansibaba would say about that. No matter. How was she going to get out of this? "Wait a minute. Why me? If she wants to experience a great spa treatment here for *research* for a book, then why me? I'm not even qualified. Switch one of the other therapists around. I can cook and run the eatery. You go." Marco frowned. "You're not going to give me some B.S. line about your phobia, are you?" Marco didn't respond. "Jeesh, you and Simon really need some help, my friend. Okay, so you won't do it, then why me?"

"I told you, two of the therapists called in sick and I only have one other available. And, with Charlotte quitting on us after the murder, we are shorthanded."

"All right, then I'll switch with the other person. I can't give Renee Rothschild a massage."

Marco looked down at the ground. "It's her or Derek, who is in the other room also waiting for a massage."

"What? Oh my God." Nikki turned around, arms out, and looked skyward, muttering the word *why* repeatedly and feeling as dramatic as her two gay friends. She sighed. "Couldn't you tell her another time, or day?"

"No. Derek says that she's going back to the city this afternoon and he insisted we get her in. He loves the idea of the book."

"Of course."

Marco pressed his hands together in prayer. *"Favore, Bellisima."*

She sighed and hung her head. What a week. Could she get any lower? Doubtful. "We're so even after this. No, you know what, you owe me."

His mouth dropped open. He stared at her and then nodded. "I owe you."

She shook a finger at him. "You and Simon will have to go and see a shrink and fix your problem or nudophobia or whatever you want to call it."

Marco shrugged in defeat. "I know you do not want to go in there, *Bellisima*, and do this massage, but please. You must go now. Renee is waiting."

Nikki didn't answer, but turned on her heels and headed toward the spa. Marco shouted after her that the woman was in room two. Perfect. She opened the French doors to the spa. The smell of lavender and neroli oil enveloped her. Oh sure, calming scents. Right, about as calming as three cups of java straight up, black, and throw a Metallica record into the mix. White candles were lit throughout the hall of the spa, and lily, freesia, and rose floral arrangements adorned the waiting area, placed perfectly on the wooden tables. To top it off, Enya's melancholy sound floated through the stereo system. It had a far more grating effect on her than surely was intended.

Nikki washed her hands and put on one of the white coats used by the therapists. Quite the fashion statement.

She tapped on door number two, her hands shaking. Stop it. Go in there, rub the woman's back with some hot oil, and get the job done. No big deal. Why had she ever decided to give up Xanax? Oh yeah, because she'd found yoga and kickboxing to relieve her anxiety instead. She took in a yogic breath all the way to the diaphragm and let it out. Not quite what an antianxiety pill would do, but a good effort at utilizing the tools at hand—air, lungs, and mind over matter.

She turned the knob and entered the room. More lavender, this time mixed with eucalyptus. Ah, the energy massage. Yes, Nikki had had one of those herself.

There on the table lay Renee Rothschild, caramel hair flowing across her back—across that perfect beige skin.

Thank God she was facedown. Ooh, maybe she'd fallen asleep and Nikki could stand in the corner and in an hour mumble thanks and leave. The woman would be convinced that the massage was so relaxing she'd fallen asleep.

"Hi," Renee said. She started to turn over.

"Oh no, on your stomach please," Nikki said, purposely finding her Southern roots and utilizing the accent she'd long ago lost. Amazing what those formative years will do for a kid: set you up for life with an identity from where you came from, making it impossible to ever really erase it. Someday she knew she would have to confront both the demons caused by her roots, but not now.

"Okay. I like the pressure somewhat hard."

Nikki didn't respond. She figured the less she said, the better. She found the jojoba oil, poured some in her hands, then took some of the aromatherapy oils and mixed them together.

She started rubbing Renee's back, who complimented her almost immediately. "That's great. Right there. I am sore there up near my neck." She kind of laughed. "I was kissing a wonderful man last night." Nikki pressed harder. "Ouch!" Renee yelped.

"Sorry."

After a few seconds Renee went back to her story. "Anyway, we were kissing and I twisted my neck ever so slightly and pulled a nerve. Derek told me I needed a massage, and that's when I started thinking about a book idea. I'm sure you were told that's why I'm here. To do a little research for a book. I didn't intend to come out here for that reason, or even stay for more than an afternoon, but things worked out that way, and now I have another great concept for a book."

Okay, now didn't most people shut up when they got a massage? What the hell was wrong with Renee? Blab, blab, blab, blah, blah, blah. Ugh! All Nikki muttered was, "Uh-huh."

"But this place is so lovely and the man behind it, he is

incredible. I even like his dog. Ollie. I don't like dogs, but
Derek's dog is wonderful. He licked my hand and I didn't
even care."

Ollie. That traitor. And, Derek's dog? Derek's dog!
And, *Ollie*? Okay, now Ollie was the nickname Nikki had
given the dog. Derek had always called him Oliver until
she'd started calling him Ollie, and now he was sharing *Ollie* with *her*? With Renee? Wait a minute, Ollie was also
her dog. Wasn't he? I mean it was the vineyard joke about
the two of them sharing the dog and how he couldn't make
up his mind as to who he liked best, Derek or Nikki, and
now Derek was sharing *their* dog, her dog, with Renee
Rothschild, who he'd only known for what, two minutes,
maybe?

Renee sighed. Nikki turned and grabbed for the oil.
When she came back around, Renee had flipped over. Thank
God the sheet was covering her. Nikki didn't think she
could take any more exposure of Renee Rothschild. She'd
already had way too much. "Oh, Nikki. I didn't know you
were a therapist as well. I thought you were the winery
manager."

Crap. "I am, but yes, I also can give a good massage
and things have been crazy here since the murder and the
fire and everything, and well, Marco and Simon needed
help today and they asked me if I could come and help,
and wow, that is so great about Derek and Ollie and everything." Why oh why, in those moments where she needed
to be her most pulled together self, did she always blow it
and fall apart? It was like Cupid also had an idiot bow and
he followed her around and when he thought he'd have
some fun, he'd shoot her with it and she'd turn into exactly what she was at that moment—an idiot. "But not
your neck. No, that is bad. Sorry about the neck." Okay,
major idiot!

Renee laughed. "You know what, it feels so much better
now. You *do* give a great massage. And let me tell you,
woman to woman, that kiss was worth any pain in the neck

I might have briefly had. You know, you might want to consider switching job positions and come over here to the spa full time. You would rake in the tips."

Nikki couldn't respond.

"Shouldn't you do the front now?"

"What?"

"Massage. Don't you do the stomach and front of the arms. That kind of thing? My regular masseuse in the city does that."

"Oh. Ah. No. See, this was the energy massage, and you know energy, it travels quickly and therefore this is only a thirty minute massage and it's designed to align the chakras." Whatever those were. She knew Simon and Marco referred to them all the time. "So, you see, the chakras release your energy field and it has to all be done in the back, and now if I work on your stomach it will basically neutralize what I just did."

"Hmmm. Interesting. Can I quote you in the book on that? I'll be sending a writer out. Unless." Renee's eyes bugged out. "Wait a second, you would be the perfect person to write this book."

"Oh no, no, no. I'm not a writer," Nikki replied.

"Sure you could do this. It doesn't matter that you're not a writer. Not for this type of book. Plus you would be the perfect person for this. You know the winery, you're Derek's right hand. You even do spa treatments. You would be fabulous. I can edit you, so you wouldn't have to worry so much about the writing. Heck, I've even seen some of your writing and you're good."

"What do you mean?"

"Weren't you the one who compiled all the notes for Derek for the book with Georges?"

"Yes. But I gave them to Georges."

"Who do you think Georges gave them to?" Nikki didn't reply. "Me. That's who. Georges didn't write all the text in the cookbook. He did the recipes, sure, but like Derek and then you, he gave me the notes and I pulled it together."

"Oh."

"Oh, nothing. Your notes were by far the easiest to work with. Really, you could write this book. Come on."

Was Renee for real? Or was she yanking her chain? "Um, you know I am so busy and I think I may be going to Spain." Oh boy. Did she really say that? Yep. The words *going to Spain* had escaped between her lips, and oddly enough, for the first time since Andrés had presented the idea, her stomach didn't turn over in a wave of nausea. The idea almost settled right there and felt, hmmm—okay.

"Great. That would be a perfect time to write the book. You would have the distance a writer sometimes needs to get it done without the distractions here at the winery."

Nikki shook her head. "No. I would probably need to be here. You know, for research."

"No. Not at all." Renee sat up, her sheet nearly dropping off of her. Oh God, Nikki thought she might have nudophobia at that moment. "It's perfect, and I bet I can get you a decent advance. I do know certain people in high places at the publishing house."

Yeah. Daddy. Nikki glanced at the clock. "I am so sorry, but I have to get going. I need to make sure an order is going out. Um, it's a very important wine dinner and it would be disastrous if the wines don't get there. You know, big client and everything. A real disaster."

"See, you are so perfect to do this. You've got your finger on the pulse of this place. I'm going to talk to Derek about it. And, I'll get you the details for tomorrow night when we do Georges' dinner. Super. This is so awesome, Nikki."

"Right, awesome." Nikki closed the door behind her. Solving murders and arsonous fires, that was one thing. But how was she going to get out of this one?

Chapter 24

After Renee's massage, Nikki put her foot down with Marco and refused to play spa lady any longer. She'd had more than enough. She checked her cell phone messages and there was one that made her change all of her plans to help Marco out.

It came from the Chowchilla prison, and the warden told her that she had permission to come down and speak with Bernadette Debussey. When she'd made the request, she'd used the pretext that she was a writer and wanted to do an article on prison life for women. Obviously, it had worked.

But, the case was a done deal, right? Granted Moran was still on the run, but Bloomenfeld would surely cop to everything eventually. However, being curious, she did want to meet Georges' ex, find out if she was as crazy as Janie said. Detective Robinson had spoken with Bernadette and she'd told him about the huge insurance policy that Baron had on Georges.

She made the decision to visit Bernadette, if for nothing other than the three-hour drive each way, which would give her plenty of time to consider her life and whether she should change it so drastically by taking a chance with Andrés and moving halfway around the world.

She headed back to her room and changed into her jeans. She opened the closet and grabbed her tennies. There was the bag that Robinson had given her. Her stuff. Marco had it sent up like she'd asked. Well, no time for that right now, not if she wanted to make it to the prison in time for visiting hours.

The drive was nothing short of boring. She decided to call Andrés. Surprisingly, he answered. "Hey," she said. "You stopped ignoring me?"

"Hi you."

"Didn't you get my message the other night? I wanted to see if you could meet me at the wine bar."

"I did," he replied. "But I thought you needed time to think without me pressuring you."

She could almost see the smile on his face, because he wasn't saying it in a mean and condescending way. He got to her like that. "Hmmm. Is that what you thought?"

"Didn't you tell me that's what you needed?"

"Yes. I guess I did."

"Uh-huh. And, you missed me, didn't you?" Andrés joked.

She couldn't help but smile herself. "You got me."

"I did, didn't I? If you don't go to Spain with me, think how much you will really miss me then. Do you want to put yourself through that?"

"You're good. Why are you so good? Huh?"

"I can be bad if you want me to. That might be fun. It might be even more fun than being good. What do you say, come to Spain and be bad with me?"

She sighed and bit her lower lip.

"You're chewing on your bottom lip, right now, aren't you?"

"Mhhm."

"It's okay. You take some more time. No pressure. I'll let

you miss me some more. But you do know you only have a day left to decide. No pressure. *Adiós mi amor.*"

"*Adiós.*" She clicked off the phone. Men like Andrés only come along once in a lifetime. So why was it so hard to go and be bad with him? Take a chance. Say yes. It's easy—a three-letter word, *yes*. She still didn't have an answer to that as she arrived at the prison in a little over three hours after making a coffee stop and filling up. She walked through the front doors of the cold and foreboding building. The place felt sterile, like most institutional buildings. It smelled of cleaning fluids, but not in a good lemon-fresh way, but rather a wipe-off-the-germs way.

A guard thoroughly checked her purse after she walked through an x-ray scanner and told her to sign in and wait in line with the other visitors, that they would be taken to the visiting area in fifteen minutes. The fifteen minutes almost felt longer than the three-hour drive, and Nikki started questioning why she was even there. Finally another guard appeared and checked everyone off the list as they proceeded single file. There were men and women of all ages, probably mothers, fathers, sisters, lovers, husbands . . . and there were also a handful of children. She shivered at the thought of what it must be like to have a mother behind bars. A brief thought of her own mother entered her mind, and then of Janie and the loss of her mom. All were different situations, but the children in line going to see their moms did have something in common with both Nikki and Janie. There was a loss.

In the visiting room there were small tables and chairs set up and everyone in the group knew right where to go. Nikki leaned in and asked the guard who Bernadette Debussey was. The guard pointed her out.

Bernadette was a petite woman with curly, long, dark hair that she must have straightened prior to her incarceration, because it was super curly now, the kind of style most women who had it hated. She looked up at Nikki with big brown, almond-shaped eyes. Nikki sat down and introduced herself. There was a hardness in those eyes, and she couldn't help wondering if it had always been there, if the thirty-year-old woman was the sociopath everyone claimed her to be, or if that hardness had developed during her so far six-month stay in jail.

"Do I know you?" Bernadette asked, a curtness in her voice.

"Actually you don't."

"Oh, I get it. You're a new attorney that dipshit Don Sanders sent over, right?"

She shook her head. "Uh, no. I don't know any Don Sanders."

"Be glad you don't." She tossed back her curls, offering a glimpse of the glamour she'd likely once exuded. No room for glamour in the slammer. Bernadette crossed her arms in front of her and leaned back in her chair. Yep, she'd gotten the inmate protocol down. Tough gal. "He's a moron. That's what I get for signing a prenup, huh? No cash to get myself a good lawyer, not like I had a prayer anyway. Everything was stolen from me and I was set up good. No one believes me."

"I'd like to talk to you about why you're here." Nikki took out a notepad from her purse, going with her plan of being a writer. She figured it might sound insane if she told her she was there out of curiosity. Could it be more than curiosity? Something still nagged her about Georges' murder. She didn't know what, but something bugged her, maybe the ghost of the chef himself.

"You never told me who you were."

"I didn't, did I?" Nikki asked. "Forgive me. I'm terribly sorry." If Aunt Cara knew her ploys, jeesh . . . "I'm doing a story. Actually a book. A nonfiction book. I'm not published or anything, but my aunt was a homicide detective in LA and she raised me, so I've always been interested in crime." *Okay, now that was good. The total truth right there.* "And writing." *True, too. Acting and writing went hand in hand. Before going to work for Malveaux she'd thought about writing screenplays.* "And, I got to thinking that it might be interesting to get a handful of stories from women in jail who claim they were falsely accused but were still convicted and are now doing time. I found your case interesting because considering who you were married to I would have expected it to be a huge story."

Bernadette was studying her. Was her radar up? Was she completely transparent? "And your name is?"

"Nikki Sands." Bernadette kept staring. Nikki nodded, and decided to jump on in. "For starters, as I said, I'm unclear why your situation was kept out of the press as much as it was. You were married to Georges Debussey. And now with his murder, do you think your story will come up again?"

"I don't know. I doubt it. I heard that they caught the guy who killed Georges, at least one of them. I'm not surprised about that slimeball Henry Bloomenfeld. I never liked that guy. Some cop came here the other day."

"What did you tell the police? Why would they question you here about Georges' murder?"

"My kid brother, Johnny, the pain, he's in a gang up in the city. I guess this cop might have thought retribution on Johnny's part. The cop wanted to know where Johnny was, and I told him that I had no clue. Then he asked me a few more questions about Georges and who might want him dead. I told him that I knew Baron O'Grady, that chef Georges was working with, his pal, had a *grande* life insurance policy on Georges. But I liked Baron. Good guy. He never rubbed me the wrong way, like Bloomenfeld did. I'm not happy Georges is dead even though he helped put me here, but since he is, I'm glad it was that creepy agent of his that did it and now he'll pay for it."

Nikki nodded. She got the distinct feeling that this was exactly what Bernadette Debussey needed—someone to listen to her. "Let's backtrack a bit and talk about why you're here in the first place, and as I asked before, how did

your story remain out of the media? There were a few articles, but it never became a huge story."

"When this thing with me went down, Georges was just
starting to go big. Yeah he was making money and people
knew him. We lived a great life. That man knew how to invest wisely and make money, but his popularity didn't take
off until the release of his first cookbook, about the time I
was convicted. Then he started working on that deal with
the winery out in Napa, but I obviously didn't see that finished."

Nikki shifted in her chair, feeling uneasy at the mention
of the winery. "Good deal for him, huh?"

"I'll say. Sure we were rolling in cash, but him closing
that deal out in the wine country was a great thing. Then, instead of me winding up between hills of grapes, I wound up
here. You asked me why the story about me being arrested
wasn't a big deal? Well, you know, a restaurateur's wife going to jail for arson makes the local news and the papers, but
it's not CNN material. I'm sure now with the book thing
and all, it likely could have, but Georges had himself a very
protective staff. That Lauren Trump for starters. She had
her own connections on how to keep things quiet about me
and my supposed crime."

Bernadette had some interesting things to say and Nikki
wondered if she'd spilled all of this to Robinson, or if he'd
simply followed the lead of Baron O'Grady's insurance
policy. "You say that you're innocent of starting the fire in
Georges' guesthouse? That you're not an arsonist?"

"That was *our* guesthouse. And, I'm not just saying it.
It's true."

"Of course. I'm sorry." She wanted to remain on
Bernadette's good side.

"I didn't start the fire. So, maybe I did go in and destroy
that slut's stuff, the one who was living in there."

Nikki flipped the page and pretended to read notes that
were not there. "That would be Jane Creswell?"

Bernadette nodded and turned away for a second. When she looked back at Nikki a bit of the hardness was gone and now confusion and hurt replaced it. Not for long. As soon as she started telling her version of the story, that stone-cold look returned.

"Yeah. Sweet Janie. The crazy thing was, is, that she was my friend. I liked her. I felt freaking sorry for her because she lost her mom. We all had a good thing there. She had her place, we hung out like sisters, and Georges loved me, until she had to go sashaying around in tight jeans and half shirts. Not cool."

"I should say not." Nikki had a hard time picturing the ethereal looking Janie in bimbo-type outfits. Had her initial approach been one of wanting to be the other woman and get ahold of some of Georges' money? Maybe that was where a lot of her pain and guilt was coming from, especially after finding out who Georges was.

"No. Not cool. Anyway she and Georges started hanging out a lot more and I know they were screwing around."

"Did you have any proof?"

"No. But a woman's intuition is solid and I knew."

"So you destroyed her stuff?"

"Hell yeah. I am not the kind of woman who sits by while some other chick tries to steal her man. She *used* me. Pretended to be my friend while she was trying to back door it—get out of the guesthouse and into *my* house. I'm sure she's hanging by the pool as we speak, sipping Vueve Clicquot."

"Right, but didn't Jane have a boyfriend? It said in the paper something about that?"

"Oh that Trevor dude? Whatever. She was using him, too. I'm telling you she's the one who should be in jail. She knows how to work and manipulate people to get what she wants. First she starts letting my man at her while she's working me and that poor Trevor kid so it all looks benign, then she sets the trap."

"Trap?"

"Trap. You do speak English, don't you? Janie knew I had

a temper, and she continued to hang on Georges, laugh at everything he said. It pushed me over the edge. I cut up her stuff, he kicked me out, and then she burnt down the guest-house, and somehow got my fingerprints, maybe from a glass, I don't know, and planted them on the lighter the fire Marshall claims was used to start the fire. I had nothing. No one to back me. No alibi. I went to our cabin in Monterey. I still had a key and I thought maybe Georges would cool off, come to his senses. I came back two days later and the cops arrested me. The place was burnt down. The lighter, which I hadn't used in God knows how long, was in my luggage. I was framed. I'm telling you."

"No one saw you in Monterey?"

"No. I packed up stuff before I left. All I took was some wine, bread, and cheese. I think an apple, too. Trust me, I wanted to get loaded and pretend he wasn't upset with me. That our love would win over whatever he was feeling for Janie."

Yeah, well, he was feeling something other than what Bernadette assumed—fatherly love.

"Crazy. I really loved him. I wouldn't have signed a prenup if I didn't, and I wouldn't have gone nuts when I re-alized that the two of them were up to no good."

Nikki sighed. The woman had a right to know the truth, but she'd promised Janie that she wouldn't tell anyone, and she'd already told Simon. But Bernadette was not exactly her close friend. Besides, it might make Bernadette feel even worse to know that her crime was totally in vain. Nikki still didn't buy that she hadn't started the fire. She was off her rocker with the jealousy thing.

The guard signaled that there was only a few minutes left. Bernadette leaned on the table now and gazed intently at Nikki. "I don't trust too many people these days, and I don't know if you're really writing a book, but you seem nice enough. I swear to you that I did not start that fire. I loved my husband and I did not do that. If you can help me prove it, you'd get an innocent woman released from jail."

With that Bernadette stood and got into line with the other inmates. Nikki walked out of the penitentiary with a gazillion thoughts running through her brain. Was she being duped by Janie? Was there something sinister behind all that innocence? Why was it that Bernadette believed so strongly that Janie and Georges were having an affair?

But her main question, which she kept repeating in her head during the three-hour drive home, was did the police have the real killer in jail? That nagging feeling sat heavy in her stomach. She still couldn't put a finger on it, but as she replayed Bernadette's story over and over in her mind, the feeling sank even deeper, and she started to think that this thing wasn't over yet.

Chapter 25

Nikki came home to a handwritten note taped to her door from Derek asking her how she was feeling and if she needed anything. He claimed that he'd called but she didn't answer and he didn't want to disturb her. He also reminded her of the dinner tomorrow night for Georges, and the last thing in the note was a question: *Have you decided about Spain? I spoke with Andrés and know the plan is for the two of you, if you decide to go, to leave on Saturday. I need to know to adjust duties around the winery accordingly.*

Nikki crumpled up the note and tossed it in the trash. She was exhausted and didn't even bother with dinner, knowing a night of good rest was what she needed.

She poured herself a glass of Pinot Noir left by the cleaning staff on the coffee table and grabbed a good book to take her mind off things. She wondered if Robinson had any leads on Moran. Where could the guy have gone? She wished Ollie were around just to prove that he still loved her best. But there was no sign of the Ridgeback. Surely he was tucked away at Derek's, maybe licking Renee's hand off. Did the dog miss her the way she missed him? Did his owner even care what she or the dog needed?

She changed into a pair of Andrés' sweats. Comfortable. Warm. Secure. Call him. She took her phone from her purse and called his house and then his cell. No answer on either. He'd probably gone back to his ploy of making her miss him. And, know what? It was working.

She snuggled up on one of the oversized chairs with the latest Evanovich novel. She thought for a moment about getting the bag Jonah Robinson had left for her, but the thought of looking in it still made her queasy. Why was it so difficult to confront the past? Was it simply that whatever was in the bag would cause her to remember that she really had lost most everything precious to her? She'd hold off a bit longer.

She started reading and although the book was entertaining, sleep took over shortly after she'd curled up in the chair.

She didn't know what time it was or if she was dreaming at first, but she soon discovered that she was not.

A guitar? Outside her room. She stood and peered out the window onto the porch. Andrés. Playing "Every Little Thing She Does Is Magic" by The Police. She opened the door. He smiled at her. Yep—warm, comfortable, secure. No doubt what's in store when it came to Andrés.

She sat down on the lounge chair on the porch, pulled her blanket around her, and listened to the song. Absolutely gorgeous. He finished and bent down and kissed her gently on the lips. She didn't pull away from him. Not this time.

He pulled away first. "Not here. Not now. There is a perfect time and place for us. In Spain." He turned around and picked up a basket of flowers and handed them to her. "Your ticket is in there, too. The flight leaves Saturday at three. I have to be in the city tomorrow to sign some more papers for the vineyard and to take care of some other business. I'll be staying at a hotel overnight. If you decide to join me, I made arrangements for your car. There's an address in the envelope with all of the information, in the basket. There's a garage near the airport where it will be stored. If you do not come, I will have to understand your decision. For me this is good-bye for now. If you decide not to join me, I want these few moments as a lasting memory. Stupid sounding, I know, but, it's the way I feel."

He smiled and tried to laugh, but Nikki knew he spoke the truth. "I, I, uh, I . . ."

Andrés held up a hand. "No. Don't say anything. Not now. You will decide and you will know, and so will I, soon enough." He kissed her again and walked away, whistling "Every Little Thing She Does Is Magic."

She fell asleep with the song in her mind along with Andrés' proposition. She tossed and turned all night and didn't feel rested at all by the time she crawled out of bed Friday morning. She felt weary and weighted down.

She thought about tonight's dinner and wondered about Janie. She hadn't seen her or Trevor since the other night at the wine bar. Had they done as she suggested and spoken to an estate attorney yet, and had Leonard Kinsgton made contact with them?

She took a long hot shower and thought about Bloomenfeld's dirty secrets. He'd committed some major crimes for chump change. Ridiculous what people would do for money, even for only a little bit of it. And considering all Georges was worth, Bloomenfeld and Moran had only pilfered a small amount. But maybe there were plans to tap into more of the millions Georges had, and through Moran that was possible. And Georges caught on so they had to do away with him. And, what about Rick Moran? Come on. The man was a financial advisor. How had he gotten sucked into Bloomenfeld's gig? Whatever the reasons, Nikki was certain they had to do with Bloomenfeld's side business or weird obsession. She went through all of what had happened in regard to Georges' murder over the past week, and even though the relationship between Moran and Bloomenfeld was odd, and Bloomenfeld had a falling out with Georges, and they were on their way to Mexico with a couple hundred grand of Georges' cash, something did not completely click for her. And, the question remained: where was Moran?

She dried off, opened the closet, and took out one of her new outfits—classic and cute—a light pink button down that pinned in tighter around the waist, so much better than the old-school, boyish button-downs she'd worn in the early eighties in high school. She pulled on a light gray striped pencil skirt and matching jacket, and for good measure she even went à la Sarah Jessica Parker, donning the pink carnation pin that came with the suit. Nice. She took it one step further and put on her size seven slingback Via Spigas. She looked at herself in the mirror, pulled her hair back into a sleek ponytail, lined her blue eyes in an espresso colored eyeliner—that's what the girl at the MAC counter called it—and matched it with a cream and then a mocha colored eye shadow in the crease—again, mocha was the salesgirl's name for it. Nikki thought it looked like tan to her, or brown. She put some lipstick on—Spirit, now there was a name to get with—and studied herself for a minute. She still had it. Not bad at all, as she climbed the ladder to forty. Besides, wasn't forty the new thirty? That meant her best years were only four years away. Thank God for Terri Hatcher and those *Desperate Housewives*.

But as she stood there in front of the mirror she had to wonder: who was she trying to impress? There was a man who loved her any way she was. He'd played the guitar for her just last night and he wanted to take her away and love her. She went back to the closet and opened it again. Did she really want to go to work all dolled up today?

The phone rang while she wrestled with this decision. She picked it up. "Hello?"

"Hi, Nikki. It's me, Robinson. We found Moran."

"You did? Where?"

"Floating in the bay this morning."

"Oh my God."

"I know. I'm on my way to the scene and then back to put some more heat on Bloomenfeld. I'll call you later."

She hung up the phone, stunned. Bloomenfeld must've killed Moran. Was he that stupid? That greedy? Well, that solved that. Time to move on, she figured.

She went back to the closet to rifle through her clothes. There was *the bag* from the fire. Screw it. Look inside. Move on. She bent down and opened it. A few items she had no real feelings about—a sweater, a dime-store vase, a few trinkets. But one of the items stood out, and she pulled it from the bag and examined it.

Oh my God. Bloomenfeld hadn't murdered either Georges or Moran. But Nikki suddenly knew who had. The cops had the clue to the real killer all the time. But of course, what she held in her hand they couldn't or wouldn't have tied to the killer's identity. Why would they? Blood rushed to her head, which started pounding. She couldn't believe it. She blinked her eyes several times, and then closed them. Yes, she knew who the real killer was, and she also knew why and how it had happened. A memory from the other day stirred in her.

She went to the nightstand, took out the phone book, and placed a call confirming that the killer would be at tonight's dinner.

Chapter 26

The table was set and so was Nikki. The evening had arrived. Renee Rothschild came into the restaurant on Derek's arm, dressed to perfection. When she spotted Nikki she let go of his arm and rushed over to her, as if the two of them had been the best of friends for years. "Have you thought any more about the book?"

Derek came up behind Renee. He put an arm around her. Nikki could hardly look at him. Mr. Dapper in his tuxedo. Did Renee know that Derek hated wearing what he referred to as monkey suits?

"I'm happy to see you feeling better. Renee tells me you're interested in writing the book about the hotel and spa. I think that's a great idea, and she mentioned that you were going to do it while in Spain. I take it that you've decided to go, then."

Nikki looked at them. "I don't know about that."

"Which part? The book or Spain?" Derek asked.

"I don't know."

"Well, all right. I think we'll go and grab a glass of wine. This just came up this morning, but I'm leaving for

Australia tomorrow for a couple of weeks. I figure it's time to expand the Malveaux dynasty. The Aussie wines are gaining in popularity, and I received a call from a colleague about a hot piece of property, so I thought I'd better take advantage."

Renee rubbed his arm. "I'm going, too." She eagerly looked up at Derek. "In the jet. I'm so excited. It'll be great. When Derek told me, I said that I had plans to go there next month. I've got two great authors doing a 'shrimp on the barbie' kind of cookbook. They were thrilled. The Aussies are so hospitable."

Nikki looked at Derek. Was he thrilled to have her company? He must be. He wasn't the kind of man to take a woman halfway across the world without meaning it. "That's great. Oh, looks like a few more people have joined us. I want to make sure they get a glass of wine and find their seats."

Derek nodded and Nikki hurried off. Good for them. New love, going to Australia to stoke the coals on the barbie and drink Aussie liquid grape. Lovely. They were perfectly suited for each other. Both beautiful. Both from money. Both highly educated. Yes. Perfectly suited.

Nikki walked over to Baron, whose eyes hadn't lit up since Georges' death. "Hello, Miss Sands. How are ye?"

"I'm good, and you? Would you like a glass of wine?"

"No. Thank ya. Whiskey, though. That would temper the ole tummy a bit. I may have wine with dinner, though. It is always nice."

"I'll get you that whiskey." Nikki turned to go to the bar. Baron reached out and grabbed her arm. "Wait a minute. I owe ya an apology."

"You do?" Nikki fidgeted with the clasp on her purse.

"I do. I was mighty testy with ye the other night in the church and that is no way for a good Catholic to act. Ye see, I have done some horrible things recently. I was in church for forgiveness and the priest reminded me of what I needed to let go of, and knowing that be the truth, it was still hard for me to take." He glanced toward the front door. In walked Lauren. He looked back at Nikki. "I do apologize."

She touched his arm. "These things happen. No worries."

She went for his drink and when she returned he was talking with Lauren. Nikki overheard her say, "I understand. Ireland is the best place for you. Certainly. But it was fun while it lasted." She took the whiskey from Nikki and passed it on to Baron. "Hello, Ms. Sands."

"Hi. Enjoy, Baron." Nikki turned around, knowing that Lauren Trump would soon be in bed with a new man in hopes of finding something she'd never had. Poor Baron with all that guilt.

Five minutes before seating time, the last guest hadn't arrived. Nikki took her seat. On one side sat Trevor and next to him Janie. The seat to her left was still open. "Did you get ahold of the estate attorney?" Nikki asked the young couple.

"I did," Trevor said. "Everything is good to go."

"That's great. So you'll be able to get the DNA samples?"

Janie nodded eagerly. "Yeah. The attorney told Trevor that he'd contacted the morgue and that before my dad's body is shipped back to France next week, they'll be able to get a sample. I just have to go to Georges' attorney's office and have a sample taken."

"You may not have to go that far," Nikki replied. "Here's Georges' attorney now." She stood. Everyone else had taken their seats. The waiters were getting ready to serve the first course of pan-fried crispy calamari with pancetta and pesto with a glass of Malveaux Fumé Blanc. "Oh, Mr. Kingston. Right here." Nikki walked around the table. She caught Simon's eye. He gave her a dirty look. She hadn't been able to get ahold of him to explain why Kingston was here. He'd understand later.

"Excuse me, Ms. Rothschild? I'm here to meet Georges

Debussey's other attorney. I got a call today from a Nikki Sands. I was unaware he had any other attorneys."

Nikki stretched out her hand. "Good evening, Mr. Kingston. I'm Nikki Sands."

"No. You're Renee Rothschild." Kingston's light blue eyes formed into slits.

"No she isn't. I'm Renee Rothschild," Renee chimed in.

Kingston's head snapped around to see Renee seated next to Derek, both of them looking rather confused. In fact, they all appeared confused.

"Nikki, what's going on? Did this gentleman just say that you're Georges' other attorney?" Derek asked. "And, why does he think you're Renee?"

She shook her head and smiled. "I can explain everything. It's not what you think."

"I don't know what to think," Derek said.

"Me neither," replied Renee.

"This is going to be good. You go, Doris!" Simon exclaimed.

"What the hell is your name? Renee, Nikki, Doris?" Kingston asked.

In unison everyone at the table answered, "Nikki."

"It's an amusing story and there is a point. I promise," Nikki said. "So, please have a seat, Mr. Kingston, and enjoy our honorary dinner for Georges, and let me explain."

"I don't appreciate shenanigans, Miss . . . whoever you are," Kingston replied.

"I assure you, Mr. Kingston, this is not a shenanigan. Now have a seat."

The lawyer sat down apprehensively next to Nikki.

Waiters brought the first course. "I don't know what you're pulling here, Ms. Sands."

Nikki picked up a piece of the tender calamari and followed up with a sip of the Fumé, enjoying the way everyone was beginning to squirm.

"Nikki, we are all waiting to hear what you have to say," Derek said.

"Of course." She set her wine down and stood. "Mr. Kingston here is quite an intelligent man. So smart, in fact, that he planned and helped to carry out the murders of Georges Debussey and Rick Moran."

"What in the hell? This is ridiculous! Who is this crazy broad? Why in the hell would I want my star client dead? And, Rick Moran? I only met him one time."

"Money. Georges was worth more to you dead. He was worth lots of money for you . . . and your son." Nikki shot a glance at Trevor, who buried his face in his hands.

"What is going on?" Janie asked.

Nikki put her fingertips on the table. She faced Janie, who deserved the truth more than anyone she'd ever known. "Trevor is Mr. Kingston's son."

"What? No. His parents died in a fire," Janie insisted.

"No. His mother died. But not his father." Nikki took out a photograph from her purse and handed it to Janie: the same family photo Kingston had in his office that she and Simon noticed the other day while in the attorney's office, only smaller. On the back the photo read: Trevor, Mom, & Dad '90. The same year Mrs. Kingston died. The picture was scorched around the edges, but it was still clear, and Nikki knew when she pulled it out of the bag Robinson had given her the other day why Kingston's eyes reminded her of someone else. Leonard Kingston and his son, Trevor, both possessed those same ice blue eyes.

Janie looked at Trevor. "What is this all about?"

"You moron. Can't you do anything right?" Leonard Kingston bellowed. "Why does she have that?" He turned to Nikki. "This means nothing."

Nikki shrugged. "Whatever. I would sit down, Mr. Kingston. You can tell it to the police." Jonah Robinson and two uniformed officers entered the building.

Nikki had phoned Robinson before the guests started arriving and told him it was important he show up at the dinner and at what time. At first he balked, but she told him it was of the utmost importance he come over.

"Janie, do you remember the other night after Georges was killed and you were on the phone with Trevor? I overheard your conversation about which suitcase you were using, and you told him his. Well, that photo was in the suitcase. I assume tucked in one of the smaller side pockets that you probably didn't use." Nikki looked at Kingston. "It bothered Trevor, and he didn't want to take a chance on you finding the photo and asking questions about it. Plus, he knew that eventually you would be meeting dear old dad when you went to sign the papers regarding Georges' estate. Trevor knew that he should have destroyed it; that's why he burned my house down. But as luck, karma, or whatever might have it, the suitcase made it through the fire. The police returned it to me. The photo was in a plastic baggie. I'm certain the police and fire marshall assumed the suitcase and its contents were mine. For all they knew, Trevor, Mom, and Dad were my relatives. So they gave it back to me. Suffice it to say, Mr. Kingston also has that same photo in his office. I'm certain he would have removed it before you came in to claim your money. By the way, Janie, your DNA is a match with Georges'. Dad and son were able to confirm this when you had a blood test to get your marriage license. Before that, they were hoping you were Georges' daughter, but once it was confirmed, I'm sure Trevor rushed you to the altar."

Everyone at the table watched in awe, not taking their eyes off the scene. Jonah approached the table.

"I did some further investigating and it seems that Trevor here has a problem with matches. He burned his house down the night his mother was killed in that fire. He was a juvenile and his father helped build his defense, saying it was an accident. But I wonder if it was an accident at all, and I wonder if the Debussey guesthouse fire was also his fault, and not caused by Bernadette Debussey."

"You are insane, lady!" Trevor stood up.

"No. You are. You and your dad planned this entire thing. You would woo Janie once Dad put you to it, after discovering that she was indeed Georges' daughter, and continue to do so after Georges placed her in his will. Seems daddy's business has been suffering some. A few million would help.

"You knew exactly where Georges would be the afternoon you killed him, because Janie kept detailed schedules for herself and Georges in her notebook. You drove out here, located the bath area, climbed up onto the verandah, hid behind the plants on the balcony, and waited for the moment you could take him out.

"And Moran? That was dumb. He was just a pawn. Were you afraid he'd stumble onto the money trail and figure things out? Or was Georges on the phone with Moran when you came into the room, and you picked up the cell to see what number he had just called? Oh, and by the way, another thing—finals were over two weeks ago at all the local colleges and universities. You never told me where you were going to school, so I had to make several phone calls. I thought it was a few weeks past graduation. Makes me wonder if you graduated or if you were even in school, Trevor. My guess is no, that you were too busy devising your wicked scheme with dear old Dad."

Trevor's eyes bulged and the veins on his face stood out as he looked at Kingston, who bowed his head.

Nikki continued. "So, you sweep Janie off her feet, murder her father, and you and Dad have yourself a nice stream of cash. Just when did you plan to burn the house down with your wife in it?"

Trevor lunged at Nikki and grabbed her around the neck. Janie cried out, "Dammit, Trevor, stop it!"

Robinson drew a gun. "Let her go. I *will* shoot."

"No!" Trevor screamed. "Dad! You said that it would work! You always mess things up for me."

"Let her go," Robinson yelled again.

Nikki's stomach clenched; her mouth went dry. Then everything slowed down. She could hear screaming, and suddenly Trevor released her and she dropped into her chair as he crashed to the floor. Had Robinson shot him?

Renee Rothschild stood over Trevor, a broken wine bottle in her hand, the other half of it on the ground. She laughed. "I couldn't let the man kill my next star author, could I?"

"Oh, God, can someone get me a drink?" Nikki exclaimed.

Chapter 27

After Kingston and Trevor had been carted away, Jonah Robinson returned. He shook a finger at Nikki. "You are sneaky, girl. Sneaky. Why didn't you tell me about all of this until an hour ago?"

"What if I was wrong?" She picked at the Salad Nicoise, which one of the waiters brought over. It was meant as the second course.

"That's right. What if you were wrong?"

"I probably would have lost my job or at the least looked like a fool," Nikki replied.

"Uh-huh. But you knew, didn't you, that you weren't wrong?"

"Maybe." She picked up her wine glass. "Don't go giving me any lectures. I know what I did was dangerous. I'm sorry. Okay? Besides, something you said the other day tipped me off. In reality, you did help figure this out."

"How so?"

"I know you can't forget our encounter at Derek's place after my cottage burned down. You mentioned the theory someone torched it to destroy evidence."

"I did, didn't I? We'd make a good team, Sands. Why don't you join the police force?"

"Nah. I like it on the down low." She figured Mr. Cool knew what she meant by that. It was like being covert, quiet about shifty operations.

He laughed. "You're not only sneaky but a nut. I'm gonna have to keep my eye on you after all, like your friend Mr. Malveaux asked me to."

"Derek?"

"Oh hell. Yeah, him. I figured you knew. The way the dude looks at you, it's obvious he has feelings."

Nikki set down her glass. "He doesn't look at me any *way*. Besides he's got a new friend."

"I see." Jonah glanced at Derek and Renee. An officer was taking their statement. "You be careful around these vineyards."

"You're telling me." She laughed. "Hey, you know, we didn't get off on the best foot. Want to share dinner with me? There's plenty in the kitchen with the party not going exactly as planned."

"Are you asking me out for dinner? Like a date?"

"Not my style. Besides I've got my hands full in that department, and something tells me you're nothing but trouble, Detective."

"I'll take a rain check. Listen, thanks for . . . well, you know."

She nodded, knowing exactly what he was thanking her for—finding the real killer.

"I'm going to get on the horn and see about opening Bernadette Debussey's case again. I'm thinking I can get Trevor to admit to the guesthouse fire and get the poor woman out of jail."

"Good. Thank you."

Jonah stood. "Be good. 'Cause I'm still gonna be watching you."

"Something tells me that you will."

"Well . . ." Robinson stood up and stretched. "I got

work to do." He pointed at her and winked. "Catch you on the down low."

Nikki chuckled as she watched Robinson leave, then looked at Derek sitting by Renee's side. She thought about Andrés. Nope. She did not need any more guy troubles.

Chapter 28

The next day, Nikki watched Derek and Renee leave the vineyard in his Range Rover. After they left, she made a phone call to personnel and left a message for the gal who hired the pourers in the tasting room, asking her to phone Alyssa on Monday about the position and highly recommending her. After that she called Alyssa, who was ecstatic over the job and thanked her a dozen times.

Nikki then took a walk and found Ollie next to the old oak tree that stood near what used to be her cottage. "Hey, you do miss me. Don't you?"

Ollie stretched out and rolled over for her. "Sure, you'll lick Renee's hand, but all I'm good for is a stroke on the tummy. Some loyalty." She rubbed his belly for a few minutes.

Marco and Simon approached. "We saw you with the doggie," Simon said. "You know my brother asked us to take care of him while he was gone. Good thing I'm taking my allergy pills."

Nikki knew Simon was allergic to dogs. When she'd first come to the vineyard, Simon wouldn't go near Ollie . . . or her, for that matter. Funny how at the time she'd pretty much decided that the two men in front of her were her enemies. One thing to always count on—life changed on a daily basis.

"I love you guys," she said.

"We love you, too. We have news."

"You do?" she asked.

Simon nodded. "We are going to Europe next month. Sansibaba will be in Italy doing a special, weeklong, intensive seminar on confronting your fears."

"We want to address our nudophobia," Marco interjected. "You were right when you told me I was a hypocrite for telling you to live a life of passion when I hide behind my own fears."

"I didn't call you a hypocrite," Nikki replied.

"But it is implied and you are right."

"We will be hanging by the chandeliers, Goldilocks," Simon said. "You want to join us?"

Marco clapped. "*Sí, Bellisima*, come to Italy. I will show you around and we will go to the vineyards and drink *vino* and face our fears under the teaching of Sansibaba."

She laughed. "I have no fears."

Her friends looked at her and then at each other. "Goldilocks, please."

She kissed them each on the cheek. "I'll be fine. You two will have a wonderful time in Italy. I'm proud of you. Be good." She turned around and headed back to her room. Ollie remained with the boys, as Simon took over rubbing the dog's belly. Typical dog—loyal to the tummy rubber, no matter who he or she may be.

In her room the basket with the information about Spain was still there on the coffee table. She'd put the roses in a vase and they had blossomed. Their heady scent spread throughout the room.

She picked up the letter Andrés had written her and read it again.

Nikki,

I want you to know that you are the one. You are my magic and I am in love with you. I want to be with you. I can't imagine my life without you in it. I want children with you, a family, a life. Come to Spain with me. I'll give you the world if you'll let me.

Love,
    Andrés

She looked at the airline ticket. The flight would be leaving in a little less than four hours. She closed her eyes. He loved her. He really loved her. She *could* make it to the airport in an hour. She *could* make the plane.

She noticed the blinking light on her answering machine. It had to be Andrés. She went over and played it.

"Nikki, it's me, Derek. I, well, I, God, I don't know what the hell I'm doing. I, dammit, I love you, Nik. Not like a friend, but, well you know, I do, I just do, okay? And, I told Renee that nothing was going to happen between her and me, and now I'm here at the airport with a plane ready to go to Australia and . . . Ah hell. Come with me, Nikki. Let's go together and see if we can't figure this thing out, get to the bottom of what's between us."

Nikki pressed rewind and played the message again. Still holding the letter and ticket Andrés had left, she read it once more.

She smiled, grabbed her purse, locked the door to her room, got behind the wheel of her Camry, and headed to the airport.

Author's Note

It has been a lot of fun to watch Nikki and her friends change and grow from when she first moved to Napa Valley. If you have followed the Wine Lover's Mysteries, then you know that the triangle between Nikki, Derek, and Andrés has evolved, and now you may be frustrated with me for leaving you hanging. Not to fear, I assure you that Nikki will either wind up in Australia with Derek for book four, or in Europe with Andrés. Of course, that doesn't necessarily mean it will be a "happily ever after," especially when there is murder and mayhem involved. As the author of the Wine Lover's Mysteries, I would love to hear from you as to who you think is the best man for Nikki, or who you would like to see her with in the next book. If you're interested in putting in your two cents, then please go to my website at www.michelescott.com and click on the poll. The results will be kept secret until book four where you will find out who the majority of you want Nikki to be tasting wine with as the sun sets in either the Australian wine country or the Spanish wine country.

RECIPE INDEX

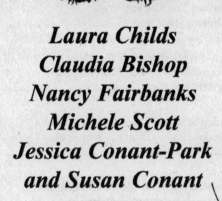